THE BIG JANGLE

THE BIG JANGLE

ROCK NEELLY

ISBN: 978-1-958414-96-5

Enigma House Press

Enigmahousepress.com

Little red wagon, little red bike,
I ain't no monkey but I know what I like.
—Bob Dylan

Never hold discussions with the monkey
When the organ grinder is in the room.
—Winston Churchill

This book is dedicated to Ezekiel, first of a new generation.
I will call you Easy, Zeke, and EZ.
Take it easy, little man, but take it with gusto, love, and happiness.

NATIONAL SECURITY AGENCY
CLASSIFIED (TOP SECRET)

Communique from British Consulate, Athens, Greece (Decoded and redirected from State Department to Central Intelligence Agency)

Occurrence Location: Istanbul Grand Bazaar. 41.0107° N, 28.9681° E

Relaying that a terrorist cell termination occurred in the city of Istanbul. 01 October 2019, at 1:49 am (GMT+03:00). British intelligence monitored the event's radio and telephone transmissions from the Athens British Consulate.

Casualties initially reported by Turkish police after large explosion in a subterranean cistern. Structure collapsed. Now no comment from Turkish Gendarmerie and Millî İstihbarat Teşkilatı, MIT, Turkish Secret Police. News stories quashed. Revised officially to description of a small fire causing minor damage to a warehouse. No diplomatic reply to our inquiry on the firefight and military grade weaponry discharged at street level in minutes prior to explosion.

British Secret Service, MI6, remotely monitored the event in progress and best analysis is at least one side of the combatants were American. They were on coms and speaking English. Definitely Yanks, according to our source who was listening to the event in real time. We have audio recordings and are clearing them through London for your review. Will expedite.

Our assets were on site (unofficially) within minutes, and to our knowledge, none of the Americans made it out before the explosion leveled the structure. However, we stayed strictly at a spectator's distance. Our relationship with the Turks is no better than yours these days. No American chatter after explosion.

No more intel is available at this time (recordings as mentioned to follow). MI6 is still investigating. Did you have operatives in the Grand Bazaar on night in question? We have no information of enemy combatants or your assets in Grand Bazaar. Usually, we'd receive a head's up from CIA or NSA of a cell's termination. None was forthcoming in this case. Please advise.

Handwritten Note from Director: Forward to Field Officer Scott Grace: Did this rogue action involve your brother Clayton Grace once again? Please advise.

THE BIG JANGLE, PART I

Maybe you care about me, Roddy O'Malley, and my partner Clayton Grace. Maybe you don't give a flying forsythia. If you don't give a rat's rump, just skip my little nine-page ramble here and get on the first case in this collection, "Monkey Bidness." Don't let the screen door hit you on the butt on the way out.

However, nobody has posted anything on our hidden blog for going-on three years, so I thought I'd give ya'all a quick Christmas letter fill-in on the fam. You know those kind of letters—Jarbo still has a rash on his Jolly Rancher, Ma is due out of county before her next court date, and a lot of you have asked about Aunt Nawleen. The Z packs didn't work, but they finally did give her a stronger antibiotic so now she can finally sit down without making that sound. We're all happy and looking forward to the new year!

Some of you just start the fireplace with those misbegotten missives. Others are gluttons for punishment and read every word. If your mantra is "Don't bore us, just sing the chorus," I get it. If that's you, move on. My feelings won't be hurt.

As you may have noticed, it's still Roddy writing here. Mr. Suave and Sophisticated. The one who can't tell a story without a few swear words and wise cracks. My partner Clayton Grace remains missing out there somewhere, fighting terrorism—mostly likely in an Arab land. My daughter, Gracie, named after him, has never seen her godfather. Clayton Grace is, to her, a fabled hero. There is Superman. There is Santa Claus and there is Clayton Grace. Mythos for the midget—that is his legacy in our house.

He would also be *numero uno* on the Most Wanted list if Iran is printing the circulars. It's been more than thirty months since he got word from the CIA that a jihad had been issued for his head by a mysterious mullah with deep pockets and a penchant for vengeance. Clayton Grace has been on the run ever since (btw, isn't *Penchant for Vengeance* a Guns and Roses album?)

There is no news on my partner. In the press and to local police, Grace is a person of interest on the run. But on the QT, he's a contractor for the CIA, NSA, or WTF—somebody, some acronym. And the men behind the curtain aren't telling me jack. But Clay does have a benefactor paying his way. At least that's something.

I've spent his time away raising my daughter Gracie. Karen, Gracie's mother, and I still aren't hitched, but she's wearing a rock these days. Karen is liable to set a date and tell me to get her to the church-on-time any day now. Gracie is looking forward to her third birthday (wants a boombox—

old-school soul, her), and that little monster rules the roost. For now, the ladies both still let me live here. It's all good.

Professionally, my fiancé is starting to bring in some big bucks as a Hollywood agent. With Netflix, Hulu, Amazon Prime, Paramount Plus, BritBox, HBO Max, Fox, Disney+, Google, Applejacks, and my Aunt Edith and Uncle Claude all producing original programming, it's not a bad time to be an agent who specializes in bringing new talent to the fore. Karen paid her dues. Now she's reaping the rewards. My baby's come a long way from being an office manager to that creepy magician back when I met her (as detailed in *The Purple Heart Detective Agency*). Good for her. She loves her job, and we're cashing the checks.

As for me, I've gone legit, at least as legit as I can get without having to take a drug test. Hey, with both legs gone and diagnosed with phantom limb pain, I still get scrips for painkillers now and then, but I no longer spend my days in a haze with dilated eyes behind dark Ray Bans. I still puff a bit of the Devil's Lettuce, although that's legal in Cali these days, but not copacetic if you have a conceal-and-carry, and I do.

I'm a security consultant now. My biggest client is—don't be surprised—Welmar Industries. The Dark Side, the Evil Empire, yeah, I know. It's a toxic relationship, but I just can't quit them. Welmar is funding Clayton's adventures out there wherever, so that keeps me in line. David Welmar, the company owner, is also Secretary of Defense for our current Prez. Cream and bastards rise, they say. I don't much like David Welmar or his company, but we're beholden until Clay comes home in one piece. I mean, he's already missing one piece, a left leg below the knee, but you know what I mean.

I'm not one to make fun of an amputee, except for myself. I'm missing some Lego parts below mid-thigh, but I have some particularly bad-ass prosthetics at this juncture and I no longer walk like Frank N. Stein. I might dance like Franky after a beer buzz if you crank up some Los Lobos, but don't we all?

Welmar sells ammunition to third world nations in proxy wars—the U.S. against Russia or China, except we have our farm teams battle it out. It's ugly but profitable and not personally dangerous. You know, like having a fight with your worst enemy, but having your little brothers do the fighting while you drink bubbly. Welmar is also a pharmaceutical provider for the Pentagon, making pills and potions that would never get past Food and Drug trials. The Welmar crew, I admit, can likely be found pictured in your dictionary when you look up the expression "evil incarnate," but I turn the other cheek and take the money. Welmar greatly overpays me (I know too much and like to kid myself that I am too tough to kill). They also underwork me. My boss, Bob Lee, an eye-patch-wearing corporate pirate hard-ass, says to consider myself on retainer. For what he has never told me. With my skill set, any assignment would not be legal or pretty when they "put me in, coach" off the bench. Mayhem would ensue. I am known for my skill with weapons, my tendency toward violent acts, and my distinct lack of subtlety. There are jobs calling for that combo plate in this world, I assure you. It is sometimes called "wet work."

So far in the last three years, Bob Lee has not put me in the game. These days, I provide a couple days of security review for software systems, monitor the burglar alarms at various warehouses filled with guns and ammo, and rarely I am called upon to shadow some titan of industry who wants extra muscle on a security detail. I have about three days a week free, never work weekends, spend most days with my daughter poolside, and still pull down enough jack to make the house payment. We thrive on Karen's income. It would be sweet city if Grace were back. But we've not heard a peep since his goodbye letter (as detailed in the end of *The Babylon Blues*).

The Purple Heart Detective Agency is closed. The IRS audited us, and the word got out to the press from the people at Welmar that Grace was laundering dough through the detective agency for something hinky. But of course, the IRS found nuttin' honey, so we're off the hook on that. By then, our doors were closed, and my partner had skedaddled.

Surprise! That audit, our closing the agency, and the subsequent news story were all just a cover. Grace's disappearance was engineered to place him into a black ops team trying to find the mullah who had ordered a hit on Clay's life (because of craziness detailed in *Prince of the Border*). All-in-all, it was disruptive to my buddy's life up in Topanga Canyon, his relationship with his gal, and our business.

Grace went with three other men. Unofficially, they kill for a living for our government. There are certain men you simply cannot arrest and bring to the Hague for a NATO tribunal. You just rid the world of their evil and move on. Grace and his companions are the tip of the spear for American values—execution-style.

However, hiding out and taking assholes off the terrorist roster is not good for anyone's mental health. My boss, Bob

Lee, told me Grace is still on the reservation, meaning he's following orders, but he is not a well-adjusted camper at this late date. It appears that thirty months into the maelstrom my brother-from-another-mother is still out there, a marauder for justice but with a chip on his shoulder. The little news I have is Grace now has a piss-poor attitude. Go figure. Won't you come home, Bill Bailey, won't you come home?

Our band of brothers, after serving together in Iraq, has pretty much gone its own way. I mean, it's been almost a decade since the war was over, and most of our platoon of crazies have rejoined the human race—if they are capable of doing so. The whole cast of characters is gone. I haven't talked to any of them since the shit with Grace and the jihad went down. There was simply too much heat to continue. The cops know our crew is responsible for an exceptional number of assholes meeting their grizzly demise, but there remains no solid evidence. No arrests. Trouble is already busy with weaker men, as The Who might say. The cops moved on, and we are just another cold case. Detective Harry Bosch is probably reviewing evidence against us as I write these words. Bring it on, Harry! See if you can bring us in. Break the case wide open, beer bottle in hand, staring over the LAPD's files on us while listening to Art Pepper! LOL

So that's it. It's just me, Karen, and Gracie against the world. The worst jam we get into is on the 405. I try to keep it that way. The ole days are not good ole ones to my way of thinking. I see none of the wrecking crew. It's better that way.

Except for Rat. I do still hang with him. He's a buddy from my Army unit back in the sandbox. Rat is now my part-time partner in whatever security detail work I do when called upon to protect some rich guy. So far, our work together has been uneventful. Guns have remained concealed. Copacetic.

Rat still spends his weekends playing high stakes poker with his ever-present toothpick stuck in his mouth. When the world gets weird, the weird go professional, and that is where Rat is. He's a professional gambler making most of his income off the books. Rat is good at stakeouts for the same reason he's good at poker. People don't take notice of him until he has the drop on them. He has quite a financial nest egg these days and is waiting for a real estate crash to buy property. Southern California, to this date, has not decided real estate should get cheaper. Therefore, his mountain of chips continues to build.

As for RoBo and Penny, other buddies from Iraq, they are in communication with Rat. He says they're incorrigible and still at their criminal ways—running guns, providing protection for very bad guys, and occasionally whacking some asshole whose only contribution to society occurs when his undiscovered body fertilizes a sapling planted over an unmarked grave.

RoBo and Penny are still in the game, violent as it may be. Not me, Jack. I have a family now. Mama, put my guns in the ground. I can't shoot them no more, right? When it comes to our old *modus operandi*, those were the dark days. I just want to put that chapter permanently to bed—without a lullaby. I want Clayton Grace to come home. He's paid long enough for our sins. It's all quiet on the west coast/ gold coast, and so far, if the phone don't ring, I know it's Grace. I deal with the phone's stony silence by not dealing with it. Sometimes avoidance is an excellent communication strategy. Sometimes, not so much. I try to remain chill. I like it quiet. Karen and Gracie like our life. Every day for a long time has pretty much been like the previous one. Until one wasn't.

It is Sunday 6:00 am when the phone rings. It is boss man Bob Lee. Apparently, he has decided to call my jersey number. The shit has hit the fan. I am getting a call to the big leagues.

THE BIG JANGLE, PART II

I just showed Karen my opening salvo and she says I got the start all wrong. Karen calls bullshit on my point-of-entry into our new adventure. Karen says this story starts eight days before that Sunday phone call from my boss Bob Lee. Yeah, a different call, but it rings our chime at the same time—6 am, the previous Saturday. It isn't even from a human. It is a monkey on the line.

Take two.

MONKEY BIDNESS

Karen's voice. And it's her "do it or die" tone. I am asleep, but even from slumberland, I jump to. Sleep is vital when you've got a hyperactive two-year old, and Karen is taking no prisoners from the sound of her voice.

"It's your monkey buddy," she says. "He says he didn't get his newspaper again."

It is just after dawn a.m. on a Saturday. Karen is shoving the receiver from our land line into my mug. I almost inhale it as I roll over. I take the receiver from her and she gives me the death ray look before she rolls over, breaking eye contact.

Yes, I still have a landline. My missing partner, Grace, has that number memorized, and with him off radar, if he needs my help and calls, I don't want him to get Estephan's Escort Service, Willie Wacker's Tree Trimming, or something, so I keep the landline.

Barely conscious, I take the call. It *is* my monkey buddy—

Jerry, the one-armed savant Rhesus monkey. He is bitching and moaning as I put the phone to my ear. I let the little guy go for a bit as I wake up, then respond, "Yeah, third time this week. I'm sure that is aggravating. But it *is* just the Saturday paper. Sunday would be a bigger deal."

Jerry goes into a string of obscenities. I remove the phone from my ear for his hot take on service in America these days.

Okay, a talking monkey will take some explaining. Jerry is an eight-year-old monkey who was once in an animal testing lab for phantom limb pain. The lab was run by, you guessed it, Welmar Industries. They were searching for meds to assist with phantom limb pain during the aftermath of the Iraq War. The bastards cut off one of his arms, him along with dozens of other poor primates, and gave him wicked-ass pills to see if his brain waves could bypass his mind's pain receptors for that missing limb.

I'm not sure that pill ever worked on phantom limb pain, but a side effect did greatly enhance Jerry's ability to communicate with humans. Once, I thought he delivered a message to me telepathically, but I smoke a lot of pot.

After testing was discontinued and the evil scientist was unmasked in a *Scooby Doo*-like denouement, Jerry was determined to have twice the vocabulary of Koko, the famous signing ape. More about his ability to speak in a bit.

Jerry is one smart monkey, but touchy about his paper getting delivered on time. I listen a while longer as I slip from bed and move like a gorilla on my knuckles and my two stumps for legs. I maneuver down the hall, quietly peek in on my still slumbering, sweet daughter. Seeing the kid asleep, I descend the stairs as Jerry rants on.

More background. Koko, if you don't follow popular science, was a female western lowland gorilla born in the San Francisco Zoo. She lived in northern Cali, not far from Jerry's current residence until just this June when she died at age 46. Koko, the "talking ape" lived in San Raphael at The Gorilla Foundation's preserve in the Santa Cruz Mountains. Koko was reported as understanding two thousand spoken human words and having the ability to sign over one thousand symbols into complex sentences and words.

Jerry, as I said, has twice the lexicon of Koko, but signing is a bit of a problem – the assholes at Welmar cut off one of his arms. And any public knowledge of Jerry's impressive mental acuity has been very hush-hush. David Welmar is Secretary of Defense now. Anybody saying a member of the Cabinet okayed cutting the arms off scores of monkeys has been discouraged. No news on that kind of cruelty is good news.

However, a new cast of scientists at Welmar see the benefit to keeping Jerry around. I suspect they are researching those pills and their communicative side effects on animals somewhere unbeknownst to me. The benefit of talking monkeys for the military industrial complex is lost on me, but if it can be monetized, I suspect Welmar is interested. However, like I say, I have no knowledge of such research, and when I've asked, they say it is not my concern. And above my pay grade. According to Bob Lee, fearless leader, all animal testing has been discontinued. He is, for the record, a skilled liar.

To enhance Jerry's "speech," sans the one arm, the tech folks at Welmar have provided a LED screen and keyboard with a speaker on an arm band wrapped around his stump where Jerry can punch in his thoughts. Using GSL (Gorilla Sign Language) symbols tapped into his armband from a keypad, my buddy can form sentences. The arm band mechanism then issues audible speech. Jerry doesn't have the vocal chords of a human, but he can talk up a storm, typing with flying fingers from his scrawny right hand onto to the keypad fastened to his left stump. Currently, the things he is saying about the *San Francisco Chronicle* should make the circulation editor blush.

"Butt holes make late after. Talk paper no here. Three times after last funny paper day. Butt holes."

I understand from talking to the Welmar techs that Jerry's combination of symbols creates the above message on his arm band. The speech it actually produces is more smoothly delivered. This is what I hear: "Assholes are late again. Newspaper not here. Three times since last Sunday. Assholes." Perversely, the Welmar people armed (pun intended) the device's synthetic voice with three mood possibilities—normal, excited, and sad. Hilariously, in pitch and intonation, Jerry armband speaker sounds just like Pee Wee Herman. So, I wait for coffee to brew at 6:15 on a Saturday morning, listening to a pissed off Pee Wee Herman.

Oh yeah, one more thing. Jerry has an audible reader, like what visually impaired folk have. He can't read but has become very adept at scanning his roller over the text of the newspaper. The device, like a narrow rolling pin with a handle, scans the copy and reads the newspaper copy aloud.

Jerry is a fanatic about scanning the newspaper. He reads it cover to cover every day. Jerry has a mania for the classified ads. He also had a mania for committing to buying things through the classifieds. Craigslist finally blocked him for non-payment and breach of contract. We had to limit his phone to calling me and a very few other numbers. He was harassing dog breeders and anybody selling old vinyl. More on that later.

After his rant, Jerry pauses. Then asks, "What you doing?"

"Getting my first sip of coffee."

"Jerry already drink too much coffee."

"No shit."

"I was going to call you today. Even before newspaper."

"What about?"

"I need hire you. You still no badge policeman, right?"

Jerry's device obviously does not have a symbol combination for the word "detective."

I groan. "Yeah, I'm still a licensed private detective, but I'm not coming up there to take the case of the missing newspaper. Just call the newspaper delivery service. Order Uber or Door Dash to bring you one. I got the Welmar people to add those numbers to your phone access."

"Okay, I call. But that not why I hire you."

I take a drink. "What then?"

"My pain pills no good. They look different. They taste different. Pain in my no arm is back. I can't sleep. Wait on newspaper too many times awake. Hurt. Get angry,"

"Yeah, you ain't shitting me on that. You are definitely

cranky. Listen, you can't call so early. I have a two-year old baby. She needs her sleep."

"Smile. How is little Roddy child?"

"Good, Jerry. She slept through your call, but you woke Karen. She also 'get angry'."

"Sorry. Can you come here and help me with pills? Pain bad."

"I'll call the people at Welmar and have them check your prescriptions. How about I start there?"

"Okay," Jerry pauses, then the voice changes intonation to calm. "Hey, did you read that End of the Line, the Allman Brothers Tribute Band, is playing the Funky Biscuit on New Year's?"

I laugh. "No, but I think the Peacheaters are the better tribute band anyway."

"They never play West Coast. Maybe they will put a show on the internet?" Jerry has learned to raise the pitch of the last word of a sentence to create questions. Smart little monkey.

"You research that, and I'll check on your pills."

"Goodbye, friend. Hug both Roddy family."

"Hope you get the newspaper thing figured out. I'll call later today."

I shower, then after checking on my girls again, I leave a message for my contact at Welmar, knowing it is Saturday and I might not get an answer until Monday. That means Jerry, if he is in pain, will suffer a little this weekend. A little later, I get a text from Jerry. His arm band can also send a text rather than speak.

"Newspaper here. Vintage vinyl sale in Larkspur tomorrow. You should come here, take me. Plus you should take my case. I am good to pay your too-high dollars. Fix pills. I hurt."

I reply that I'm checking on his pills. He says he is day drinking Coors Light. I tell him it can't hurt.

Later, Gracie wakes and I snatch her up, trying to let Karen sleep, but my steady gal stumbles into the kitchen a few minutes later. I pour her some java. My cell is sitting on the counter. Gracie hits the screen and Karen reads it.

"Jerry wants to hire you? You going up?"

I laugh. "His thought, not mine. Just a medication prob. I'm hoping the Welmar folks can get Jerry an appointment with his vet. Balance out his pain management." I nod down at my stumps encased in hemmed biking shorts. "What can I do? Peeps can't get access to pain killers without a prescription."

Karen laughs. "I remember days where I would have called bullshit to that statement."

"The bad ole days, babe."

Gracie says, "Bullshit," and I give Karen a look.

Karen and I move on, ignoring our child's curse. The two of us drop more f-bombs than the Enola Gay over Japan, so the kid has a potty mouth. It's an inevitable outcome unless we clean up our language, and there is no fucking way that's happening.

Karen nods at her daughter and then shrugs. "Hey, I'm supposed to go to that premier at the Balboa in San Francisco on Tuesday anyway. We could go up early. Gracie has been wanting to meet your monkey friend. And Jerry does seem to be in distress."

"Family vacay?" I ask.

Karen nods. "Plus, you might get Jerry to chill. That monkey does jangle my last nerve. We've got to get him calmed down. Six a.m. phone calls suck. Totally jangles my day."

"The Big Jangle," says Gracie. "That's what Tom Petty calls Mike Campbell on guitar.

We all laugh.

Karen says, "Yes, but we girls prefer Derek Trucks, right?"

"Yep," pipes the three-year-old. "Derek is *the* man."

"Jerry prefers Duane Allman," I say to our daughter.

Gracie looks up from her oatmeal and screws up her nose in disgust. She shakes her head in disapproval but then says, "I wanna meet your monkey, Daddy."

The boss has spoken. Family vacay on the docket.

"Gracie, meet Jerry. Jerry, this is my daughter, Gracie."

If monkeys can blush with joy, Jerry is definitely there. His eyes glisten with happiness. He extends his one spiderly hand, and Gracie takes it. I have taught her how to shake hands. She does me proud.

We are in Jerry's condo at the assisted living center. He has a standalone unit as far as possible from all the retired geezers living there because my monkey man plays his stereo too loud for anybody to be next door. He owns a vintage system with a Kenwood amp and some big ass Cerwin Vega

12TR floor standing audiophile speakers. He can make your ears bleed if he wants to, and sometimes he does seem to want to. Not now. He is on his best behavior with Gracie there. Jerry understands the significance of her visit.

"It is a Your Honor to meet you," he types and the arm band above his stump gives audio to the words.

Gracie's eyes dance hearing it. She laughs and dances a little jig, which makes Jerry positively gleeful.

I correct him, though. "Your Honor is a judge."

Jerry types. "Judges are assholes."

Gracie raises her eyebrows. "Assholes. Jerry talks bad like us too, Daddy."

I have to smile and Jerry shrugs, then types, "Sorry, I have met just one. He did not allow me to testify in court. Would not allow monkey take the oath."

I shrug, then go to his fridge and fix the three of us each a small glass of Sprite. Jerry's caffeine load is too high, and I've asked the grocery delivery to cut his Coca Cola to a twelve pack of minis a week. Anything else has to be caffeine free. But then he got a Crups and makes his own single serving brews. His little overworked heart will blow up someday.

We go outside to the deck. Monkey man has a bench seat and two chairs. For whom, I don't know. He gets no visitors to speak of, except me, his vet, and GrubHub. I don't think he has made friends with the geezers, but I don't know for sure. Jerry sits in a chair while Gracie and I sit on the bench. It doesn't take long for Gracie to be bored – even in the presence of a talking monkey. She looks across the lawn. Two old ladies are playing croquet, using mallets to inefficiently move wooden balls around the emerald lawn.

"Can I go play ball with the biddies, Daddy?"

I nod yes, and she wanders over. The two old birds are delighted. They wave at me, hand my daughter a mallet, and I watch Gracie, hoping she doesn't whack one of them on the noggin.

Jerry goes inside and brings me some pill bottles. He sets them down and types, "Take a look. They are... hinky."

I smile in spite of myself, having convinced the boys at Welmar to put that word in Jerry's vocabulary mix on the arm band.

I take off the lids and spread the pills from each onto the bench. I take one of each and smell it. The color is a distinct gray, not the sterling white I myself am used to. I take the pill and put it on my tongue. No bitterness. More like flour or baking soda. Definitely hinky is my take too.

I reach into my pocket and take a two-compartment pill dispenser and hand it to Jerry. He takes it greedily and sets it on the seat next to his skinny little ass.

"Thank you." The look on his face is pure Gollum from *Lord of the Rings*. I am surprised he doesn't whisper, "My precious," upon seeing my pharma stash.

I am a little annoyed at Jerry's obvious greed at seeing the pills. I respond with a raised eyebrow. "I am not taking them every day. I checked. My dosage is twice yours. Take one of mine and it will fuck you up or you'll OD. Bite them in half."

Jerry nods. He uses a foot to hold the dispenser down and opens the lid with his one hand. He takes a pill and using his incisors, busts it in half. He swallows one half and puts the half judiciously back in, clicking the lid.

I nod at him, my eyes on Gracie as she is running those

old broads ragged with her red ball and mallet. I can hear all three of them cackling. I wish Karen was here to see it, but she is getting her starlet ready for a press conference tomorrow.

"Jer, my first take is your pills are imitations. They have the same shape and the right markings, but I would say they are placebos at best, fakes most likely. How did you come to get these?"

"Same. Delivery once a month. Van come. No words on side. I scan bottles. Desmond Pharmacy. Same bottles, different pills."

"How long?"

"Second month."

"Same guy?"

"Different guy. Rude asshole."

I nod. "I know a chemist here in town. I'll see if I can get him to analyze the chemical compounds in the pills they gave you. Find out if they are old or fake or whatever. I'm going to take them with me. Okay?"

He nods. "Not worth bowel movement."

"Gracie can't hear you from over there."

Jerry smiles. "I watch my typing around her. Behave gentleman."

"Thanks. Just remember to take it easy on the pills."

He nods and the smile on his face is one for the ages. "Wait," he says, then goes in the house. In a moment, Jerry comes out grinning, wearing a red MAGA hat. He types, "Surprise!"

We laugh hard. Jerry dances a bit. Maybe the half pill is hitting him a little already. However, he could be high on life.

"Where'd the hat come from?" I say, smiling at him.

"Made in China?" he asks, and we laugh even louder.

"Seriously, where did you get it?"

He nods back toward the care center's apartment. "Old codger die. I steal it out of his room when the ladies cry at his now-dead ceremony. He no need it. It look good on me?"

"You look very MAGA to me," I laugh back.

He frowns. "No, Jerry smart."

We laugh so hard the old ladies stop losing at croquet to watch us.

"Time to go," I say, giving him a hug. "I'll be back before I head south. Sorry I didn't get here in time to go to the record sale."

He waves it away as unimportant.

I scoop up the gray pills and put them back in their respective brown receptacles. Then I retrieve my daughter and thank the ladies before the trip back over the Golden Gate Bridge into the city.

That night, Karen and I take Gracie to a ramen joint in Chinatown. She loves trying to eat noodles with chopsticks. However, she is not very successful at getting much nourishment. We end up cutting the noodles into edible lengths with a knife and eat them with forks.

With full bellies, we head back to the Hotel Emblem, which is a cool place—decorated with posters of Beat poets and books by San Francisco authors stacked around. The bar is dimly lit and looks inviting, but Gracie is jabbering about a chopsticks-and-Cheerios challenge when we get home, so we whisk her right up to the room for jammies and a little reading. We're lucky. She is asleep right away.

We are fortunate enough to be in a suite on the seventh floor, the topper-most, popper most, and have two bedrooms. Karen and I share a little alone time. Later, good sleep by all three Roddy family, as Jerry would say.

In the morning, Karen is busy on the phone preparing her starlet for the big interview, so I got the kid. Gracie and I eat downstairs and unsuccessfully try out chopsticks on scrambled eggs and sausage patties. Then we're off to the chem labs. I know a guy who owes me from way back. I hand off the pills for analysis, and then Gracie and I are tourists. San Francisco can break your heart with cold, gloomy weather on a summer day, but not today. We ride the cable cars, go to Pier 39 with a million other folks to watch the seals, and later, we take a taxi winding down Lombard Street, leaning out the windows, gob-smacked with grins, which is Gracie's favorite thing. After a lunch at Ghirardelli Square at a Johnny Rockets where they dance on the counter for us, much to my daughter's delight, my phone chimes.

"Roddy."

"Rod, Mercer here."

That's the chemist.

"Yeah?"

"You're right. No active ingredients in those pills. Pressed flour and corn starch. Fakes. Pretty good imitations, stamped right, a little off in color."

"What do you know about Desmond Pharmacy? Why would they sub out pills on a one-armed monkey?"

There is a pause. Mercer once worked in the monkey lab creating compounds from hell to test on primates. He knows Jerry's story and I get a click of his tongue, like he is still dealing with the guilt of being involved in monkeys losing arms. I like that he feels bad about it. I like Mercer. He is a man of many talents and a keeper of many things the cops should not know about.

"I don't know," he says, "Gimmee an hour. I'll research them a little."

I take my girl back to the room. Karen is there banging away at her laptop. Gracie is too tired to lift her head off my shoulder. I take her into the far room and put her on the center of the bed.

"I got to see a guy," I say, entering the room.

"About a dog?" Karen asks without looking up.

"Monkey," I say, and I'm gone.

Mercer is waiting for me with a report. He has a Cheshire grin on his face.

"I take it you found something interesting," I say.

"Desmond Pharmacy changed hands two months ago," he says, lifting a printout.

"Jerry said he had a new delivery boy."

"New owners out of Philly. Beneficent Pharmaceutical of Philadelphia."

"And who owns BPP?"

"Murky at best. Most of them guys with a lot of vowels ending their names."

"Any in particular?"

"Otero."

"Johnny?"

"His nephew, Burt. No arrests, but big ambitions."

I nod. "So it ain't just Jerry getting fake pain pills?"

"Desmond delivers to 105 rest homes in the Bay area. Services over 15,000 clients."

"What percentage of old folks get a pain killer?"

"A goodly number, I'd say. Maybe a majority. And mostly more than one a day too."

"We're guessing ten thousand old folks around the city are experiencing joint pain and getting no relief today?"

Mercer nods.

"What's the street value of an Oxy right now? Or a Percocet?"

He shrugs and raises an eyebrow that I should know.

"I'm clean these days, bro. I really don't know."

Mercer nods, not buying my denial. "Let's say forty bucks."

"Do the math."

Mercer grabs a calculator. "Street value of eight hundred grand a day."

"Won't be able to get away with it very long. Somebody will catch on. Close 'em down."

Mercer sips an energy drink. "They are two months in." He cranks on the calc once more. "Maybe 48 million street value stolen so far."

I reach down and take a cigarette out of the pack in his front shirt pocket. "Gimme your lighter."

Mercer shakes his head. "You can't smoke in here."

"You can't smoke in San Francisco," I say and take the lighter which he is offering despite the warning. I laugh. "You own the joint. Gonna throw me out? Give me a ticket?"

"Don't own the building or the smoke detectors," he says, shrugging. Mercer then laughs too. His backroom is off limits to his employees at his little chemical company. I hand back him the lighter and he lights one too. Then he turns on a Dyson floor fan. There are no blades. It is both cool and it sucks. Get it?

I think for a second. "Fucking Jerry has me in deep shit with the Otero's again. Can I dip into your weapon bin?"

Mercer nods. "Take what you need."

I enter the safe room at the back of his shop. A nightmare of weapons dangle on trigger guards from hooks. I take a Springfield Armory Hellcat niner down and hold it in my big mitt. It looks kind of insignificant.

Mercer looks over his shoulder. "I have an extended mag for that. Thirteen plus one."

I nod and he indicates the drawer on the desk. I take the extra magazine and two boxes of shells.

"You got anything really off the books?"

Mercer laughs. "Everything hanging there is really off the

books. What you looking for? Nuclear weapons, flame throwers?"

"Bad shit. I'll know it when I see it. Whatcha got?"

Mercer's eyes light up. "You know what? I do have something for your sick, little, twisted mind. Got a couple flash bangs."

"What?

"Grenades. Just firebombs. Not fragmentation. No kill radius to speak of. Just concussion and then they kindle a flame to whatever is close. Old Army stuff, AN-14's, burning incendiary devices according to the label. A local guy in the National Guard liberates unneeded materiel for me on occasion."

Mercer goes to another drawer, this one locked. He opens it and takes two metal cylinders with the all-too-familiar Army script on their sides. "You're not fucking around, I see," he says, as I examine the grenades. "Why not call Johnny Law?"

"Might end up doing that. Best to be prepared. Can you bill Welmar for my order?"

He nods, laughing. "Anything for Jerry's kids."

I call Jerry and tell him his pills are bogus. He swears for a while, saying I told you so. I reply by asking him what he wants on his salad from Panera. Again, Jerry's wound up, and I can tell he's more than a little high, so I know he took a whole pill this morning. He goes on an obscene tear. I decide to ignore him and order two salads with the Fuji apples on them. I tell him I'll be there in two hours.

When I get there, he is literally bounding around the joint.

I look at him, amused. "They're just salads. Cool your jets."

"You late. We have meeting with the Desmond Pharmacy men. I call them from game room phone. Old lady help me find number and dial them. I tell them we knew the pills were bad. I told them we needed a sit down. We to meet down the hill in the park ten minutes ago."

"Jerry, that's nuts. Those guys are bad people. They are mafia," I say angrily. "They are criminals. Really bad guys." I pause. "Did you decide on the location or them?"

Jerry beams. "Them. They say very secluded. We talk freely there without worry."

"Very secluded, eh? Sounds like they mean to shut you up for good."

The monkey's face changes from glee to concern. "Kill Jerry? Think I should have consult you first?"

"Yeah, I think. Did you give them your name and address?"

"No, just Gerald Munk like on my prescriptions."

I drop my head. "So they have your address too. Well, we'll just leave. We no-show the meeting and get you somewhere safe. I guess we head back to my hotel. We can stash you there."

"Can't cancel. The press already be there."

"The press?"

"I invite *San Francisco Chronicle* attend meeting. Big news."

It is not getting any better. I put the salads I'd been holding into the fridge. I need a moment so I don't totally lose my shit here. After a couple of deep breaths, I ask, "What reporter did you call to attend the meeting?"

"Just name on the card I got if I have paper trouble—*San Francisco Chronicle*."

"Let me get this straight. You invited your paper boy to a meeting with the mob?"

"Yes." Jerry nods, smiling. "Timmy Jorgensen. He very responsive when I contact him about the late deliveries."

"His name is Timmy?"

"Yes, we ten minutes late."

"Go get in the car."

Jerry streaks out, jazzed for an outing to see the Oteros. I am less so. I turn off the lights and lock up. It doesn't look like we'll be back for a hot minute or two. And those salads looked delicious—and just out of reach. Damnation. Hungry again.

Let me set the stage. We're at the top of one of those big ass hills the region is famous for. Think of it as a big, inverted parabola. We're on the northside at the crest looking down into the park. Past the valley's bottom, perhaps a third of the way up the next hill's rise, there's a kid sitting on a picnic bench with his bike. Timmy from *The Chronicle*, no doubt. I watch the boy shift around at the table, rubbernecking the surroundings. Looking for Gerald Munk. I am hoping the boy leaves, but for now Timmy's a gamer, waiting to deal with a difficult customer on the path of his nascent business career.

Further on up the hill, just at the edge of the forest beyond, two black sedans are parked off the road. A man stands at each vehicle's passenger side. They look to be smoking. There are obviously more guys inside the vehicles. I inspect the surrounding hillside, but I don't see anybody out and about. There might be a sniper up in the trees, but that seems like a lot of trouble to go to for a geriatric Gerald Munk. They're just hoping he drives up and asks to get popped all by himself in the park. I'm pretty sure they have no idea he's a Rhesus monkey.

The two cars are separated by a telephone pole. High above them a transformer hums at the top, audible even from our distance. I see the trees beyond the wise guys and the access road beyond that. An idea forms and then I abandon it. Too cra-cra even for me.

Then I decide. What the hell? It's me, Timmy the news-paper delivery boy, and Jerry the one-armed talking monkey against the Otero mob. If ever there was time for cra-cra, this seems to be it.

I drive away from the park, circle the mile section and head down the access road behind the forest. I give Jerry his marching orders. He smiles broadly.

"Remember," I say to him, "just climb the tree closest to the telephone pole. Stay in cover in the limbs of the trees. Get as close as you can without being seen."

He nods. "No trouble climbing trees with only one hand. Easy Jerry."

I tie my jacket double around his skinny waist. I cinch it tight. Then I show him the grenades in the pockets.

"Just remove the grenades, pull the pins, and let them drop on the slope of the hill. When you pull the first pin, you drop it immediately. Got that? Pull pin. Drop. Pull second pin. Drop. Just stay in cover and climb back down the tree. Stay hidden up there until I come get you. If it gets hairy, then head back to your place and keep all the lights off. If I beat you there, where is your hidden house key? You have one?"

"Hidden in tin skirting around chimney on roof."

I sigh. "Your hidden key is on your roof?"

He shrugs. "Easy Jerry."

I nod wearily. "Okay, we're not going to fight these guys. You're just a diversion. When the grenades go off, I'm going to go grab Timmy and get the fuck out of there. Okay?"

"Pull pin and drop."

"Yes, you ready?"

Jerry smiles. "Born ready."

Of course, it goes down without a hitch. And you know that's bullshit. Total cluster. And I mean *total*.

Jerry is to wait until I get back in position with the rental. He doesn't, and he doesn't stay in the cover of the trees. The little dork monkey-walks, for lack of a better description, across the line out to the telephone pole with the transformer. Jerry makes his way there using a guidewire above he can hold with his one hand. His feet grip the line below with each step. I note his tail is also wrapped around the line above as he progresses out into full view.

"You stupid little bastard," I say under my breath, arriving back at the crest on the other side of the valley. I hope none of the three men will notice Jerry up above them as he is. All heads are down, watching the access road. They seem to have noticed me, but not Jerry. So far, so good—kinda.

Once safely on the pole, my monkey friend is all business. Jerry takes the first grenade from his jacket pocket. He looks across the way toward me with a shit-eating grin on his face. He waves stupidly at me, grenade in hand. It makes me flinch. Gleefully, Jerry places the grenade between his feet as he sits on the stand holding the transformer. Then the little fella, like a champ, pulls the pin and drops that grenade from both feet like the hot potato it is.

The incendiary device bounces once on the slope, descending in one hop where it actually goes under the car on the left. The explosion is massive. The gas tank must have combusted in sync with the flashbang. The concussion from the grenade almost knocks Jerry off his perch all the way up there. It definitely fucks with the guys standing there smoking cigs. They go flying like the Wallendas. If there was anybody in the car, say on a cell phone, their service was interrupted permanently.

I am already speeding down the hill in the rental. Timmy is now standing up on the picnic bench, staring wide-eyed at the conflagration. Stretching out, he is offering the biggest target his four-foot frame can muster. I floor it and streak down the hill.

The wise guys exiting the second vehicle have moxie. They are still all about me and remember there is the distraction of a car burning right beside them and three of their buddies toppled into the ditch. Two get out and begin to blast my way. The slowest man, maybe their leader, is last out of the not-flaming car. He looks up at the telephone pole. Jerry has recovered from the first explosion and has the second grenade in his fist. The guy on the ground sees the monkey and decides to inflict damage on my little compatriot. How many times he shoots is difficult to distinguish due to the frequent shots at me by the other two. All I know is I can see the man firing up at Jerry.

I slide the rental to a stop near the picnic table. Timmy looks terrified. I leave the car, exiting the driver's door, running around the backside of the vehicle. There is no time even to reach for my weapon. I gallop toward the kid. My stride is big, but on my metal stilts, I lumber along. Nobody watching would actually call what I am doing running, but I make good time crossing the thirty feet to the kid. I snatch him off his pedestal, slide down the bank, and hustle us into the trees.

Jerry has pulled the second pin, this time with his teeth, but a bullet slams into the pole next to him. He falls back in natural reaction to the velocity of the round and the splinters flying from the post. He loses his grip on the grenade. It topples backward into the gap between the transformer and the pole.

I'll say this: Gerald Munk has good instincts. It is no time to think about whether to reach in and try to recover the grenade. Nope, it is time to get out of Dodge. Jerry vacates the pole and hurries out on the line. This time he is down low, hand, both feet, and tail all wrapped around the single line below him. He scurries away down the line. Bullets ring out. One second, then two, pass, then the blast. The transformer, of course, goes too. It is a terrific concussion. The line Jerry is on bends low and then whips back like a bullwhip. It separates into two strands and Jerry is on the downward side of the break, much to his benefit. He is ass-first at the end of the string, arcing out along the pendulum of the freed line. It swings him roughly into the trees, and Jerry's voice rings through the cacophony, "Motherrrrrr-fuckerrrrr!" in Pee Wee Herman's excited tone.

I laugh in spite of myself, and Timmy looks at me like I am insane. I will have to trust his judgement.

Meanwhile, Jerry begins to bounce off tree trunks like a pinball on the bumpers as he reenters the foliage. I lose sight of the little bastard, marveling that he is still alive at last glimpse.

I am holding Timmy close to my chest. He is crying.

Otero's thugs decide to cut their losses. They inspect their three guys in the ditch. They pick up two, both injured. After looking at one, they leave him. The one viable vehicle screams out of the park and heads south toward the city.

"What happened?" Timmy asks me through his traumatized breaths.

"Are you okay?"

He blinks. "What happened?" he asks again.

"Didn't you see those guys up there drinking booze? They

were drunk and had guns. They shot up at the telephone pole. The transformer blew up. Wow, what a big explosion! Did you see it happen?"

Timmy of the *San Francisco Chronicle* nods, accepting, even believing, my explanation. "Yes, I saw it." He does not mention any monkeys and I omit Jerry from the story.

The cops arrive after we have our story straight. They interview us together and apart. They can't shake us. "Bad guys with booze and guns shot a transformer on the telephone pole and it blew up. Something fell and the car blew up too."

The story will run the next day with a decent photo of the kid's mug. "Paper Boy Witnesses Explosion." I bet Timmy will be a big hit with the girls in home room after that.

As regards the story, Timmy is branded a hero. I am not mentioned by name and noted only as a security guard for the nearby convalescent care facility. Welmar Industries is responsible for the omission. They have that kind of pull with the press, but I get word Bob Lee is not happy. I tend to do lots of stuff that makes the boss man unhappy, so it is just another day. Night falls. I will live to fight again tomorrow. Jerry too.

I find him in the woods and take him back with me.

Morning. I will find out just how unhappy Lee and his one unpatched, jaundiced eye are in just an hour. Mr. Lee's personal secretary (a solemn man named Orson who carries a tiny .28 caliber in his shoulder holster) calls before I go to bed and tells me curtly to be in Welmar's offices at eight a.m. in the morning.

I am awake already when the newspaper is delivered to our hotel room just before dawn. I order coffee via room service while Jerry lies in bed beside me. Karen and the kid slumber in the other room. I have been banished to the room for animals. Gracie's words, but Karen's sentiments. Jerry scans Timmy's article with his roller and I listen.

"I go back to sleep after newspaper read. Jerry sore as hell from hitting trees. Take full pill today."

I nod vacantly, heading for the shower, noting the other bedroom door is still shut and all is quiet. Karen's last nerve was definitely jangled by Jerry and me being in a gunfight, but what's a guy to do?

"Roddy, what the hell are you thinking?"

Bob Lee's voice is loud and angry.

"You take that damn monkey with you to participate in a hair-brained adventure facing off with armed criminals. Don't you realize our goal is to keep Jerry out of the press? Guns, kids, mobsters, drugs, and explosions. Jesus, Roddy, what the hell? You're not even legal to drive a rental car. Your license is restricted to hand-control vehicles. And you rented it using your corporate credit card."

I sit back in Lee's deep wingback chair in his comfy office on Russian Hill. The coffee is full eclipse black. The view is spectacular. The chair's leather is supple. The room is bathed in a soothing light. Bob's suit is tailored and his tie knotted perfectly too. In fact, everything is perfect. Well, not Bob. I noticed his face is mottled red except for the white-as-marble tip on his nose. I think to ask him if it is just cartilage or if it gets cold because of poor circulation. I decide now is a bad time. Mulling my observations, I realize with a start that my boss has continued shouting at me. I look attentive. He goes on a while about me driving a car with my prosthetics.

Finally, Lee's diatribe is slowing. He looks at me to respond.

I laugh, "Really? That's your take? The Otero crime family is running a twenty-five million a month scam on old folks in the Bay Area, they stage a meeting in a secluded spot to kill Jerry and me, a little kid's life was in jeopardy, a man dies after an explosion, telephone lines are out of service for over three thousand customers, the old folks up the hill don't get cable TV for a whole night, and you're concerned I rented a car without proper credentials?"

Bob shrugs angrily. "A good deal of that mayhem was either because of you or that troublesome chimp."

"Not really a chimp. Actually a monkey. Rhesus monkey, Jerry." God, I am starting to talk like the little bastard.

"Shut up, Roddy."

I nod.

"Anything else you were planning on springing on me"" Lee asks as he stands and moves to the window. The lawn of the tiny park across the street looks manicured. Gardeners probably trim it with nose clippers.

"I paid to have Jerry's pills analyzed. I also bought a few things out the backdoor of the shop. Told them to bill you."

"Who?"

"Mercer Chemical Labs."

Lee nods. He knows Mercer. "What did you buy? Drugs?"

I lean back, giving fake offense. "No, of course not. An unregistered niner, an extra mag, two boxes of shells and stuff."

"Stuff?"

"A couple of incendiary grenades. They were old. Army surplus, or maybe plundered."

"I take it the transformer didn't just blow up after an errant shot by the Otero boys?"

"Oh, it blew up big time. It just had different help than we told the cops."

Lee considers these new facts. "I didn't think you got close enough to throw a grenade. Weren't they a couple hundred yards away from the kid? How is he anyway?"

"Kid is fine," I say, leading with my strong suit. "As for the grenades, Jerry came in through the trees on the telephone line. He delivered the payload." I smile broadly and circle back to the positive. "Our newsman Timmy is fine. Enjoying elevated status in his fifth-grade class as we speak. Suddenly he is visible to the popular girls. And boys, I guess. Let us not judge orientation harshly. It *is* San Francisco."

Lee does not speak. He just leans back and shakes his head. "I never imagined I'd be debriefing an operative about a monkey with grenades. Well, at least you didn't discharge your firearm. The police have listed the decedent's cause as death by misadventure—discharging a weapon while intoxicated. Stray bullet hit the transformer. Mayhem ensured. We've avoided a national news story."

He turns to me. "Where is Jerry?"

"I left him in the hotel room with Karen and my daughter. When I left, he was teaching Gracie to make fart sounds with his underarm. They are fast friends."

Lee forces a smile, although with trepidation. "Okay, keep him under cover until the feds close this thing out. They are at the BPP pharm distribution center as we speak. Shutting it down. Arresting anyone who's still around. Unfortunately, your antics probably spooked the Oteros, and they'll have vacated the premises already. That's just my supposition. If you would have come to me..."

I cut him off. "It was not my intent to engage the Oteros. Jerry called them to complain about his pills. They decided to silence him."

"After which, you armed him with grenades," Lee retorts.

"There is that."

"Go back to the hotel. Stay in for the day. Let the FBI and the DEA close down Desmond Pharmacy operations. Can you do that?"

"Absolutely. These days I don't look for trouble."

Lee grimaces. "That doesn't mean it doesn't still find you."

I don't go to the movie premier with Karen. Having me at her work events with all the pretty people just doesn't work out. I put on a silly suit, tux and tails, whatever, and I look like Peter Boyle in *Young Frankenstein*—sleeves stretched tight over my bulging biceps, tux pants tucked into combat boots. If I stand next to her, Karen fields questions all night, like:

"Why do you need security?" or "Have you received threats?" So, we agree. I stay at the hotel and watch the kid.

That Tuesday night, Jerry is also with us. For entertainment, I buy three elastic hairbands and a deck of cards. I also get three rolls of pennies from the desk. We eat pizza, drink Sprite, and play "no-peek-'em" poker in the hotel room. All of us have headbands on, a single card stuck on our foreheads, and fifty pennies to bet. We each have to ante and then bet based upon the cards on our two opponents' heads. Low cards on your opponents' foreheads means drop a heavy bet down.

The game does not go well. First Jerry cheats with the mirror outside the bathroom. He keeps peeking at it to see what card he has stuck to his forehead. Then he either folds or doubles down. Cheating little punk. I have to cover the mirror with a sheet. Next after losing, he refuses to accept that an ace is high card. It is lower than the deuce, he insists. Gracie is getting unhappy as Jerry is winning with rule changes. When she ends up with a joker, Jerry demands both jokers should have been removed from the deck. His ten high should win. There are nine pennies in the pot, so it is a big deal.

Gracie pushes the large pot of pennies off the bed onto the floor with her feet. "This is bullshit," she says. The lady, just shy of three, folds her arms as she leaves us to go to the TV. She grabs the remote and turns on *Nick at Night*.

Jerry looks at me. "Little Roddy girl, like you, too competitive."

I laugh. "Swears just like you."

Jerry grins.

"But you're right," I say, "She's definitely my gal. I think I'll keep her."

Jerry looks concerned. "You have considered selling?"

I am saved from having to explain by the phone ringing.

It is Bob Lee.

"It's done. You were right on the major details. The pharmacy workers were in a large, unmarked building near the Embarcadero. The prescriptions were filled by machines. The pills are in huge dispensers. The dispensers arrive in unmarked trucks with armed guards. No one tests product efficacy at the facility. They just maintain the automation filling the dispensers, and the scripts for each care facility end up packaged together. Nobody knew anything. Pain killers tested in the dispensers on site are indeed fake. Also, some very expensive cancer treatments were bogus too. Patients have died as a result. It's good we shut them down.

"But thanks to you and Jerry, all the pharma management is already gone. We're looking at the manifests for today's flights to Philly, but no dice. Those involved have gone to ground. No arrests."

I thank him and hang up the phone.

It rings again not fifteen seconds after.

I pick it up. "Yeah, Bob. What'd you forget?"

"I ain't Bob. We ain't met."

"Gotcha. Who are you trying to reach, kind sir with the East Coast greaseball accent?"

"You, smart ass. Got a message for you. This is coming from Philly. From the top."

"From Johnny or from Burt? Who's running things for the Otero's out here in Cali?"

"Smart ass. Too smart. Gonna get you in trouble. Already did."

"You're not the first to say that. What's the message? Do I need a pencil?"

"Understand you were involved in causing folks in San Fran to shut down operations a few weeks early. Million dollar a day operation."

"Not me. The FBI and DEA did the closing."

"Nah, we got the straight stuff. It was you and a guy from the old folk's home. Some geezer named Gerald Munk. We got a real problem with your actions. Him too."

"I have to insist it was not our doing. And Gerald Munk is just an old guy who got bum pills from you. He complained. You had to know people would eventually complain when you take their candy away."

There is a laugh on the other end of the line. "Yeah, somebody always wants to get numb on pills. Bitching about hurting. I got no sympathy for drug users."

"Bad take for a pharmacy owner. How many chains have you owned? I take it this west coast business venture was not your first foray into pharmacy fraud?"

"Smart ass. We can shut you down too. You tell that old fart Gerald Munk to be careful answering the door. We might come visit."

The line goes dead.

Jerry looks at me. "Who that?"

"Room service. Wanted us to know they have ice cream if we want some."

Jerry nods with a shit-eating grin. Ice cream, it is, then.

~

The next morning, Karen is alternatingly beaming with joy at the reviews of her starlet's performance in the film's premier showing and frowning at me for the request I make of her. The frowns eventually win and she takes Gracie alone to the airport. The two of them fly the shuttle home. Jerry and I drive the rental car back to L.A. We arrive six hours after the girls. We listen to the Allman Brothers' *Eat a Peach* all the way back.

I drop the rental car at the airport, but Karen tells us to Uber our monkey asses home. The car is tiny and I don't fit in the backseat. I think the model is a Chrysler Crouton. It's a tight fit, but the So Cal night was perfect on the ride, windows down, to *mi casa*. However, upon arrival, Karen is still irritable. Nice night, chilly inside. But what's a guy and a monkey to do?

I make Jerry comfortable in the old servant's quarters room off of our kitchen. Karen suggests I bunk on the couch for the night. I get extra blankets because, buddy, it is cold on the home front. However, my gal and my daughter both give me a peck on the cheek before they head upstairs for the night. I know my banishment is temporary. Jerry watches the girls disappear. Then he asks, "Got any weed?"

As a matter of fact, I do have my one-hitter. That's how we roll in Cali, I tell him. Again, Jerry with the shit-eating grin.

And that, boys and girls, is the story of how Jerry came to live with us.

THE BIG JANGLE, PART 3

Bob Lee's call is at six a.m. the Sunday after Jerry comes to live with us. I answer. There is a solemnity in Lee's tone that makes me roll out of bed and head down to the kitchen before responding.

"Okay, give it to me," I say, looking out the window at the pale dawn. I am still not ready for the straight shit, whatever it may be, but I am fully awake—every nerve tingling, every sense heightened.

"Need you to go to London," Lee says.

"Okay, why?"

"Need you to identify a body."

I pause, knowing I could get a call like this someday, but I still can't believe it.

"We sure it's Grace?"

"If we were sure we wouldn't need you to identify the body."

"They send a photo?"

"No, this is all back channels. No documents, no photos. This never happened, okay?"

I nod, then realize he is waiting for a response, so I say, "Yeah. Got it." I then ask another question. "Grace and his team were working in Great Britain?"

"No, MI6 retrieved the body in Istanbul. There was an explosion at the Grand Bazaar, terrorism related."

I seem to remember seeing a news story and google it on the iPad.

The Grand Bazaar in Istanbul is one of the largest and oldest covered markets in the world, with 61 covered streets and over 4,000 shops within a total area of four-square miles. Up to a half million people a day go there. I find a small news story, but there are no details of the explosion. Nothing in the two paragraphs describe the event as involving terrorism. There are no forthcoming details.

Again, I realize Lee is waiting for me to speak. "What about the rest of his team?"

"Not on a landline. St. Clair will meet your flight and fill you in."

That answers one question. St. Clair was one of the team. At least all four aren't dead. Bob and I discuss logistics for a moment, but I'm not really with him. We hang up, and I just sit there with the phone in my hand for a good five minutes. Bad dream? Nope. I am fucking awake.

I wake Karen and we both cry for a moment, having had our worst worries about Grace seemingly realized. Then I'm all business. I pack a bag and grab my passport. Bob Lee made the arrangements. A limo picks me up an hour later. I am in the air in two.

I review what I know about Grace's team while in flight. There had been four of them in a "cell," modeled after the use of a small team of men who move independently and without connection to a larger unit. The separation made them hard to track, hard to betray, and hard to find. Unfortunately, it also made them hard to protect.

Grace's unit included St. Clair, a mercenary from France, although of Scottish lineage. St. Clair is a weapons and tactical specialist. His husband, Taymur, whom we call the Moor, is a giant of a man. A true one-man wrecking crew on the battlefield, but a kind and soft soul off of it. Two gay mercenaries might wrinkle people's brows, but not folks in the business of violence. It would not be the first time I had met the two men, partnered in life and in the field. I saw them in action once, and they are the real deal.

The final member of the cell was Grace's personal bodyguard and the unit's language specialist, William Twelve Moons, a diplomatic officer in the Iraq war and a native American from the Rincon Band of Luiseño tribe. Twelve Moons' job was to keep Grace alive.

St. Clair, true as the North Star, is waiting on my flight at Heathrow. He nods as I clear customs. Expedited by Lee's influence, I walk right through with a wave of my passport and visa. St. Clair's husband, Taymur, is not with him. I look for signs of sorrow on his face, but his visage is stone. Unyielding of any news of my friend.

St. Clair is Scottish and his bloodline royal, but his family had long ago moved to France because of their Catholicism during the reign of Elizabeth I. Evidently, the St. Clair's were more the Mary, Queen of Scots sort—vengeful and prone to attempting to kill those who crossed them. St. Clair is a good friend and a bad foe.

St. Clair looks different than when I had last seen him. He is a pale ruddy man normally, but not now. His face and arms are darkened, too deeply bronzed to be called tanned. I remember he and Grace were using skin dye to better blend in with the population in the Middle East. St. Clair's normally red hair is long and dyed black to match an equally black beard. A ponytail trails down his back. He is wearing dark Persol sunglasses, though it is now night in London. Eleven hours have passed since I left Los Angeles.

"What happened?"

St. Clair only nods, taking my duffel. "Tell you in the car."

"Where's the Moor?"

St. Clair lights a Dunhill and offers me the pack. I take it and light up as well. He doesn't speak until he pulls the black Land Rover from the curb where it is illegally parked. "Taymur is fine. He's in Belgium. We weren't there for the explosion. Your boys at Langley pulled the two of us." He raises an eyebrow. "A week before."

"You left Grace behind in Turkey? The CIA pulls you out and then Grace gets blown up just days later? Sounds hinky. I don't believe in coincidence."

St. Clair shakes his head. "Maybe it was just that. I don't know."

"Why?" I ask, frustrated with St. Clair's reluctance to part with information. To show my pique, I lean in and blow a mouthful of smoke into his face. He grimaces at the childish act and responds by switching lanes. More silence. But eventually he speaks.

"Why? Why were we pulled from the team? Because of the Moor. Taymur is too easy to identify. A six feet-nine monster weighing nearly three hundred pounds? Word started getting around that a 'jinn,' the Islamic term for a huge creature essentially like the Jewish golem, was arriving in Arab cities like an angel of death." St. Clair blows out smoke to match mine. "And wherever we went, believe me, we left death."

"They left Grace with just one guy. Just Twelve Moons? The two of them uncovered and exposed?"

"No, they brought in two good guys. Two Chechen mercenaries, twin brothers. Real pros." St. Clair looks at me. "I wouldn't have left if I thought they weren't up to the job."

I nod, but I am not happy.

"Khasan and Vakha Bahaev. Islamic, identical twins," explains St. Clair. "They speak Arabic and Farsi perfectly. Khasan, an explosives specialist, and Vakha, a gunner. Perfect for the kind of shenanigans we were up to, which was not good stuff at all. We did bad shit, Roddy."

"Where did you last see Grace? In Turkey?"

"No, Egypt. The two Chechens arrived just before the Moor and I rotated out. But I knew them by reputation before then. Total pros. We met them in Egypt. Hurghada, the Riviera of the Red Sea. A resort town. A private villa for the assassination team, a little down time."

"And?"

"We got word the jihad on Grace was being paid for by a mullah hiding out in Malta. Just didn't know a name or address, but Malta is small. We were working on how to locate the mullah when the CIA sent word that Taymur and I were out. I don't know why the team went to Turkey. These things are always strictly need-to-know. I would have thought the next move was Malta, but once I was out..." The French/Scot shrugs.

"They went to Turkey because the CIA needed one more terrorist dead before Grace came home?" I say bitterly.

St. Clair turns his head toward mine, noting my cynicism. He stares at me long and intensely as we sit at the light. "Could be," he finally says. "Yeah, that is probably it. Just one more job before they let Grace off the hook. Grace's brother Scott was our handler at the agency, and he's a brutal SOB, a real bastard. I can tell you that."

"Where we headed?"

"To the rendezvous. MI6 sent coordinates."

"Their HQ?"

"No." St. Clair smiles grimly. "They don't keep dead bodies at Vauxhall Cross, 85 Albert Embankment," he says. "They're finicky about dead people laying on slabs over there. It messes with the buffet. We're to visit an afterhours coroner they keep off the books. The lads're expecting us. Just minutes away. I pray they've made a mistake."

"Yeah, me too."

We cross the Thames at Hammersmith and entered Battersea. We arrive at a non-descript gray stone building with no identifying markings, other than the street address. St. Clair parks along the curb. We leave the vehicle and mount the long-mottled marble steps in front of the building. As we approach the front doors, I can hear electronic locks release. They are obviously watching and expecting us. I estimate they knew when I exited the plane as well. St. Clair pulls the door open. The air inside smells of Pine-Sol floor cleaner.

Inside, the two of us are alone in a lobby. Two elevators wait with infinite patience, and there are no designations of offices or occupants listed on the empty tenant board. No furniture. Nothing on the walls. Mahogany panels rise above marble floors in silence. I can see dust clinging in long tethers out of reach of the cleaning staff. Smoke has tinged the walls higher up, yellow gray on white stone near the ceiling. Just for fun, I press the elevator buttons, trying to light up every floor. Neither set functions, and I notice a card reader below the buttons. Secured floors.

We wait. Figuring we are on camera, St. Clair makes an obvious point of lighting two more Dunhills, offering me one. We smoke, finish, and stub them out with our heels on the shiny marble floor. We consider lighting a second, but then the elevator dings. A tall drink of a man in a dark suit and red bowtie steps free of the doors.

"Thanks for arriving promptly," our liaison says, nonplussed, with a crisp accent. "I'm Wilson-Davies. Before I

take you down to the morgue, I'm to brief you. We'll go up to
five to a conference room, then to the basement."

I nod. "Thank you, Mr. Davies." I begin to introduce the
two of us, but he cuts me off.

"I'm sorry. My last name is Wilson-Davies. My first name
is Brian." Then he smiles sadly and shakes our hands. He
only says, "Bloody awful business, this." He asks of us, "You
are O'Malley and you are St. Clair?"

We nod. Wilson-Davies steps back into the elevator and
bids us to join him. The elevator doors close, he inserts a
card, and we are whisked away.

Upstairs on five, we are ensconced at a long table in a
conference room. Wilson-Davies presses a button on the
microphone device. "Three cuppas," he says into it.

The British agent turns and reaches into a side table's top
drawer and sets an ashtray on the table. "You can smoke if
you like. Noticed you light up while you were waiting. We
really don't mind. Concerned with larger matters. I'm sure
you understand."

A younger man in a similar suit to Wilson-Davies' arrives
momentarily with the tea and service. In his early twenties,
he is well-trained to avoid any eye contact with either St.
Clair or me. The youngish man moves with traditional
British stiffness as he delivers a kettle on a cozy, cups, and
cream to our table. His banded tie I recognize as one from
the colleges at Oxford, but I am not knowledgeable on which
one. I note his one furtive glance at my legs. He's obviously
been briefed that I am a double amputee. I nod at his peek,
and the young man blushes, returning his gaze to the floor.
He seems nothing more than a younger version of the man

seated in front of us. He will be Brian Wilson-Davies in two decades. When the rookie leaves, Wilson-Davies drops a sugar cube into his cup and motions us to drink. He takes a sip, returns the cup to its saucer, and finally looks as if he is getting down to business.

"Yes, I trust your journey was pleasant," he says to me.

"Cut the bullshit if you don't mind," I snort. "I've been in transit for half a day to identify the body of my best friend. Let's get the show on the road if you don't mind." I motion to St. Clair to pass me the smokes. I light one and blow smoke across the table. It seems my only move is blowing smoke at people's nostrils.

"Certainly," Wilson-Davies says, raising an eyebrow as if I had breached the etiquette of his Etonian code. "I understand these things tend to be personal, as it were."

"What happened?" I ask.

"Yes, well, we only know a little."

"Give me what you got."

"MI6 has interests, as does the U.S., in Turkey. We have agents on the ground in Istanbul. We have known in the past of Iranian teams operating out of the market and its chaos. Last week, our surveillance, electronic and on the street, started picking up chatter of activity in the Grand Bazaar."

St. Clair sips his cuppa and offers a Dunhill to Wilson-Davies. Surprisingly, the agent takes it, lights it, and sucks smoke into his lungs.

Breathing out a cloud, the British spy smiles. "But chatter is hardly enough for anyone to go on. The Grand Bazaar is nearly as big as the island of Manhattan in your New York City. We hardly have enough manpower to even monitor events as they take place. We were, however, at the ready with our coms at this occurrence."

"When did the shit go down?"

"Last Saturday evening. Reports began to arrive at the consulate of a firefight taking place in the bazaar in the northeast quadrant. The 'shit,' as you say, was indeed going down."

Wilson-Davies smiles as if pleased with himself and his use of American vernacular. He continues, "Of course, we had no idea initially that Yanks were involved. It could have easily been an Al Qaeda attack. We initiated observation teams to adjacent locales and began electronic surveillance within fifteen minutes of the first signs of altercation. Quite a lot of gun play, even before the bomb went off. Imagine our surprise when the communications taking place on radio frequencies were in English!"

"Do you have a transcript?"

"Sorry, security clearance issues there, but I am allowed to tell you that it appears to have been an American team going in to eliminate an Iranian Shi'a cell."

"And things went sideways."

"Indeed."

Wilson-Davies takes a sip of tea and puffs his cig for a moment before he continues, "The head of the cell was cornered in a subterranean series of tunnels. Istanbul is filled with cisterns and wells, sometimes three levels below the street. It is an ancient city built on top of many previous incarnations of itself."

I nod, understanding. "Grace and his team trap the bad

guys below ground. The *numero uno* bad guy figures out he is a goner and he lights up the whole block."

"Yes, that is essentially it," Wilson-Davies says and sits silent for a moment, letting it sink in. He puffs on the Dunhill with diligence.

"Did you confirm the kills?"

"On the Shi'a side? Oh, no. The tunnels collapsed. Later, they filled with water from Istanbul's water mains. We're fairly certain no one survived."

"But you recovered at least one body?"

"Just the one we thought to be on your team. Armed with Western weaponry. There were others, distinctly Turkish, that we left behind, all those at street level. Actually, near the dwelling's entrance. The rest was not navigable."

"Any chatter afterwards?"

"Oh, radio silence from our Shi'a friends. Americans went silent too. Plenty from the Turks."

"And from the Turks? What did they say?"

"From the police, mainly crowd control, investigating the explosion, which, by the way, has been explained to the press as a gas leak."

"And from intelligence?"

"Turkey's MIT intelligence agency has also been mostly mum, but we did learn they have at least one, perhaps two, prisoners. American team or Iranian cell, we do not know which. The Gendarmerie in Istanbul reports to the Minister of the Interior, which would be like having your Secretary of the Interior control your intelligence services. Our relationship there is not good, not with the Minister, and not with the MIT, which is like your FBI."

"Except the MIT is much more uncivilized than the FBI."

"If you say so." Wilson-Davies smirks.

"Are either of their prisoners Americans?"

"We honestly don't know. Nothing in our reports, but our knowledge is limited. MIT is not forthcoming, as you might imagine."

St. Clair speaks for the first time, "The bloody Turks have the worst prisons on earth, bloody bastards."

"Yes," says Wilson-Davies, notably surprised at St. Clair's Scottish lilt. "Metris Prison in Istanbul is far from the worse of the Turkish centers of incarceration, but it is bad enough. We think that is where the two prisoners, if there are two and they are both still alive, are being held. Our sources say a Colonel in the MIT named Aksoy Demir, a brute even by Turkish standards, has been the officer-in-charge of investigating the explosion at the Grand Bazaar. He has been on our radar for a good bit. Not a likeable bloke."

"Anything else?"

"No, I believe you now know what we do. Except, to view the body. We recovered it before Turkish police arrived. He carried a B&T APC9 Pro-K Sub Compact 9 by 19 dangling by a strap around his neck," Wilson-Davies pauses. "That is an American-made submachine gun."

"We know what kind of gun it is. Both of us are experienced with firearms," I say.

"Yes, I've read your file," Wilson-Davies says. "You definitely know guns." He turns to St. Clair. "However, it says you are French. We seldom make errors in our background checks." The spy raises an eyebrow at my companion.

"Scot at one time," St. Clair says, but then adds, "Only on my mother's side."

Wilson-Davies shrugs. "As for the dead man," he says, "it looks as if the collapsible stock of the weapon penetrated his abdomen from the force of the blast. Death would have been painful, but quite quick if that is any consolation. I read the coroner's report personally." He smiles awkwardly, showing his discomfiture.

"We removed the body and stored it in our temporary morgue at the consulate in Istanbul. The day afterwards, we received word from your CIA through channels that you were looking for a yank operative missing a left leg. Your Clayton Grace." The MI6's officer's face shows his remorse.

"Unfortunately, the body we had in the cooler was missing a leg as well. We contacted your agency, agreed to transport the body by embassy plane, and here you are."

My heart sinks with his words, but I steel myself, nodding and doing my level best to show no emotion. "Okay, let's do the deed."

"Yes," says Wilson-Davies rising from his seat and stubbing out his cigarette. "Shall we?"

THE BIG JANGLE, PART 4

"It's not him."

It's difficult to feel elation looking at a dead body, but that is my emotion. I look to St. Clair. His expression is different than mine. His frown is pronounced. The Brits don't serve their beer cold, but they certainly keep dead bodies on ice. The place is freezing, and I can see St. Clair's breath come from his open mouth. His sorrow is palatable. St. Clair's face has a tint of blue on his lips, like the body in front of us, yet I feel like doing a cartwheel.

"You know him?" I ask St. Clair who is silent.

"Ay, it's either Khasan or Vakha."

I take the sheet covering the body from Wilson-Davies' hands. I pull it back past the gaping wound in the abdomen when the gun's machine stock penetrated. I proceed until I can see the corpse's single leg. Where the second should be, instead I saw a wound torn and raw just below the left knee.

A new wound, and most likely, a mortal one. Without help, a man would bleed out in a minute or less from such an injury.

St. Clair explains to Wilson-Davies, "It's not Clayton Grace, the American. It is, however, a member of the team. He's either Khasan or Vakha Bahaev; they are, er, or were, Chechen contractors. Identical twins, so I don't know which it is."

Wilson-Davies raises an eyebrow. "The Americans are hiring Chechen rebels these days? I heard there was a labor shortage, but I had no idea."

I don't dignify his words with an answer. I am too happy, and there is no reason to stay in this frozen morgue any longer.

We thank Wilson-Davies on the elevator on the way up from the dingy freezer below the street. In the lobby, we shake hands and quickly depart, ensuring him that the American Embassy will be in touch about taking possession of the deceased. Then it is goodbye.

Before St. Clair pulls away from the curb on the way to our hotel, I am on the phone.

Bob Lee is as relieved as me that the stiff on the slab isn't Grace. I tell him what I need. Lee asks me to give him until morning to secure permission. I suggest we proceed and apologize later. He disagrees. Secretary Welmar will have to be briefed at Defense, and my requests will also have to be channeled through State. I hang up, impatient and wanting to fly to Turkey and find my friend.

Once in our suite, St. Clair orders a bottle of Lagavulin 16-year-old scotch whiskey. He pours three fingers in each of two glasses. After a swig, I call Karen. I tell her it isn't Grace and she begins to cry with relief. I ask her to get hold of Rat and let him know. He can let the rest of our band of brothers know. However, I warn her that the news is not good, just not the worst. We still have no information about Grace's whereabouts. He is missing, maybe dead in a pile of rubble three floors down underwater, or he may be a prisoner in one of the worst prisons on earth.

Our situation has changed markedly. We know the dead body isn't Clayton Grace, but we still have no idea where Grace is. But I have a sneaking suspicion that a Turkish Colonel in the MIT named Aksoy Demir might know.

By the time St. Clair and I arrive in Istanbul, diplomatic channels are transacting at full bore.

Turkish officials first assure the American diplomatic corps they have no prisoners apprehended from the Grand Bazaar, then after the British intercepts are injected into the conversation, they admit to having two prisoners. However, the Turks insist neither is American. By evening of the second day, after Secretary Welmar threatens to cease all arms sales to the Turk army, the American Embassy is okayed to send a medical team to the Metris Prison to tend to the prisoners.

Clayton Grace and Vakha Bahaev are released before nightfall. Both are in rough shape. Despite my protests and

St. Clair's choice words, we are not allowed to see either man that night. Doctor's orders.

Morning. In a ward at the Turkish American embassy, a doctor and two nurses hover over our two heroes. It is first light. I enter the embassy way before dawn. I begin pounding on the infirmary doors at 4:30 a.m. They finally open the door to tell me to be quiet at five. The looks I am getting tell me I am not their favorite American, not at this hour.

Shortly thereafter, looking cross and tired, the ambassador arrives at the patients' door, insisting we leave there and join him at his office. I refuse, so he shrugs, goes inside the patient ward, closing the door behind him. In a moment, St. Clair and I are escorted to the small medical wing.

The ambassador says to us, "The doctors say you two may have five minutes. But let's be clear, both men are very ill, not only from their injuries in the explosion, but secondarily at the hands of their Turkish jailers. Keep them calm. The next forty-eight hours is critical for both Clayton Grace and Vakha Bahaev. There is time down the road for their debriefs. Are we clear?"

We nod and enter.

Grace's face is thin. His skin is very dark, so dark that Vakha Bahaev, who seems in better shape than Clayton, tells us the Turks believed Grace to be North African. After capture,

Grace refused to speak at all, not wanting to give himself away. His Arabic was still poor. Grace was attuned to the fact that Turkish Gendarmerie might figure out he was an American spy, making him a prisoner too hot to handle. They might have disposed of him to avoid the shitstorm they eventually did get anyway. Grace, says Vakha, decided silence as a North African rather than execution as an American was the better option.

However, staying silent resulted in, for Grace, an extreme reaction by Colonel Aksoy Demir's men. They tortured him. Grace has a blackened eye, a missing tooth, and two of his fingernails had been removed. The index fingers of both hands are bloodied and swollen. He is covered with bruises.

I look at his wrecked body and whisper a curse, promising vengeance as I stand over my unconscious friend. I place my hand tenderly on Clay's left cheek. He shudders a little and then opens his eyes. Grace shows fear for just a moment, then confusion. I realize he believes he is dreaming or hallucinating.

"I'm really here, compadre. We got you out."

Clayton looks from me to St. Clair. "The rest of the team?"

"Khasan is dead. Bled out after losing a leg in the explosion," St Clair says with gravity. "Vakha is right over there."

Clayton attempts to raise up to look over, but he cannot. The pain in his ribs, likely broken, is too much. "Twelve Moons?"

"We don't know where Twelve Moons is. He might have drowned after the explosion. The sub-floors filled with water."

Grace shakes his head. "He was outside. Sniper rifle, night scope. He was outside."

I nod at this new intel. "Bob Lee has already authorized teams and any and all resources to finding Twelve Moons. I'll let them know. But we don't know where he is," I say. Tears have found their way onto my cheeks.

I long to take Grace's hand as he had me when I awoke after losing both my legs long ago, back at Landstuhl Regional Hospital on Ramstein Air Base, but my partner's hands are so mangled from Turkish plyers I dare not. "I do know this much, buddy. You're coming home. It's over. For now, we're going to let you sleep. Heal up. Right now, the nurses want us out of here. We have to go.

"Rest assured this nightmare is over," I say, "You are coming home. Is there anything you need? Is there anything you want as soon as we get back to Cali?"

Clayton tips his head forward. He grins with false bravado. "A Whataburger double on the way to a Prince concert. Or maybe to Tom Petty. I haven't seen live music in so long." He attempts to laugh, but that is a bridge too far. The nurses both leap to Grace's aid after his grimace.

I don't have the heart to tell him both bits of bad news on the music front. The doctor then herds us out.

Penny and RoBo, two members of our band of brothers from back in Iraq, arrive the next afternoon on an American cargo flight with sealed information for the American ambassador here in Turkey. The two assassins are to be provided arms and any other necessary materiel of war needed to facilitate their dastardly deeds. They have been tasked by Lee and Welmar as contractors to terminate a certain Colonel Aksoy Demir of the Turkish MIT. The ambassador wants nothing to do with them but shrugs as he approves their requests for arms and vehicles.

Penny is dressed in a dark suit, white shirt, and a skinny black tie. He wears boots to increase his height, but he is still only a single cent taller than the minimum army reg height—5 foot tall. However, he is nearly as wide as his height at the shoulders. His muscles ripple, visible through the Italian fabric. His hair is long again, down along those incredibly broad shoulders. Now it has blond highlights and is tucked behind his ears. Sunglasses are pushed up to the crown of his head. He is clean shaven and his eyes are blue and intense. He looks like a *Miami Vice* extra, but I know he is a real player in the real Miami vice scene. A killer.

RoBo, Penny's partner in crime, wears a leather bomber jacket, brown slacks and military boots, desert camo in design. A goatee graces his slim southern face. His eyes are green and lazy; they have led many a man to underestimate him. Many have mistaken that southern drawl for stupid. Those men are no longer breathing. Grace always said it was RoBo's sleepy eyes and drawl that suckered them—like a cobra's taunting dance. They hide a predator within. RoBo, if he had not lost use of an arm in Iraq, would have likely been a general at the Pentagon by now, such was his military prowess. His injury, however, got him flushed from the service. Now he runs his own business, one catering to those who need military expertise to protect operations usually outside the law.

RoBo always wears a sling for his damaged right arm. Today's sling is black like his jacket. RoBo's enemies would do well to remember that although his arm does not work, his hand inside the sling works fine. Inside that gathered fabric at his wrist, RoBo keeps a weapon within his grasp. He is quicker with it than his namesake, William Bonney—Billy the Kid. Robertson Bonney, aka RoBo, is a quick and deadly shot with his hideout pistol.

The two men are able to see Grace but for a moment. Clayton is worse today. The wounds in his fingers are infected and he is feverish and unresponsive to all but the doctor's entreaties. He is receiving intravenous transfusions of both antibiotics and plasma. He remains severely dehydrated. His health status is downgraded from stable to critical, but the doctor maintains he does not believe Clayton's injuries to be life-threatening. We just need to give his body time.

Penny, always one step away from violent outburst, is furious after seeing Clayton in such bad shape. "Is this the work of Colonel Aksoy Demir, the man we're to take off the board?"

St. Clair nods. "Yes, at least British intel tells us that he is responsible. The CIA isn't talking. No help at all, other than to bring you in. Bob Lee is asking the Defense Department to open its files to us, but so far, the intelligence services have given nothing to Roddy here."

I nod, confirming St. Clair's words. The four of us have a drink, and then St. Clair says his goodbyes. I have asked him to meet Taymur, the Moor, his partner and husband, in Malta. One more man, the mullah, has to die in Malta for all of this to be over.

Any intelligence I can get from Bob Lee is to include the whereabouts and identity of the mullah who ordered the jihad on Grace over the last three years. Malta is a small island. A sheik walking around like a king on a small Mediterranean island should be easy to spot.

I have no information yet, but I want boots on the ground in Malta by the time Bob Lee relays whatever intel is available. I also reach out to Scott Grace, Clayton's brother, an officer in the CIA, and a hard-nosed asshole if ever there was one. I figure Scott, who sent his younger brother into the Grand Bazaar in the first place, ought to be here. Clayton is his only living relative and vice versa. It is the least he can do, and Scott is really good at the least he could do.

After meeting there at the embassy, Penny and Robo crash at the hotel, having been in transit for twenty straight hours—Marathon Island to Miami; Miami to New York; New York to Paris; Paris to Istanbul. As they sleep, I email Bob Lee, hoping to receive information to achieve our vengeance.

However, even before Lee's intel arrives, Penny and RoBo receive help from an unexpected source while casing Istanbul's Metris Prison. My two assassin buddies insist on seeing the prison where their target, Colonel Aksoy Demir, works. They sit in silence in an Embassy limo with tinted windows. They stare. They clean their weapons. They stare some more.

Far down the block from the prison entrance, vagrants, the homeless, the blind, and the diseased lepers beg those coming out of the business district to the south. Taxis wait at the boundary of the prison's giant courtyard, hovering about like vultures. Few taxis arrive there with passengers, but some depart, carting away those who have business at Metris and are lucky enough to be allowed to leave. Along that straggling line, Penny and Robo sit with their driver in a Mercedes sedan. Their windows are dark enough no one can see in.

Metris Prison is not a place decent people of Istanbul go. Those who must go there, many of them guards, exit quickly without looking over their shoulder. Often, those who exit the looming structure head straight to the cafes of downtown. They pass, unseeing, past the beggar line. Few take pity on the city's refuse. No one pays them any mind, and these miserable souls seem to be the only segment of society who may walk on the bricks of Metris' haunted courtyard. No one but the unwashed whose lives are without value dare walk there.

Penny and RoBo, protected from scrutiny inside the dark tint of their windows, stay in their hired car, their driver in the taxi line, much to the consternation of other cabbies. One ventures to the rear window of the limo to complain with a loud rap of his knuckles on glass. He is greeted at the rear window, which is lowered just enough—only an inch— but enough for Penny's gun barrel to wave the complainant away. After that, no one else bothers them. No one, except one bum, dressed in rags, who ambles to the same window. This time, the Embassy driver opens his door, stepping forth to curse at the dirty vagrant who dares approach the Mercedes.

Undeterred, the bum taps the rear window once again. Penny lowers the dark glass minutely. The business end of his sidearm extends an inch from the tinted pane.

The bum still does not hesitate. He leans close. "Hey, it's Twelve Moons. Open up. I've been waiting days for someone to show up. They got Grace and one of the Chechens in the prison."

It happens quick. Penny pops the door, and much to the surprise of the cabbies, who are smoking by their vehicles, the beggar stoops and is allowed to enter the backseat of the sedan. The door closes with a hefty thud, and the limo roars into the evening's falling sky. Metris is left behind like Dracula's tower in the gathering gloom.

Penny and RoBo catch the Rincon tribesman up on news on the ride back to the hotel. Twelve Moons is ecstatic to learn Grace and Vakha are alive. He is even more excited they have been released. Despite the good news, Twelve Moons is saddened to hear of Khasan's death. He had only worked with the man for a week but had liked him. Good soldiers are always missed when they make the ultimate sacrifice.

Twelve Moons, after being hustled up the freight elevator at our hotel, is allowed a shower and is given a set of RoBo's clothes. He is not too much worse for wear. The Rincon wolfs down a sandwich and a quart of milk before explaining his whereabouts for the last week. He tells his tale as he sits on the sofa in the antechamber of our suite of rooms. He looks exhausted, but the food revives him a bit.

We learn Grace was right in telling us that Twelve Moons had been outside the blast zone during the firefight. The Rincon had been on a second story roof in the market, waiting for a clear shot at one of the members of the terrorist cell. But then the building his friends entered exploded. The size of the explosion was incredible. The earth shook. Twelve Moons nearly fell to the street. Within moments, hundreds of Turks arrived to inspect the catastrophe. Flames licked at the destruction. Long before the Turkish police arrived, the Native American ditched his sniper rifle and climbed off the roof into the crowd. As uniformed officers scoured the crowd, he beat a hasty retreat into the night.

Twelve Moons pauses in telling his story. RoBo and Penny take a detour to their mission of revenge. We discuss strategy in eliminating Colonel Aksoy Demir. It has only been a minute since Twelve Moons took a break in his story. I look over. He is asleep, still holding a bit of crusted bread in his hand. I let the Rincon sleep on my couch all night.

In the morning after coffee, RoBo and Penny join us. Now after sleep and an espresso, Twelve Moons looks remarkably better. He is ready to finish his report. It is less rambling than last night's. Twelve Moons today is more soldier than survivor, and this morning his words are more debrief than story.

Twelve Moons tells us that the morning after the firefight in the Grand Bazaar, he went there again. He bought a used Arab thobe, dirty white with the cuffs soiled with food. He found a scarf, a jubba, a kaftan and a thawb. Sandals too small for his large feet completed his outfit. Then he changed behind a restaurant's refuge bins. He threw all of his belongings away, except for his service pistol, two loaded mags, and a serrated blade. He hid all three in the folds of his clothes. He rubbed dirt on his face, hands, and feet, and then took to the street. His Rincon face, bronze and ruddy, his jet-black hair, and his none-too-clean Turkish attire, allowed him access along Istanbul's streets. No one seems to notice him. Just one of a million homeless men living hand-to-mouth. No one notices him, but he notices everything.

Twelve Moons is watching. Watching, ever watching. For days, he huddles among the beggars, the lepers, and the maimed along the plaza outside Metris Prison. Twelve Moons had been a language specialist in Iraq. He speaks Turkish, Arabic, and even Zazaki without accent, well enough indeed, to not incur suspicion, but he does not speak.

Instead, he listens. And listens some more. He listens to guards and employees as they enter and exit the prison. He hears them talk as they pass him by, one of the invisible—Istanbul's unwashed. He follows behind as they enter the cafes. Unable to enter, he stands in the alleyways, or sometimes sits along the rail of an outside café. He hears the guards talk. He hears them gossip. They speak of two special prisoners. Terrorists. Captured terrorists. Two special prisoners guarded by the most feared man inside those walls – Colonel Aksoy Demir, head of prison security and the man who oversees its torture chambers. The guards shudder as they mention Demir's name.

Once at a smoke shop, he hears a shopkeeper curse

Demir as a devil. Sensing a comrade in spirit, he watches until the man leaves the market. Twelve Moons follows at a distance until the man is alone in the street. Sliding up beside him, the Rincon speaks for the first time in three days. He leans close to the man and whispers in harsh Turkish.

"My brother, I heard your curse. Colonel Demir is my enemy as well. He holds my brother inside Metris' walls. I have no news."

The shopkeeper looks about before speaking. "If your brother is inside, then he is a dead man."

"Most likely true. I pray for his safe return. And if he does not return, I pray for revenge."

The man smiles. "One such as you cannot harm Demir."

Twelve Moons pulls back the fold on his kaftan to show his Walther. The shopkeeper's eyes widen. Twelve Moons can see the derision leave the shopkeeper's eyes.

"Why did you curse him?" Twelve Moons asks. "Has he wronged you?"

The sight of the gun and now these words have the man truly frightened. He begins to walk away. Twelve Moons keeps pace with him.

The man stares at him. "Leave me be. Are you a devil come to vex me?"

"Indeed, I am a devil, but the man I come to vex is Colonel Demir," Twelve Moons answers.

The shopkeeper stops then in his tracks. He nods, somehow understanding that fate has dealt him into matters better avoided. "Colonel Demir is responsible for the death of my daughter's son. He had done nothing. Demir is wicked."

"And thus, he shall be punished," says Twelve Moons. "What can you tell me about him?"

It turns out the shopkeeper has damn good intel.

Later that evening, Twelve Moons speaks to both St. Clair and Taymur by phone. In Malta and undercover, Taymur cries upon hearing his friend's voice on the phone. The two had been together in harm's way for more than two years. They are blood brothers. St. Clair promises a reunion once they each find their prey.

After the phone call, Twelve Moons insists he assist RoBo and Penny in their assassination of Colonel Aksoy Demir. I agree. I can hardly turn him down. The shopkeeper's intel lets us know where Demir lives, where his concubine resides, and the restaurant the colonel frequents most evenings.

It seems I, Roddy O'Malley, father, fiancé, semi-retired private detective, legless wonder, and a chill dude, am now in charge of two assassination teams. I am the big boss man in charge. Nobody can tell me what to do.

Bob Lee has other ideas about my decisions by morning. Including having Twelve Moons on the hit squad. Lee orders me to have the Rincon stand down.

Twelve Moons is understandably upset when I tell him.

"I want in on taking down the colonel," Twelve Moons insists.

"Bob Lee says you're to come home with me and Grace when he's ready," I reply.

We are drinking beer on the roof of the hotel. I finish mine and notice that Twelve Moons is down to backwash. I open two more. He curses but takes the beer.

"It will be days before Grace is ready to go stateside," he says. "Clayton is in rough shape. He may have to go to Ramstein before heading home. He may need that kind of care."

I nod, agreeing. "That's actually in the works. I'm going with him. There's somebody there I need to thank."

Twelve Moons nods too but is undeterred. "I know this city. I speak the language. Let me be the ferryman. Let me take your assassins to the banks of the River Styx. There, we will assist Demir across."

I smile both at his passion and his allusion.

"Penny and RoBo can handle it. Thanks to you, we have Colonel Demir's address. He has a tight-knit security detail. He always travels with as many as four guards with him. Lives in a walled compound. It's a secure building. He lives on the third floor. Covered windows, probably bullet-proof. We're trying to find a way in."

"I can be their chauffeur."

"Vakha Bahaev is out of the hospital. He has already filled that position."

"I insist on being in."

I shrug, knowing I will not be able to stop him from trailing them if I don't include him or lock him up. "Okay, you're in. But when Grace is ready to leave, we leave. No bitching."

Twelve Moon grins.

We now have another four-man assassination team in Turkey, just like Grace's had been. His did not fare too well. But now, I am their handler. I don't like it. I don't want to be involved in this kind of gig anymore. I lose sleep over it, I admit. But there are bills to be paid. And retribution to mete out.

It only takes two days before the four show back up with smiles and two bottles of Wild Turkey from the duty-free store in the lobby of our hotel.

RoBo sits down on the couch across from me. He removes a double-barreled shotgun pistol from the folds of his sling. "Got the bastard."

I show my surprise. "It was that easy?"

Penny pours shots for everyone. "That easy? We're that good."

"How'd it go down?" I ask, taking the whiskey from him.

"The colonel went to his restaurant, just like Twelve Moon told us. The place is right on the river. Kind of a dark and mysterious place. Casablanca stuff. It's this old Roman era building on the Bosporus. Demir goes in before sundown."

Vakha Bahaev speaks for the first time to me. "We were waiting before they even arrived."

"Uhuh," adds RoBo, "but it was too dangerous in full light. We waited until after Demir ate, and after his team had a few nips at their own bottles outside. They get comfortable, waiting for the Colonel and his best gal to come back downstairs."

"By then it was full dark, no moon," Twelve Moons says.

"And?"

"I snuck up and asked the limo driver, who was standing next to his vehicle, to not participate in saving his boss," Penny said.

"Really?"

Penny laughs. "No, I put my hand over his mouth and punctured his kidneys a bit. Come on, Roddy. We're professionals. I don't leave things to chance when I can ensure that guy is out of the game permanently."

"Duly noted. Then what?"

"Twelve Moons clipped the man posted across the street from a couple hundred yards away with a Blazer 93 Tactical equipped with a silencer," RoBo replies. He looks to Twelve Moons. "Nifty shot, that."

Twelve Moons bows slightly. "Used a German weapon, left it behind, no prints. I wore gloves."

"Let me make sure I got it straight," I say. "The colonel is just coming out with his two bodyguards and his lady friend? But nobody is left alive outside to rescue him?"

"'Correct," says Vakha.

I nod, grim-faced. "How'd it go down?"

Penny says, "I stung the first man out with a Taser, just to slow him down."

"Really?" I say, surprised.

"Fuck no," Penny snaps back at me. "RoBo blasted him with his little baby shotgun while the guard's gun hand was still holding the door open for his boss."

"Three down, one guard and Demir to go."

"Right," Twelve Moons says. "I'm not sure whether it was my shot or Penny's that took out the last guard."

Penny smiles. "It was mine. I was using a Sig MCX Rattler. I fired about twenty rounds. Took out the last guard and the doorman."

"And I killed the colonel," says Vakha. "He died with my first and only shot. I did not try for the heart since everyone knew the colonel did not have one."

We all laugh.

Penny illustrates the point and takes his index finger like the barrel of a gun and puts it right between his eyes. He goes cross-eyed and puckers his mouth up, mouthing the word, "Pow."

Everyone laughs again.

"How about the hooker?" I ask. "Did she see any of you? Were there any other witnesses?"

Penny smiled. "Jeez, Roddy. You *have* been out of the game too long. We're professional hitmen. I did mention I gave the doorway a spray of twenty rounds, right? I'm afraid the prostitute's clientele will find she will miss the rest of this week's appointments."

I nod. Another one chalked up to collateral damage.

"Okay, mission accomplished, five enemy combatants down." I don't mention the doorman and the hooker. "You are all out of country tonight on a diplomatic flight. Showers and civvies for everyone. Carry nothing out, except your passports. I'll order room service while you are preparing to leave."

We all drink one more shot. The four leave the room,

smiling from successfully killing seven people. Mission accomplished. I slap their backs and congratulate them on a job well done. I can hear their happy chatter down the hall. I know the jubilation of surviving a firefight, even one in which the enemy does not get off a shot. Those are actually the best kind. There is a rush after a fight when you are still alive. The rush of still living. It is the ultimate high. And I am an expert on high.

I call Bob Lee's service. "Done," I say into the receiver. "Four outbound, stateside. Out." I make the decision that Twelve Moons gets out with the rest. Grace does not need additional security inside our largest military hospital. I will do just fine.

Afterwards, thinking about the violence I ordered to take place, I feel a shiver as I know I have let evil back into my life once again. There will be hell to pay.

Grace and I leave for Ramstein, Germany the next day. There, Grace has surgery on his hands to repair the damage his torturers have inflicted on his two fingers. The next day, he spends time with soldiers who are rehabbing. There are always wounded soldiers at Ramstein.

In the day room, a poker game has been going on since 1966. Grace cannot yet hold cards, so he merely sits at the table, listening to the laughter for an hour or so. I watch him. Grace is there but not fully. Every little bit, he stares into space or perhaps into the horror he has seen, forgetting the other men at the table with him. One of them snaps his fingers in Grace's eyes, ending his trance. They all laugh. Then at least for a bit, he is with them. The injured but alive. To be among the living is a new sensation for him. For more than two years, Grace had been assigned to be the angel of death. He is just now waking from the bad dream.

Eventually, he nods over at me that he is tired and wants to leave. He did not play poker today, but he has gambled enough over the last few years. A very high stakes game. It will be sometime before he will be able to deal when it comes around the table to his turn. He is not yet dealing with anything. I roll his wheelchair back to his room. Grace is ready for a nap, and I help him to bed. My best bud is lights out in two minutes. I leave him slumbering peacefully without medication required.

As for me, I head into town to find Eric, the defrocked priest, who was with me in 2003 when I came out of my induced coma, having lost my legs. I asked him that day for a handgun to end my life. Father Eric did not assist me with that request. Praise the Lord.

When we last heard from him, Eric had lost his faith and left the church. He was also out of the closet. When Grace found him, he was a drunk holding court at The Golden Bull, a tavern on the *Mainstrauss* of Kaiserslautern. Eric all but slept there, drinking beer all day, reading detective novels in his regular booth until he passed out. The local family he lived with there in the village were called each day to retrieve him after he passed out. They were Catholic and believed it was their job to help Eric until he again found his faith.

I do not find Eric. I inquire at the bar, and amazingly find out Eric nearly a year ago declared he was bound for the City of Angels and the land of Raymond Chandler novels. He is now, the bartender tells me, a success coach in Redondo Beach. He has also married a martial arts trainer named Lars. Laughing, I write down Father Eric's return address off the letter the bartender shows me and promise to look up Father Eric, newly-minted success coach to the stars, when I get back to Cali.

When the going gets weird, the weird go professional. Right.

The day Grace is set to fly stateside to Walter Reed for a final check-up from the neck up, I get a call from St. Clair.

"It's over."

"Team status?"

"We are all fine. Full team is out of country already. Leaving stateside from Rome tomorrow."

I am amazed. After all this time, the man who put the contract on Grace is dead. "Details?"

"Rocket propelled grenade from the top of a double-decker bus, The Moor at 6'9" could see over the wall."

I laugh at that absurd mental picture. I have questions, but too much has already been said over an open line. I do ask, "Who was he? Give me at least that much."

"An American gone Muslim radical. Went by Mohammed Abdullah Khan. American name of Silva."

I nod. "Mariyah's man from her L.A. days."

"The Black Queen," says St. Clair. He was there (as detailed in *The Prince of the Border*).

"Silva was Mariyah's man back when they were both in the Latin Playboys. You know Grace took her child. Saved him from that crazy bitch."

"I know, but it's an open line, Roddy. We can discuss it over scotch in L.A."

I tell Grace it's over on the flight to Germany. He smiles and then sleeps for eleven straight hours.

SAY GRACE

S till Roddy speaking. Two weeks back in the states. My buddy Clayton Grace is here in Cali and out of hospitals—two since I wrote: Walter Reed for a psychological eval. Then a full physical at the VA here in L.A. He is signed up for both rehab on his hands and for some counseling with a shrink. Hopefully, both will do him good. His artificial tan is starting to fade, but the light in his eyes is still hazy. I see no fire, no verve for life there. He is tired. He is beat up. He is depressed. I totally get it.

Grace is installed in the spare bedroom upstairs at our home in West Hollywood. Karen insists, although our little bungalow feels packed. I admit I'm a little claustrophobic in my own home now. But my phobias aside, there is an upside. Clayton Grace being in our upstairs bedroom is like having Santa or the Easter Bunny come live with us. Our daughter, Gracie, named after Clayton, is in awe. I don't think she really believed Grace was real. But he is ever so real. And currently, that realism is taking the form of showing mortality. He is frail, beat up, depressed, and sad. Maybe sad most of all.

Karen and I have the Master Bedroom. Gracie has her room, a Jack and Jill, which shares a bathroom with Grace. Jerry the Monkey is downstairs, inhabiting the "maid quarters" off the kitchen in our turn-of-the-last-century Hollywood bungalow. It is a classic up/down split level common before the huge mansions of the golden era of films caused most homes like ours to be bulldozed to make way for boulevards and retreats for movie stars and directors.

Our homeplace is not fancy, but it was built in a time when Hispanic Angelinos commonly lived in and served the privileged as domestic help. Our domicile is the smallest home in a neighborhood that is being reclaimed by the Hollywood elite. I will admit that it has a pool, three orange trees, and an eight-foot wall around the yard—so I'll just shut my mouth and pay the ever-increasing property taxes. We are very lucky.

Yes, our three bedroom, plus one, is packed with folks. Full of life. Full of bluster. And that ain't great if you're Clayton Grace, just back from a two-year mission for the CIA which ended with being incarcerated in Turkey's most infamous prison. He might have wanted a bit more quiet time. However, his VA doctors think a busy household might be beneficial. I am not sure my best friend agrees.

Sometimes, I must admit the music here is too loud. I tend to crank it. So does my crew. Karen, Gracie and Jerry the monkey all like their rock-and-roll. Jerry is the worst perpetrator of excessive volume. He actually has a tiny, black t-shirt with an amp on it with the volume turned to 11.

I give a general order to the troops, including the monkey and the two-year-old, that there would be no battle of the bands – Duane vs. Derek—for the foreseeable future. Grace needs to recover.

My buddy has two appointments a week now with a shrink at the V.A., in addition to physical therapy for his hands. I drive him. Grace sleeps a lot, but I will say he is eating okay. And he swims—or at least lounges in the floatie. Once in a while, I catch him smiling at the antics of Jerry and Gracie. I also see him in reflection, thinking of the horror of the last two years. I have noticed him wipe away a tear although he does try to hide stray emotions.

Karen says I should broker a conversation. So far, I have not. I have not crossed that Rubicon. Grace, I counter, will talk when he's ready. I tell Karen that my buddy needs his space. He needs to allow his inner core, that thing we call soul, to reinhabit his body. It will take a bit. I have been there. Karen nods, remembering.

"Just keep the fridge full of anything we notice he is eating or drinking," I say. "I'll keep the maniacs in line during the day. We'll let Grace sleep when he wants, eat when he wants, drink when he wants, and walk around the perimeter of the property in the shade of our orange trees when it's not too hot. He's processing. Right now, we wait."

Karen kisses me and goes to work, making the world safe for starlets in their first feature films. In a world where Harvey Weinstein still exists, Karen has her work cut out for her.

On my end, I reach out to Bob Lee, my boss, and give him an update, making the call out sitting at the pool early one morning.

"How's our boy doing?"

"Healing. Gonna take a while. The scars are in his head."

"A-hum."

"I'm not going to be in this week. Maybe not next. You got somebody to cover my security checks?"

"What is it you do anyway?" Lee says, laughing.

"I do your dirty work and cash your checks."

"True enough," Lee replies. There is a flatness in his voice. The tone is his acknowledgement that the services Grace and I have provided over the last half decade are very expensive indeed. The price was costly for both the company and to the two of us. Sacrifices have been made.

"Look," I say, "you don't need to check in or worry. Grace is not at any health risk. He's not in any mental crisis. He's just decompressing. It can't be done quickly. Not coming up from a deep underwater dive or from a deep undercover mission. We both know that."

There was a pause. I left it be. Finally, the boss man responds.

"Let me know if you need anything."

I nod and know he knows I will.

The phone goes dead.

Inside, I refill my coffee. I can hear Jerry in his room reading the *L.A Times* classified section with his scanner. I can hear the device spout the words on the page telling him about a vinyl collection at an estate sale in Westwood. I figure Jerry and I will be going for a drive. It is Saturday morning. Karen is home, and she can watch over Grace. I'll take the little monkey for an outing.

Jerry, for a lunatic, has been pretty good since Grace showed up, but Jerry can only heed quiet time in short stints. He needs to kick up his heels and head bang to some Sabbath or something similar at least every other day. If I keep the lid on too tight with him, I fear something reckless or stupid might happen. On cue, Jerry enters the kitchen. He asks about the record show. I fuss, hem, and haw and then finally agree to take him to buy vinyl. The monkey gives me his million-dollar grin.

Jerry likes to convince himself he can bully me into trips around town. Truth is I like to take him along. It is fun to see the double takes as we pass by people in Topanga Canyon or on Sunset, playing "Radar Love" at full blast with the windows down and Jerry giving people the "hook 'em horns" rock-n-roll sign with his only hand. Hollywood has all kinds, but not any like Jerry.

On rare chilly days, like today, Jerry will wear a women's Allman Brothers sweatshirt, which is more his size, as we hit yard sales. We prepare to leave. I assess the situation. Grace is still asleep. Gracie is using crayons to fill backgrounds in a *Frozen* coloring book. Karen is checking emails. Currently, everything is copacetic, but there is no room left at the inn. I know things can't stay like this. But for now, I am happy. I am the protector of all who matter to me. I am good with that. Everyone is safe. What can I do for an encore?

Maybe it is time to get Clayton up to snuff. Maybe I'll start a conversation with my partner tomorrow morning. Maybe not. For now, all I can do is go and buy used vinyl. It ain't much, but it seems to make the little primate happy. I am content.

Dawn. I stick my head in on Gracie. Snoring lightly. Stick my head in on Grace. Snoring not so lightly. Stick my head in on Jerry. Reading with a concentration like he is cramming for the GRE tomorrow morning. Finally, at the end of the column at the bottom of the page, Jerry looks up to me.

"Got a hot lead on a big collection of records. Saturday estate sale. Six days. Pre-sale on vinyl goes up at 8:00. We get there at 7:00. Beat blue hairs. Old hippies not get up early."

I groan, mainly for effect. "I'll think about it."

"It so worth it. Say they have signed Beach Boys records. *Pet Sounds* with Brian Wilson's signature. So worth it."

"I said let me think about it."

"I been good. Grace hard to be good around. All the time quiet. So sad. Jerry tell."

"I know. You have been good. We'll go, okay."

Jerry nods. He immediately dismisses me and goes back to scanning columns of the newspaper. He is happy. He has something to look forward to. A trip to get new tunes. I leave him to his device and to his devices.

I step outside. The morning is clear. The day already warm. The sky is impossibly blue. I slip out of my prostheses and boxers. I take a skinny dip. Then I wrap a towel around me, recline in the sun which is just peeking over the east wall and look at my phone. Nothing much there. I close my eyes and even doze for a few minutes. In a bit, I hear the door from the house open. I realized time has passed. My hair is dry. Grace approaches from the kitchen, carrying two coffees.

"Thought you might need a fresh cup."

"Thanks, bro." I smile and take the steaming mug from him. "Gracie up?"

"Yeah, she's lying on the bed with Jerry. I been meaning to ask if she's potty trained?"

"Got through that phase a while back. One day she just decided she was done with diapers. Started peeing in the pot on her own."

"Hitting the mark?"

"Better than me, according to Karen."

Grace smiles, and then we are quiet. Both of us just enjoying the caffeine. The two of us are good with silence. You spend 40 hours on a weekend stakeout inside a van with someone, you get used to silence. Otherwise, it is hell. If the other guy has to fill the quiet time, just can't leave it alone, it is painful. Both of you need to just leave it be. Speak when you need to. Don't when you don't. We both figured that out long ago. Now is a time for silence. Fine. It is all copacetic.

I let Grace take the lead and keep my mouth shut except to sip the java. Finally, Grace leans toward me. His body language seems to be asking me to pay attention. His expression says this communique is beyond the norm. That he is letting me inside the wall of his thoughts. I nod and set my coffee mug on the tile.

"The floor is yours," I say.

Grace nods. He takes one last sip of coffee and then sets his mug down next to mine. "I have some things that need being said," Grace says.

"I did stuff in the last two years that I can't ever talk to you about. Stuff my brother sent me to do for the agency. Supposedly on the trail of the man who ordered the jihad on me. Who had ties in Iran with enough power to fund an endless supply of killers out to get me. Scott had me by the short ones, kept us on the trail. We were always one bad guy away from getting the name we needed to know. And the end was always the same. The CIA provided details on the location of our target, assured us they were truly bad guys who needed killing. So we did it. We killed them. It was that simple. Until Istanbul and the explosion."

I nod.

Grace sets his coffee cup down and looks at the house. "I can't live like that anymore. I'm not sure I can come back to the detective agency, and I think you want me to. You haven't said it, but I am getting that vibe. I am not sure I can go into the field again. Not now for sure, maybe not ever. I wanted you to know in case you were waiting on me to suit up and start working cases again with you."

"No, no expectations. I get it. Your own timetable. Your

own life. You decide the next step. Whatever it is, we're good. I just want you to feel better."

"Me too." Then Grace stands and strips off his sweatpants. With only his boxer briefs and one prosthesis attached to his calf, he steps to the pool. Grace releases the tension on the elastic that holds his false leg onto his stump. He lets it drop alongside the ladder. Then he leaps in, cannonball spraying me. I laugh and jump in alongside him.

When I surface, Grace says, "What is up with my trailer? Is it still there?"

"Yeah, but I don't think it is a good idea for you to be alone up there for days at a time."

"I agree, but would you take me up there? I want to see that coyote. The one I called Dapper? I want to see if he is still running those hills."

I swim over to the diving board and pull myself up onto the flat surface.

Grace looks at me. "What about Dani?"

"She married someone else. They have a kid now."

Grace nods, taking that in. Then he smiles. "Better circle back to the coyote then. Can we go up there today?"

"No worries. How about breakfast first?"

"Definitely," he says with a grin. "Thanks." He pauses. "It might be fun to take the crew along with us."

"Jerry and Gracie? Karen asked me to watch them today. She and a friend want to do a little shopping." I don't mention that the friend is Vio Landaugh, another of Grace's exes.

"Thanks," Grace says.

"No prob. A trip into the hills to see if we can find Dapper the coyote? The maniacs will love that."

"You know that coyote could communicate with me like Jerry did with you back in the day."

"Yeah, that old Vietnam vet fed him those same pills. Bad side effects to that. Gave Jerry cancer. He's lucky to still be in remission."

"The bad ole days," Grace says remembering.

"But in the past," I reply.

"Brother, I'm still having bad days," he says. His grimace is a weight in my heart.

"We're working to change that," I say forcefully. "First things, first. Let's make pancakes for the crew. Then head up above Topanga and Mulholland to find Dapper. That will be a big win."

And amazingly, we do find Dapper, but, like Grace, he is down on his luck. We are there a bit before the coyote comes down from the hills. Jerry and Gracie are cleaning dead leaves out of the tank so we can run fresh water into it. Grace and I inspect the trailer. It is dusty but fine. It gives me weird vibes, though. I can tell it depresses Grace. I tell him it's good that it hasn't been broken into. I don't tell him I find that fact amazing. Almost freaky. But that Airstream trailer is way the hell up here. Grace's land, and his trailer itself, is so far up in the boonies, you almost have to have the GPS coordinates to find it. Evidently, looters and teenagers looking for a place to party and screw hadn't been able to locate it.

After an hour, most of which we spend in the shade on

that great slab of granite that overlooks Mulholland, we hear something coming through the brush. It is Dapper. Time has not been kind to him. He looks thin and unhealthy. He is limping a bit and his fur, the color of the desert, is matted. His narrow face is directed at us. His eyes peering and wary. Grace stands and the three of us watch silently. Jerry is not good at silence, but he seems to understand the moment.

Dapper is leery of us and is staring at Jerry. Not a lot of monkeys in the hills above Topanga, I'm guessing. Grace approaches the coyote, kneels, and puts out his hands. The coyote moves his gaze from the monkey to the man. He pauses a long moment, but then comes and leans against his old friend. I hear a chirp beside me, look over and see Gracie is crying. I realize I am too. Jerry has one eyebrow raised like he doesn't get it.

Later, after we feed the coyote a can of wet dog food, Grace gives Dapper a shower. He scrubs him under the warm spray. I can tell as the coyote unwinds in the warm water that he was in distress when we showed up. He is painfully thin. It looks as if he has lost teeth. Afterwards, Grace and Gracie dry the animal. Then Dapper lies on the floor on an old G.I. surplus sleeping bag and dozes. Grace moves to the dusty bed and lies above the coyote. I give Jerry and Gracie the shush sign and we leave the trailer on tiptoes.

We move away down the clearing and I break out a frisbee from the vehicle. Jerry and Gracie get busy with bad throws and chasing after the disk. I walk back to the trailer and look in. Dapper has moved from the floor. He is now curled into Grace's side. They are spooning. I sneak back and join the fray with the frisbee.

ZULU HOUR AT ZUMA BEACH

Now is a good time to talk about monkey hygiene.

Monkeys smell bad—I mean, not to other monkeys, but to fiancés they do. Karen says she is tired of the homestead smelling like the monkey cage at the L.A. Zoo. In nasal retaliation, we've instituted a few musts for our new houseguest.

Our home is a familiar style for Los Angeles when money was flowing like water does to almond groves after a back-room payoff. Back then, even poor whites had domestic help. The house is a split level, three-up with a small servant quarters off the kitchen. Back in the Golden Age of Hollywood, even the smaller homes made room for having a live-in maid. Ours is not in use in that capacity (not since *Prince of the Border*). It was set up as a guest room, but now has become Jerry's new home. It has a bath with a shower. There is no separate entrance, only a door off the kitchen.

Jerry's use of the facilities for both urinating and bowel

movements is to squat above the pot with a foot gripping each side of the toilet seat. We have installed a bidet to clean him, and he is generally pretty accurate in peeing. Karen says as accurate as me.

The smell problem is not from his toilet training. It is a skin and fur thing. We've tried various shampoos. Paul Mitchell's Tea Tree was spectacularly unsuccessful. After his first use of that elixir over his entire body, our house reeked of the scent of chocolate mint ice cream. 24/7, I'm saying. Think about shampooing your entire body. That is a lot of shampoo and a lot of smell good afterward. End result, just a different type of obnoxious smell. No longer monkey cage. Now Baskin Robbins.

Try two. Johnson Baby Shampoo. It worked, but only for a day. Jerry complained of having to shampoo his entire body each time. Dry skin, he said. Every other day, back to monkey cage smell. Nope. Looking for another 'poo.

We did make a successful find on our third attempt. Aveeno Farm-Fresh Oat Milk Sulfate-Free Shampoo with Colloidal Oatmeal & Almond Milk, Moisturizing Shampoo for All Hair Types, Safe for Color-Treated Hair, Paraben & Dye-Free! I understand the guy who named it was being paid by the word.

Now Jerry is happily saturated. Karen's nose is placated. Gracie isn't asking for Ben and Jerry's chocolate mint from breakfast until sleep. I am happy because everyone else is happy. It's all good.

∾

Grace, still recuperating, has taken to sleeping up at the trailer against our objections. He shopped for and stocked provisions. I visit him about every third day. Rat takes a day too. So does Fortune. And Twelve Moons too. Everyday somebody is out there with him. We bring him a take-out dinner. Stay a couple of hours to shoot the shit. Clayton seems okay. He is sleeping a great deal. Healing, inside and out. Letting his neural pathways rewire. Not having to sleep with one eye open because someone has a contract on your life is a new experience to him. Grace is trying to relax his muscles. Take his finger off the trigger of his mental machine gun. I get it. He needs time. We give it. His constant companion, Dapper, the coyote, seems to get it too. They both have had a couple of tough years. Living dangerously, you need a partner. They have it in one another.

The Santa Ana winds are expected on Tuesday. It is a Saturday morning. Today is perfect. But those devil winds hang out there in the margin of our consciousness. Karen and I know kids and animals act weird during a Santa Ana. Grown-ups are worse. Ask cops.

The family decides on a day at the beach. Jerry has never been and he is excited. He wakes me before dawn.

"Wakey, Wakey! Ocean Day! Jerry boogie board today."

Karen rolls over and puts an elbow into my ribs. I roll out and follow the simian downstairs. The coffee is brewed and half the pot has already been consumed.

I raise an eyebrow. "How long you been up?"

"Did not sleep much. Excited."

"And fully caffeinated."

"Oh yes. Coffee good on excitement day."

"I'll have a cup. Then we'll get things around. Let's let the ladies sleep for a while."

"Okay. I help. Jerry got the Big Jangle after four cups."

We are on the road by nine. Zuma Beach is in Malibu and right along the PCH. The beach is the best public one in the Los Angeles area. Beautiful sand and on a late fall day arriving by ten, we should be able to get a primo spot. The sun beams down from a sky right out of a Beach Boys song. We're on a surfing safari – with a monkey.

We arrive. I bring the crew to an unloading area along Malibu Canyon Road. Our destination is the southeast side of Zuma, a place called Westward Beach. They filmed the last scene in *Planet of the Apes* here. I know that factoid, but it might upset Jerry's vibe. Mum's the word. We dismount. Jerry is jumping around like he's been bumping cocaine all the way up in the car. Gracie is always a cool cucumber and shares a grin with me. Karen smirks too. Today is going to be awesome. I got to admit the moment is joyous.

Point Dume rises above the beach to our south and gives the illusion we are away from a city of 4 million. The beach entrance is tarmac covered in sand. I unload the surfboard, a boogie board or two, the picnic basket, a backpack of supplies, and a small ice chest. Karen and Gracie plan on carrying what they can to the beach. Jerry will stay with the boards and gear until I park the car. I head back up MCR, looking for a place to put the vehicle.

Westward Beach sticks out like a thumb on Malibu's westernmost promontory known as Point Dume. It has the best surfing near the city, but there's a riptide and it is important to stay in close. There is a shallow cove wrapped on the backside of the short sandy shelf, a true and perfect surfer's pipeline, which brings surfers like bees to honey. The waves on the reverse side of the shelf are shorter than, say, any in Hawaii, but they are tall and steep. It is a quick out and a good ride. I am looking forward to it.

All of us have life jackets and will wear them in the water here. Karen and I have decided we will too as good examples, even in the shallow backwater of the cove. Jerry and Gracie won't complain that way.

I walk back, receiving looks as I come back in jams and my metal legs. I am immune at this point and pay it no mind. Jerry and I lug the surfboard and a boogie board in. I wear one backpack and so does he. We trudge through the sand. I wobble on my stilts, but fun awaits. All good. The little guy carries his own weight and does not complain with the load. In the distance, I see Karen wave from our beach blanket. She is applying sunscreen on the kid.

We arrive. Karen sprays sunscreen on both Jerry and me. I am not sure if monkeys sunburn, but we're taking no chances. I remove my stilts and jams. Under I am wearing compression shorts sewn closed at the bottom. I am now just a bit taller than Jerry, but I outweigh him by a hundred and twenty pounds. His torso is thinner than my biceps. I flex them as Karen sprays me. Gracie laughs. Jerry is prancing.

Karen, Jerry, and Gracie head into the shallows. I take photos of the three frolicking in the surf. The grins are great. Frameable, I'm thinking.

Jerry, after a short bit, returns to my side.

"Sharks here?" His eyes have the caffeinated, paranoid look.

I laugh. "Not there." I point to the other side of the inlet, past the one-foot deep channel where Gracie sits, letting the waves bob around her. "Maybe out there, beyond the breakers."

"Sharks kill more people than monkeys?" he asks.

"I don't think monkeys kill many people, do they?' I respond, smiling.

"Me no mean that way."

I nod at him. "I know what you meant, but you're safe. Sharks don't bother you if you're on a board and you're wearing a life vest."

He acknowledges that. "Let's surf, dude."

I take off his arm band communicator. And we surf.

Jerry and I are an interesting spectacle on our boards. I tow him out. He sits on his boogie board. I paddle with my arms – having no legs messes with my scissor kick. Out beyond the break, I position him on the board, squatting like he's going to pee. Surfboard, tethered to my arm, I push him onto a cresting wave, finding its curved back. I push him into the kinetic energy, and he's gone. At first, Jerry's face is one experiencing terror. He hangs onto the tip of the board with his one arm, but his monkey balance is perfect. He rides the crest in, falls as the break brings toward land. I see him ragdoll in the wake. Jerry comes up, spitting water. Smiling broadly. Clinging to his board, he gives me the finger. I see Karen in the distance laughing. I shrug at her, and Karen looks over and says something to my daughter.

They both give me the finger.

Before lunch, Jerry has actually pipelined for the first time. He is a natural with perfect balance. His tail works as a rudder, moving back and forth to keep him centered on the board. I am good on my board. Having no legs makes my center of gravity low. I hang zero on the board. It is a great morning.

But the water is cold. We tire after an hour or more. Jerry motions with his fingers like he is stuffing a folded piece of pizza into his mouth. It is weird being with him without his communicator. I am so used to him "talking" that having him not talk is jarring. Technology, you imp.

Karen and I rent an umbrella to protect us from the sun which at noon is now hot despite the early November date. The girls are soon safely ensconced in the shade. Karen is reading a book of Bob Marley lyrics to Gracie. They lounge in the sand. One or both will be asleep by the time we return with lunch.

Jerry and I rent a motorized sand trike and roll up to Spruzzo's. I order the pizza and four bottled waters. We sit on the patio while we wait, tired but happy.

"Best day Jerry new life," he says.

"New life?"

"Since baby Jerry taken."

"You remember that?"

"Yes. Sad day. Jerry."

"I'm sure. What do you remember?"

"Jerry baby. Man grab. Put in basket."

"Sorry, little friend," I say.

"Sold to white coat men. They cut off my arm. Make money."

"Yeah, I know that part. I rescued you."

"Thank you. Take in homeless Jerry."

"You're family now."

"You Jerry family too. You. Karen. Little Roddy girl too."

"Fur ever," I say.

He winks back a tear. "No more sad talk," Jerry says. "Today great day."

Just then they call my name, saving us from hugging. I go up and pay. When I return, Jerry nods a look across the shaded patio. "Bad man taking dollars off tables. Pizza lady not get her tip money."

I glance over and there is a homeless guy, gray hair and beard, grimy Adidas jacket, cargo shorts and sandals. His eyes dart away from mine as he scrambles off the patio. I can tell he's guilty of something. Jerry remains as the only witness.

"We stop him?" Jerry is on his feet.

I am holding a pizza. "No, we definitely do not stop him," I say. "He probably really needs that money. I'll tip the waitress on the way out. Make up for her short drawer."

"You no badge police, though."

"Not today. Today we play."

Jerry shrugs, but I can tell he is disappointed.

The afternoon is better than the morning if that's possible. We play dodgeball in the shallows. I give Gracie a swimming lesson while Jerry heckles her. Karen reads a good book and leaves her phone in her beach bag all afternoon. About three, everyone is tired. Jerry is lying on his boogie board in the shade. He is nodding out. I leave them there and return the trike.

Upon my return, I tell the crew to snap to. We are packing up. Soon, the four of us are loaded down and head back to the vehicle. Once there, we'll pile everything in the back. Then the other three will pile in for their nap back to town. I will have a Red Bull on the ride home while the others dream happy dreams.

At the entrance, Jerry points. "There bad man again." The homeless guy is about two blocks down. He is wearing head-phones. My headphones.

Gracie points too. "Daddy, those are your headphones. They have my pink tape on the cord."

She's right. My Sennheiser HD 280s are decorated with neon pink Xs on the earphones. No one has a pair that looks like that. Mine had been in the truck. That means the home-less guy has broken into my truck. That is NG. No Good. I have a gun safe in the car with a Glock 43X inside. The bad news is I put the key for it in my glove compartment, not wanting to take a chance on losing it at the beach. I am worried "bad man" now has my weapon. I tell Karen. Then I look to the monkey.

"Jerry, come with me. We're following 'bad man.' Karen, call 9-11. I'm just going to try to keep this guy in range. Jerry, you stay behind me about a block. Text Karen if anything happens, but I'm not going to do anything stupid. I just don't want to have my gun ending up in the hands of some vagrant liable to use it to kill a liquor store owner."

The monkey gives me a wry smile. "This very Spiderman. You no stop steal tips. Then bad man commits crime on you. Very Spiderman, but no old uncle."

"Yeah, thanks for the 'I told you so.'"

Jerry just nods. "Jerry follow. Me no badge cop too now."

Karen gives me an exasperated look and tells me to keep my phone at the ready. I nod and follow "bad man."

I stay more than a block behind "bad man" as he heads inland up Malibu Canyon Road. Jerry crosses the street and is roughly even with me. I get a text from Karen.

"Police on the way. NO HERO SHIT."

"Roger that," I respond.

Another text. This one from Jerry across the street from me. I see him sticking his head out from a rack of t-shirts at a shop catering to tourists.

"Jerry undercover."

"Stay that way" is my answer.

"Jerry hide good."

I look over and he is pretending to shop for greeting cards. Blending in with the shoppers. Like one-armed Rhesus macaques are commonly buying Christmas cards on Zuma Beach.

Bad guy in my earphones is noodling his way up MCR. One block up, he turns right, jaywalking the light. I hurry up. Get to the intersection and cross after the traffic clears. I can't see bad guy anywhere. Shit. How could I have lost him? Did he make his tail? How could he have noticed a man walking on metal legs and a one-armed monkey trailing him? What are the chances?

I go up half a block and turn down the alley. It is strewn with dumpsters for the restaurants on the front half of the street. There are apartments above the retail below. The sky above is littered with corroded fire escapes, brown with rust and disuse. The alley is narrow.

I tentatively step forward. The alley is in deep shadow. Suddenly, bad guy leaps from the protection of a stack of pallets. His eyes say, "I'm totally nuts."

"Why you following me?" he says, his voice is as ragged as his clothing.

I nod with my chin. "Those are my headphones."

He raises my Glock, pointing it at said chin. "This yours too?"

I hear sirens far down the PCH. They won't get here in time. I'm thinking I got myself into this mess, I got to get myself out. But then a deeper shadow crosses my vision path. It is Jerry. He is upside down, swinging from a fire escape's retracted ladder. His feet are gripping the bottom bar. In his hand, he holds one of those old 7-Up glass bottles with the red dot painted on it. He swings it wildly like Mike Trout fooled on a change-up. And monkey hero boy plunks me right on the back of the noggin.

Down goes Frazier. I go face-first to the pavement. I am not unconscious, but I am seeing stars like a Hollywood movie premier at Grauman's Chinese Theatre. The ladder begins to descend with Jerry's weight and torque. He releases, rolling and tumbling. Bad guy fires a wild shot into the heavens. Jerry's lithe body slams into the vagrant. It is like getting hit in the chest by a bowling ball. Bad guy falls backward on his ass and loses his grip on the gun. There is a kerfuffle over the Glock, which Jerry wins. Bad guy hightails it up the alley.

Malibu police utilize Shot Spotter gunfire detection systems and they are able to pinpoint our location within the minute. Bad guy is arrested within two.

Everybody is okay, although I see a paramedic for a concussion protocol. Karen is not too happy with me. She drives the kid home in the truck while Jerry and I face the music from the cops. I am not arrested, only detained. I use my one phone call to call Bob Lee. He does what he does... eventually. It is Zulu Hour when the cops release Jerry and me from Interview Room #1. I order an Uber for the long and expensive ride home.

At midnight, at least our ride is quick to arrive. Our driver plays disco from India on the car stereo. I actually like it. Jerry shakes his head with negativity, but he is so happy not even bad tunes can screw it up.

"Best day ever!" Jerry exclaims as we roll onto Pacific Coast Highway.

"You think? Somebody tried to kill you with a gun today."

"Jerry save Roddy life."

"Yes. Thank you."

"You owe me."

"Okay. What do you want?"

"Big vinyl sale next Saturday. Freakbeat store here in Malibu. You take Jerry. Bring credit card."

"We'll see."

"More than see. Jerry have records on hold already. Texted list to store while cops with badges talk to you."

"Yeah, I didn't get my gun back."

"Why not?"

"I can't have both a conceal and carry weapon and be in possession of marijuana. They found your grass in the truck, and I had to claim it. Bob Lee is going to make it go away with the cops tomorrow."

"You make right choice. Give up gun, not weed," Jerry says. Then my monkey leans forward and asks our driver to change the station to 95.5 FM, KLOS, Classic Rock Malibu. And damn if it isn't the Allman Brothers twanging away first thing. Jerry smiles again.

"Best day ever," I say, having to laugh.

"You betcha," Jerry says and hugs me.

THANKSGIVING'S GRACE

Thanksgiving morning in L.A. We're having a swimming party. It is 90 before noon. Ramnith "Speedy" Khuzaymah and his wife Aliza bring their kids over early. Speed has just got his Detective Three ranking, and along with it, his own squad in Robbery/Homicide. He is no longer Captain Janelle Jackson's side man. No matter, Janelle is now at Park Center, LAPD's HQ anyway, busy being groomed to be the force's first woman Chief of Police. Everyone knows it. But she is not too busy that we didn't expect her for our feast.

At ten, the keg is already tapped in the back under the three orange trees. I am frying a turkey. We have a roped off area—no monkeys or kids allowed on the east side near the open flame and grease. Only drunks.

Jerry the monkey has a DJ stand set up with a table and stool on the far west side with an extension cord (far from the pool) over the wall from the garage. He plays all the hits—off of the Allman Brothers Best of set. I have made a black dot on the volume knob with a grease pencil. No louder than 4, thank you very much. "Midnight Rider" is whipping the crowd into a frenzy at the moment.

Avengers Assemble! The whole crew is there. Rat, a little bleary-eyed from late night poker, is there, drinking a red beer (Bloody Mary mix with a Modelo), stirring it with a prawn. Alongside him, RoBo. Our southern gentleman wears a cowboy hat and jean shorts, no shirt, He is seriously day-drinking and leans back in a chaise lounge. Ray Bans, dark and mysterious-like. His arm in a sling, RoBo will not swim, but he assures me his derringer has been left in the hotel safe on this day.

St. Clair and Taymur are there. The Moor, a living giant, is standing in the deep end, head and shoulders above the water. Speedy's son is on his back. Penny, a full twenty inches shorter than Taymur, stands shoulders and head above the water in the shallow end. Speedy's daughter is on his shoulders.

St. Clair sits with an old fashioned (double cherry) facing RoBo. The two both know military history and strategize old battle campaigns, which is their version of fun.

Fortune is there. He was once a runt kid in our unit at Fort Benning, but he is now a man, racked and stacked like a bodybuilder. He runs his own security agency in Hollywood, keeping paparazzi and fans behind the rope for A-listers who can pay. Fortune dangles feet in the water, drinking Perrier water and talking with Speedy who lounges on a raft in the pool. Recently, I learned that the Speedster and Fortune are hanging quite a bit. Brothers from different mothers these days. It is good for both of them. Everyone needs a shoulder, a sounding board. Even men who carry guns for a living. I am glad Speedy and Fortune are now close buds.

Clayton Grace is there with me, cooking the turkey. He's drinking Wild Turkey. Every so often, he'll have me use my massive arms and raise the 24 pounder out of the sizzling juice. He puts the thermometer deep into the carcass and gets a reading. Not yet quite up to temp. Ten minutes to go, he estimates.

Aliza, Speedy's wife, and Karen are in the kitchen chatting over a bottle of wine. My daughter Gracie has her head in the fridge, examining the bananas and cherry Jell-O the two of us made early this morning. Is it solid yet? Yep, time to eat lunch, she declares. Where is that turkey, she asks her mom.

Captain Janelle Jackson arrives solo, says hello at the door to Gracie, and then makes the rounds. Hugs in the kitchen. Shout outs to everyone out back. Janelle is a somebody in L.A these days. She gets noticed. A lot of the guys today will notice her even more when she gets down to her bikini after we eat. She is an USC ex-miler track star with long legs and all the right curves too. She still runs twenty miles a week, predawn, with a gun on her hip. Works twelve hour days and sleeps on weekends. But today is Thursday. Thanksgiving.

Janelle enters the backyard, gives Jerry a high-five for his most recent selection ("I'm No Angel" by Gregg), and waves to everyone as she taps the keg for a beer, no foam. She eventually stops her rounds in the shade of the orange trees. Cargo shorts and a USC track team tee. Shiny white New

Balance shoes. Skin the color of pecan pie. Smiling broadly with the whitest teeth in America, Janelle shakes her old partner Grace's hand. I see their eyes meet as she raises one eyebrow to inquire without saying a word on his recovery. He nods infinitesimally. All is good in the kingdom today.

Janelle looks to me. "How long on the turkey?"

"One more beer," Grace answers for me.

Janelle points to the house with her chin. "Karen says they're ready inside."

"Still waiting on Father Eric," I say. "He's saying grace."

Father Eric is the Catholic priest who had been at my side when I woke from my surgery at Landstuhl Regional Medical Center in Germany after losing both my legs. I asked him for a weapon to kill myself with that day. He refused. I am forever in his debt for that refusal. Now I have Karen and Gracie. I want to live forever with them. Things change.

Eric is now working on a screenplay. Kind of Raymond Chandler thing, he tells me. One of a million folks in the city doing that, I reply. Janelle knows of Eric's and my stories. She smiles, perhaps with just a hint of melancholy. It is my turn to nod infinitesimally.

Clayton says, "I'll let Karen know we're ten minutes off."

He leaves us.

"I note a high ratio of contract killers at this party," Janelle says with a wry grin.

"Yep, and a low percentage of cops."

"I can fix that with a phone call."

"Hold back on that. At least until after the National Dog Show."

"Deal," she says, looking back over her shoulder. "How is Clayton?"

"Not ready to come back, although I've once again leased our office space. I hope he will be able to return soon, but he's not ready. Not yet. Maybe not ever. Janelle, he's damaged, and I don't just mean physically."

Janelle frowns. "I have tried to meet him for coffee or dinner, but he's begged off."

"It's gonna take time," I say. "Give him some space. You're important to him. He'll come around."

She nods and takes a sip of beer. It is all copacetic for now.

Inside, the doorbell rings. Gracie answers once again. The guy at the door is Father Eric to us. However, nobody else in L.A. calls him that. His Screenwriter's Guild Card says Eric Benoit. Things are better for him here. Besides the unfinished screenplay, he is a budding success as a life coach with a handful of clients. He is also a youth counselor for a non-denominational church on Hollywood Boulevard.

Father Eric has found his way out of the bottle and found his way back to his faith, sans Holy Roman anything. If you ask him why he left the priesthood, he would say molesting boys was a bridge too far for any organization he would be a part of. Eric prefers his men of legal age. Thus, he said goodbye to the church for good, but not God. He decided to separate the two. The space between allows him to smile. He is currently smiling at my daughter who opens the door.

"I'm Eric. Are you Gracie?"

"Yeppers."

Eric smiles. "I'm here for the pool party. Can you help me find the swimming pool?"

"Yeppers."

Gracie, in a white Tedeschi-Trucks tank and red swimming trunks, turns and with a wave, heads through the house. The two, one a skinny tike, the other a lumbering ex-priest in a polo shirt, cargo shorts and flip flops, amble through the kitchen, saying hello and giving hugs. Gracie patiently holds the door for her guest as he gabs a bit with her mom. The toddler sighs as Karen introduces Aliza.

Then Eric nods at the waiting tour guide and steps out the sliding glass door. Just then Clayton is arriving to let Karen know to start putting food on the table. Grace exhibits a big grin and hugs the ex-priest tightly. They step back from each other and then shake hands, eyes glistening. They speak for another long minute. The little girl gazes upon them disinterestedly.

Finally, Eric looks down at Clayton's goddaughter. "Gracie here has been guiding me to the party." Eric smiles down upon the little girl. "Maybe someday you'll come to my church and I can help you find Jesus."

"Doubt it. You couldn't even find the swimming pool by yourself," Gracie says. Then she trots off to ask Jerry to play some TTB.

Clayton hears the whole thing. Mic drop moment. Swears it happened. Says he swallowed an ice cube and almost needed Heimlich. Eric laughs until he gets the hiccups. Gracie never notices, too busy getting "Midnight in Harlem" onto the monkey's turntable.

Great line. That's my girl. We did start going to Eric's church, though. He got to baptize Gracie too.

P.S. With everyone stuffed and drowsy with booze, we watch the dog show. Thor, the bulldog, won Best of Show and it wasn't even that close.

A MAN ABOUT A DOG

Grace is still rehabbing this week. Lots of counseling and PT to attend—he is driving again. The jeep is up and running. Today is the Monday after Thanksgiving, one of those clear, blue, but chilly days in the first week of December in Los Angeles where winter means wearing a hoodie.

I decide to go to the newly leased office space since I dropped a bundle on it. Maybe prematurely, according to Grace. Karen rolled her eyes as we arranged daycare for our daughter Gracie and Jerry the monkey. For the record, I didn't even consider leaving the monkey in charge of watching the kid. It would work better if I left the nearly three-year-old human in charge. Jerry is, at best, a bit unhinged. For now, Madilyn Rose Epstein, an old Jewish lady from up the block, is babysitting. I hope she can handle the maniacs.

It will likely be a "told-you-so" from Karen—money

spent for naught. I will probably be sitting on my ass, making Spotify playlists, reading *True Detective* online, but I hit the road, running into traffic, but not minding because I stopped for donuts beforehand.

But guess what? I haven't been in the office long enough to make a pot of coffee when the phone rings. Usually, when I get a call from a potential client, I listen intently, say a-huh a dozen times, and then ask them if they would like to set an appointment. They ask how much our services are. I email them the standard contract. They take a look and that's that. People who aren't seriously in trouble don't drop two grand a day, five days minimum, which is our new rate. If they bite, then something in their life has gone seriously wrong. People don't hire peeps at our rates unless the shit has hit the fan.

However, I haven't taken many cases since Grace went walkabout after the jihad was issued on his hide. Potential clients reaching my cell after the office line had been turned off were rare. Those prospective calls have been infrequent at best. If I do get a call these days, say a divorce case, I most likely turn it down. We don't do domestic stuff. I am not sympathetic enough, and Grace isn't prurient to take photos of trysts at no-tell motels. But I do get those calls, even at home, even in the evening.

After I hang up, Karen will ask, "Who was that?"

I will reply, "A man about a dog." It is my way of telling her I've turned down a case. I spare her the dirty details if I know them. Let's face it. Most times, calls to a private detective involve a shitstorm and the details are not fit for the young ears of my daughter who is usually lurking around, listening intently. Not that Karen wants to hear the dirty bits either. No need to give details about some guy diddling his secretary, cheating on his fourth wife. One time, a guy's first mistress, who was wife-approved, wanted to hire me to see if Lancelot had a second Runaround Sue. It takes all kinds.

When that office phone does ring, I gotta say my first thought is to ask myself, "Are you sure you want to slip back into this world?"

But instead, I just pick up the receiver and say, "Purple Heart Detective Agency."

It is a woman. I can tell that, but she is crying so hard I can't make out the words. Finally, a man takes the line from her. "Is this the Purple Heart Detective Agency?"

"It used to be. I guess it is again. It's our first day back open in two years. This is Roddy O'Malley."

"Yes, hello. My name is Vinmore, Wayne Vinmore. My wife Winifred and I are up in Ventura County. We heard the agency was closed but decided to take a chance. My wife followed your exploits in the paper. Actually kept a scrapbook. Didn't ever think we'd need a detective firm's services, but we do. Desperately so."

"What seems to be the issue?"

Vinmore's tone flattens out, like he was embarrassed to say the words. "We've lost our dog. He's a Norwegian Buhund, a rather expensive breed. He is named Lassiter. He's been trained to stay close. Trained to respond to my voice. Quite an obedient fellow. We've just had him a few months, and his trainer did such a good job. My wife," he stops as if assessing what to say next, then plunges ahead. "My wife lost a child. We were six months pregnant. She was devastated. The dog, Lassiter, has been playing a role in her recovery. To get her through this delicate time. Now he's gone. Winnie is, well, she's inconsolable. You can see why it's so important to get him back."

I lean back in the chair. Shit. The Case of the Missing Pooch is not my idea of our first case back in the game. Not an auspicious return to glory, eh?

Vinmore doesn't speak further. The sorrow is deafening on his end of the call.

"Mr. Vinmore, we're not dogcatchers. I can't drive up to Ventura Country to find a dog. I'm just not willing to do that. And even if I was, I would charge $2,000 a day, plus expenses, with a five-day minimum retainer. Not to mention, as you might know, I'm not really equipped to find a dog in the wilds of Ventura County. I'm missing both legs. Hiking the back country up your way is not my strong suit. If I did come up, I would need a legs man, so to speak. It would cost you an extra thousand a day to hire a second investigator. For five days, you're talking $15,000 after expenses. If you have the wherewithal to spend that sum on a dog, you would be much better off offering a $15,000 reward. That kind of jack will generate tons of publicity. You are much more likely to get your Lassiter back in that manner than with anything I can do."

We speak for a few more minutes. Vinmore assures me money is not a problem, and they indeed wanted to hire us, spend the $15,000, and in addition, would gladly offer a $10,000 reward on top of our fee. I still turn Vinmore down. Dogcatcher is not in my job description.

At lunch, Karen calls and asks if anything is cooking. I tell her I had one call.

"You took a new case on already?"

"No, it was nothing I could help with. Just a man about a dog," I reply. We then return to our regularly scheduled programming.

Wayne Vinmore calls again three days later. It is early and Karen and I are having coffee in the kitchen.

Vinmore's voice is much different than before, tonally different, like someone in shock. Perhaps quiet fury. It is an odd combo and I perk up in listening. The Ventura resident insists he and his wife hire me and want me to be there by morning. I detect a serious concern for his wife's well-being, repressed rage, and heartbreak in his plea this time.

I cut him off a minute in. "I'm sorry, Mr. Vinmore. I just can't help you find your dog."

"We found the dog."

"I see. That's great."

"Somebody killed him."

"Not so great. I'm very sorry. Hit by a car?"

"No. Murdered. I want the son-of-a-bitch found and brought to justice."

"I'm not sure a private detective is who you need. Have the police...?" I start to phrase a question.

It is his turn to cut me off. "We found the dog. I mean a hiker found the dog's body in Los Padres National Forest. Our home *is* actually in the forest itself. The dog was found on our property, which is extensive. The sheriff's department doesn't seem interested. The Park Rangers aren't equipped to even patrol the area for the upcoming fire season. No one will get off their ass."

"I don't see..." I begin, but again he interrupts.

"No, you don't. Is this a cell phone?"

"Yes."

"I'm going to send you some photos. You look at them and call me back."

It isn't two minutes before the three photos arrived. It is horrific stuff. The three texted images are so disturbing that I walk to the backyard to make sure Karen does not see the photo's contents. The dog had been tortured. The acts are really not something I care to describe. It is beyond disturbing. It is evil. Demonic. Cruel.

I call Wayne Vinmore back.

"You got them?" he asks, answering.

"Yes."

"Then you understand. Did you see? Thank God my wife didn't see them. She has been unbalanced since the miscarriage..." he pauses, and his voice breaks. "Did you see?"

"Yes," I say. "I saw." I am also silent for a moment considering those images, finding myself changing my mind in mid-sentence. "Whomever did that to your dog must be caught. It was an evil act. One of the worst things I've ever seen, Wayne. There is a sickness there that must be culled from the herd."

"I agree."

"I will be up in the morning," I say. "I will be bringing an associate. It won't be cheap, but whoever committed this act must be found and made to pay." I search for the words, "To pay for this atrocity. We'll exact justice, or vengeance, or something."

Vinmore makes an appreciative choking noise into the phone. I wait for him to gather himself. Finally, he speaks. "I will make arrangements at the best hotel locally. I'll text you the reservations and our address. Can you send routing instructions so I can transfer your retainer? I will send the fifteen thousand. I am also offering a $10,000 reward for the capture, or 'culling' as you say, of the bastard who committed this act, who tortured and killed our Lassiter. I will look for you tomorrow around noon then."

I hang up the phone.

Karen looks across a steaming cup of joe at me. "You took a case?"

I nod but don't speak. I can't explain and would never in a million years show her those photos.

My partner Grace isn't up to snuff yet, so he is out. I need help, but who? After a bit of reflection, I call Twelve Moons. I knew the Rincon tribesman is a skilled tracker, and that might come in handy up in Los Padres National Forest. I think about what tools we might need in this investigation. It leaves me adrift. I am not really sure *I* am up to catching a dog killer.

William Twelve Moons is a lanky, 6'3" Native American raised on the reservation near Valley Center, California way east past the Palomar Mountains. He is fluent in his tribe's language, plus English, and Spanish at a young age. His mother is Navaho, so he'd learned that too. Knowing Navaho made Twelve Moons an interesting recruit for the military. Navaho is perhaps the most difficult tongue to learn on Earth, so being proficient there checked some boxes with the intelligence branches. Twelve Moons ended up as a language specialist in Iraq in the Green Zone during the war. There he learned Farsi and Arabic. Upon his return after the war, Clayton Grace recruited Twelve Moons as an operative for Welmar Security because of his ability to move about the Syrian immigrant community that had formed in Valley Center.

Twelve Moons is quick with a smile, but according to sources, he is also more than adequate in combat. Grace spent two years undercover with Twelve Moons as a contractor for the CIA. If Grace says you're a badass, then you're definitely a badass.

"I'm in," Twelve Moons replies when I ask for his help. "Where we headed?"

"Just up to Ventura. Staying in Santa Paula on Ojai Road, if you know where that is."

"The sticks."

"Yeah, the sticks."

"You picking me up or I coming out?"

"Ah, you're the wrong direction and once I pick you up, then we're in traffic."

"Okay, I'll meet you. What time?"

"6:00 am here."

"What am I bringing?"

"Clothes for five days. Be ready to do some hiking. You'll

be my legs if we have a need to head into the forest, and that's pretty likely. Sidearm, long rifle."

"We aiming to take somebody out?"

"May come to that. Bad hombre we're looking for. It's weird. I'll tell you on the way up."

When I wake up, I look out the bedroom window with the false dawn. The Rincon is sitting in the driveway, like he's slept there. I am thinking everyone in the house is asleep, but Jerry the monkey sits on a bar stool in the kitchen. I greet him as I pour two go-cups of coffee.

Jerry does not look up as he scans his newspaper. "Man in red car sit in driveway when I get newspaper."

"Yeah, I got a job. He's going with me."

The monkey nods. "Be good no-police badge man."

"I will," I reply and wave goodbye on my way out. He does not notice.

We take my pick-up which is better suited to the roads in Los Padres than Twelve Moon's new Subaru. Twelve Moons just purchased the vehicle when he came back from Turkey. He also found an apartment in North Redondo near Manhattan Beach. I like that Twelve Moons is settling in. He is still on Welmar's payroll but hasn't had a lot to do since he returned. Bob Lee, our boss, has cut everyone some slack. There has been enough mayhem. Everyone needs to chill.

My pick-up is equipped with hand controls for those of us with no legs.

I take the wheel. Once on the road, sipping coffee, I tell Twelve Moons about the gig. He is surprised we are going to Ventura to find a dog killer. I can see a bit of dejection in his eyes. I show him the three photos on my phone. He changes his mind.

"If we find this sick fuck, we kill him and leave him for the coyotes?"

"I don't think we can do that," I say. "We have clients. They'll want to know we resolved the case. If we kill the perpetrator, they'll have to know. I'm not sure about Vinmore. He sounded as if vengeance was his deal on the phone, but we can't count on him being mum about it. Plus, the wife is mentally unstable, has a therapist, et cetera. We would have to assume whatever we do, they will spill the beans."

The Rincon nodded, considering. "We turn him over to Johnny Law?"

"Maybe."

"And he gets six months' probation?"

"Maybe."

"Then why are we going to all the trouble? The outcomes are in the dog killer's favor. We just going for a quick payday?"

"No, not that."

"Then what? Even if we catch the dog's killer, he'll get a slap on the wrist."

"Maybe."

"Then why?"

"The FBI stats say that fifty-six percent of all serial killers start by killing animals. The other correlations are arson and bed-wetting after the age of five, by the way."

"You think we're dealing with a serial killer emerging from his chrysalis? Or just a jerk who kills dogs and pisses the bed?"

"Maybe both." I laugh. "But you saw the photos. Do those look like the work of someone who will say, 'This behavior was a step too far. I'm going back to pulling wings off flies, or burning ants with a magnifying glass'?"

"Not so much."

We sit silent for a while. When I pull to a stop sign at the junction of California State Highway 33, Twelve Moons reaches over and stops my hand from giving the truck the gas. I turn to look at him, surprised.

"I agree with you about how important it is to find this guy," he says. "I disagree on what we do when we catch him. This bad egg will eventually hurt people, if he hasn't already. We have to figure out a way to x-out his future."

"I know," I say. "But whacking people we don't like is punishable by long jail sentences. Execution isn't in the cards. You gotta know that our clients will dish our dirty deeds eventually after one too many cocktails at the country club. Too good a story not to tell it at least once."

Twelve Moons nods and leans back. "We'll figure it out. As long as we're in agreement with the outcome needed, we'll find a way."

I shake my head. "We are not in agreement. Not at all."

I'm thinking Twelve Moons has been desensitized to

violence in his two years undercover. That gives me pause about Grace. Hmmmm.

The Vinmores live in a Swiss chalet-type mansion on the southern flank of the Ojai Mountains leading into Las Padres National Forest. We are so far from Santa Paula we are almost to Sulphur Springs. It is high desert and is quite hot by noon. The national forest feels more like an inland desert. The whole place looks to be a tinderbox that might go up in flames. Drought in California is definitely a thing.

Like a lot of responsible owners, the Vinmores have cut the deadwood and old growth out and away from their home as they are in the heart of fire country. However, the act makes their house an obscenity. A Swiss chalet in a desert setting with cactus growing in the front flower beds. It is definitely ugly. Like watching *The Sound of Music* performed on an asphalt parking lot in Culver City on an August afternoon.

We pull into the long drive curling toward the house. Vinmore exits from the front as we stop and open the car doors. The air is fresh and clear, absent of the scent of L A. smog. I note the extra oxygen.

Vinmore himself is pretty much as expected. A software designer who'd cashed out early, he wears a golf sweater over a svelte frame from long hours on a rowing machine. His legs look like a swimmer's, heavily muscled thighs protruding from his golf shorts. His face, though, does not share the extended youth of his frame. His eyes tell a different story. They are dark and sunken like a man who is not sleeping, or maybe like a man who when he sleeps finds the devil awaiting in his nightmares.

I introduce him to William Twelve Moons. Hands are shaken. Vinmore takes us inside and has lunch waiting—quail sandwiches of all things. Winifred, his wife, does not descend from the second floor of the sprawling home. Vinmore explains she has become so distraught at even the prospect of our conversation that she'd taken a sedative.

"How will you find the son-of-a-bitch?" Vinmore asks at lunch, a mouthful of bird and bread in his question.

"We need to solicit information from every nearby law enforcement officer. I have connections with Interpol. While local law enforcement will not likely take a dog's death seriously, a request about a dog's death or similar crimes solicited from Interpol will garner more interest. I'm hoping we find other cases and maybe some leads."

Vinmore nods. "You think he's done this before? Or maybe since?"

"Probably. The individual responsible is not fully in control of his impulses, I'd think you'd agree. He's sick. I think he'll be driven to repeat his compulsion, and hopefully he's made mistakes along the way."

"How can I help?"

"Just take care of your wife. If this sick bastard can be caught, we'll catch him."

"What will happen then?"

"He'll be arrested and will go to prison."

"I checked," Vinmore replies. "Killing an animal won't get

the perpetrator a year. And the prisons are so crowded, he's likely to get a plea deal. Won't do time at all."

"It's likely if we catch him that he's guilty of more than just killing Lassiter."

Vinmore stares into my eyes and then into Twelve Moon's. "I'll double the reward from ten to twenty if at the end of this the monster who killed our dog is dead himself."

My Rincon friend nods his head, agreeing. I am careful not to react.

Late that afternoon, Twelve Moons and I check into the hotel in Santa Paula. I call my boss Bob Lee from the room to ensure he is okay with my plan to use his credentials for an Interpol information request. He is mildly amused I am in the wilds of Ventura County hunting down a dog killer, but he okays my use of his international law enforcement request for information.

I send the request. Then we walk to Santa Paula's Village Constable's Office which isn't but about three blocks away from our lodgings. Constable Mullins is more than happy to see us since the Vinmores are both upstanding citizens, and notably, the richest peeps of the township.

"Thanks for seeing us."

Constable Mullins nods and allows us entry to sit across from him at his shiny desk. The air in his office is cold after the heat of the afternoon sun on our walk over. I lean back on the chilled black leather. Twelve Moons sits next of me, his jeans showing dust over his square toed boots. Mullins slides two bottles of water across the unblemished glass top of his notably uncluttered desk. Evidently, crime is at an all-time low here or the Constable is a neat freak. I am guessing both.

"I'm glad to help. Wayne and Winnie are friends. Terrible about them losing the baby. Then this. Somebody killing their dog too. Just terrible and the way the fiend went about it." He shakes his head. "I'm understaffed. And underfunded. Most of my officers have to spend eighty percent of their time writing speeding tickets just to keep us in jobs. There's no staffing for investigating a dog's death. We've no criminalist, not anymore. No detectives. If we have a murder or a robbery, I have to put in a request to have a detective come over from the city of Ventura. And we haven't had a murder in five years. Ventura doesn't like it if I make a request for assistance either. Too busy for our nonsense. They would laugh if I put in a request over a dog's death." Mullins shakes his head ruefully.

"That's all right," I say. "We'll take it from here."

"I did at least store the evidence. We do have a refrigerated locker."

Twelve Moons gives me a look. This revelation is a welcome surprise, albeit a likely gruesome one.

"What do you have?"

"The body. The contents of the dog's stomach. The ropes with the knots. Knots are unique, I've found. I've made cases on poachers where I've been able to, say, match a knot on a tent line or a rope used to haul a deer carcass out of the national forest."

I nod appreciatively. Constable Mullins has more going on than we first thought.

"You mentioned the contents of the dog's stomach."

"Yeah, obviously meat. Beef, I would think. Lured the poor beast in with chunks of beef. Oh yes, I also have the duct tape used to contain the animal's snout," Mullins reports matter-of-factly.

Then the Constable rises from his desk. He moves to the file cabinet. On top, Mullins lifts a thin folder. "I made copies of the crime report. It's just one page, plus photos of the scene. You've seen those," Wayne says. "We haven't followed up at all. Didn't find anything to follow up with."

"Can we see what evidence you have?" I ask.

He leads us down a hallway. We enter a long closet and the lawman pulls down a cardboard storage box from a high shelf. He sets it on a table, hands us latex gloves which he also puts on. Opening the lid, Mullins removes rope, stained in places with old blood, and a cut piece of tape, perhaps long enough to have gone round the dog's nose and snout three times. I note it is cut smooth. Scissors or a knife.

We examine the meager evidence for a moment.

The Constable shrugs. "Honestly, had it not been someone as prominent as Wayne Vinmore, we wouldn't have even gathered this."

"Did you find tracks?"

"Shoe prints? No, it was too sandy at the sight. Dry as a bone and becoming the Sahara day by day. No place for a track. Only impressions, ruts, if you will, in the sand. I would guess a man's size footprint. But I'm projecting. I wouldn't stand up in court and testify I knew it was a man's foot that left the impression in the sand."

I ask to see the dog, although I dread doing so. He shows us. We stay only a minute in the morgue cooler, but that is too much. The wounds are from a knife. Probably serrated. I had seen enough of those in Iraq to see definitive indications of the type of blade.

Next, the Constable takes us to his evidence locker—which is really just a fridge with a lock on it. There he removes a glass container sealed with yellow tape. A date and two signatures are scrawled across the seal.

"Stomach contents," he says, handing me the glass jar to examine.

The contents of the stomach are interesting. The beef looks to be a steak of some kind. It is diced fine. Tiny cubes.

"Any testing to see if the food was poisoned, or maybe drugged?"

The Constable's eyes meets mine, his breath rising like fog in the cold storage. "Dog didn't die of poison, Mr. O'Malley. You may have noticed."

I call Vinmore and ask him if he will take us out to the crime scene at dusk, trying to match the light of that day last week when the dog had disappeared.

Vinmore meets us in desert khaki pants and tall boots. "Keeps the sidewinders from getting a fang into you," he says, taking off at a brisk pace. I am not worried on my metal legs.

I have trouble walking through the descending desert

canyon in the loose sand. Cactus and sage brush is pretty much the only vegetation once we leave the trees. The dog had been found by a logger who claims downed trees and drags them out by ATV. When we arrive, the site is a mile from nowhere. An abandoned place where a sick monster would have felt free from the eye of civilization.

"Lassiter always ran free?" Twelve Moons asks.

"Yeah, why not?" Vinmore replies. "He was well-trained. Never ran off. No worry about cars way out here. We didn't worry about snakes or coyotes either. He was bigger than any coyote. Tough guy too, Lassiter. Plus, he stayed close in. Knew he was my wife's dog. Was protective of her. I liked that. I sold my company, but I still have business interests in Ventura. Sometimes I travel all the way into Los Angeles. It was nice knowing the dog was with her."

"But then he disappeared that day?"

"Yeah, just at dusk like we told you."

"And the logger found him here a week later?"

"A-hum."

There isn't much to see. A wide-open place. Two trees on a stark hillside. A place where the dog's carcass could have remained for years possibly without being found. Where coyotes or other scavengers could have carted away all evidence long before the site was discovered. Twelve Moons prowls around. He finds no tracks. There is nothing to see. No knowledge gained.

～

Twelve Moons and I return to the hotel rooms and a quiet dinner. We are silent during our meal, but finally, over coffee, the Rincon speaks.

"What's next?"

"We go to the library in the morning. We look through all the local newspapers. We look for advertisements for missing dogs. Then we call the numbers and see if the owner ever got the dog back. We check the dog pounds in each local municipality and talk to the employees. See if anybody has heard about a dog tortured or killed by someone."

"Sounds like a long shot."

"Yeah, I'm hoping we get a hit on the Interpol request for similar crimes to the Vinmores'."

"Sounds like a long shot," Twelve Moons repeats.

The next morning is a bust. We discover a lot of dogs go missing in Ventura County, and most are either eventually picked up by the dogcatcher or in some cases hit by cars. No one we call who'd run a classified looking for their mutt found the dog either dead or maimed by anything other than a speeding truck on California 150 or 33. Calls to vets or kennels also gets us nothing but odd silences and then negative responses. No one has a lead for us.

Just as we are finishing lunch at the hotel cafe, two Cobb salads, thank you very much, my cell phone chimes. I open it, expecting a note from Karen. It is a response from a Police Chief in the tiny town of North Fillmore, a good fifty miles west of Santa Paula.

"Didn't find a dog tortured," he writes, "but found evidence that someone carried off a hurt dog. Maybe a dead dog. Your crime scene off of Ojai Road reminded me. Thought you might like to talk."

He leaves his name and cell number.

I call it and we arrange to meet in two hours. It takes an hour and fifteen to drive there as traffic seldom moves over fifty on the highway headed west. I let Twelve Moons drive as I think. We amble along, trailing a paneled van from a florist and a flatbed truck from a local vineyard. In town, we stop for gas and to each get an Evian. We can drink the good stuff when we are billing expenses to someone else.

The Police Department building is a squat little red brick building that looks as if it had been built to withstand earthquakes, societal upheaval, and rock-and-roll. We park and enter the building. The afternoon is hot and dry. We each carry our water bottle. Inside, the Chief looks from his glass office to us, waves he is finishing up a call, phone to his ear. He nods at our bottles of water, then opens the tiny fridge to the side of his desk and takes out a Dasani. Name brand water is today's theme.

"Howdy," says Chief Marcus, pumping our hands. A big smile rests on his mug. "Nice of you to come over. Don't have much for you, but it might help a bit. Who's to tell?"

We sit in front of Marcus's desk, and he circles around it, sits and faces us, his butt on the edge of his chair. I have the feeling he doesn't get much company and is tickled pink to see someone in the office. North Fillmore is not a crime-ridden burg, I am guessing. Introductions are cordial.

"Thanks for seeing us."

Marcus smiles broadly. "Thanks for coming over. Don't often see folks from the city. First time ever I got a request for information from Interpol. You working for someone in France?"

"Ojai Valley."

He nods, a little sad at the localness of it all. It silences him.

"What can you tell us about your maimed dog?

"It was about eight months ago. Ned Williams, a school-teacher, lost his Lab. Offered a reward and all that. His kids loved that dog, so after it went missing, he spent the next few evenings out walking after school, trying to find it. Some trace, you know?"

"And what did Mr. Williams find?"

"A pool of blood."

"How did he know it was dog blood?"

The policeman is stymied at that question. "Don't know if it was, I guess. Ned called me on his cell and I went to join him. Had a hell of a time finding him. Up in the hills behind his place. It was curious."

"What?"

"A pool of relatively fresh blood on a bare patch of sand, except in the center, there was a man's footprint. Blood all around it, but not where the man's foot had been. Like the blood was spilled while he was standing there. I photographed it." He used his index finger to swipe at his phone's screen. He handed it to Twelve Moons.

We take turns looking at it.

"Looks like the wearer would have been wearing blood all over the boot and maybe even a pant leg."

"Yeah, my thought too. I was worried it might be human blood. That we had someone hurt bad up there in those hills. Sent a sample to the crime lab. They said non-human. I let it drop. No time to look into dog deaths. We're a two-person department. Sally Mint, my lone patrol person, spends her time directing traffic before and after school. Writes a good share of tickets out on the highway. She knows where her paycheck money comes from." He smiles.

"So, you know it's not human, but not what kind of blood it is?" I ask.

"Right, non-human is all the report said. Strange, though. Vibram soled boot, Sally was able to determine, but there's a hell of a lot of boots in California or even just Ventura County with that kind of sole. Size twelve. No other distinguishing markings."

"Did you try to follow a trail?" Twelve Moons asks, reading my mind.

"Nah, not more than a few yards. A little blood in the footprints, but then that went away. Didn't try after he went toward the trees and grass pastureland."

"Any sign whoever it was killed the dog?"

"Don't rightly know the dog was dead, if it was a dog."

"Seems likely given the amount of blood, plus a missing dog."

Marcus just nods. "Whatever it was, no carcass. The man carried it away. No tracks that it walked. The boot was probably covered in blood. Had to be a messy job, carrying that animal."

"How big was Ned's dog?"

"Big. That made me think too. Must be a big man. Size

twelve shoes, carrying a sixty-five-pound dog up that hill? What for?"

"Had to be determined. Strong too."

"My first though is someone found the dog injured and carried it out of the back country to save it."

"Was the animal chipped?"

"No but had a collar with identification. No one called Ned or the vet. No one took a dog to a vet. I kind of figured someone found the injured dog, tried to carry it out. Dog died, and they left it. Maybe the dog had lost its collar, maybe it was a poacher who decided once the dog was dead, it was just trouble to let us know he was hunting out of season up in the Las Padres."

"Could be."

"I thought that until I saw your request for info."

"Now what you think?"

"Same as you. Might have a sicko out there killing dogs."

That night, after dinner, I call Vinmore and tell him about the police report from North Fillmore. He sounds encouraged until I ask about his wife. Winifred is worse, he lets us know, and he's taken her for care at the local hospital. She is under observation for suicidal depression. NG, not good.

Back at the room, Twelve Moons pours us both some Surf City California Still Works Single Barrel Bourbon Whiskey. I take a sip, breathe in the fire, and listen as the Rincon speaks.

"Seems to me, our perp changed his way of doing things.

He wants to torture dogs. First time out maybe, over in the woods above North Fillmore, he follows a dog, or maybe lures it way out with his diced steak. He stabs it, maybe kills it, maybe just maims it, and wants to do his dirty deeds back in his garage or something, but it's hard that way."

"I see where you're going," I say, liking his choice of booze.

"Yeah, he decides to carry the dog out. But it's heavy and messy with all the blood. I figure he stabbed it. No guns, right?"

"No guns. Too loud for people, too quick for the dogs, but he's armed when he goes out for his hunt."

"Yeah, I agree. In case he runs into trouble."

I nod. This guy would be very dangerous.

"So now the Vinmores lose their dog eight months later. The crime is now totally onsite. He tempts the dog with the cubed steak, drugs the dogs maybe. Dog gets loopy. He captures it. He tapes the snout shut and does the deed right there. Gets his jollies and heads home. Leaves the carcass. No fuss, no muss."

"Eight months between?" I ask. "You think he waited eight months after the first one to go out again? After a successful, although messy, hunt?"

"No fucking way."

"I agree. There are more incidents out there. We just need to find them."

I grab my laptop, add the details from Chief Marcus' report to our Interpol request and resend it to all the law enforcement agencies in Ventura County. One drink later, both of us are in a snoring contest. I'm pretty sure I won.

The next morning after breakfast, we have three hits on my new Interpol request.

The first is from north of the Vinmore place and was from six months prior. The town of record is Sitas Springs off of Cal 33, near Santa Ana Road.

The second occurred west of Santa Clarita in Pirus. It was three months ago and within thirty miles of North Fillmore.

The third is more than a hundred miles from the first instance and occurred four months after the North Fillmore crime scene was discovered. It is located along Shepard's Casitas Pass just off the coast on the way to Montecito. The address was on Cal 150.

"He's bouncing back and forth across all of Ventura."

"A new one about every few weeks," I say and then amend myself. "Truly, less than that. Almost certainly less. We more than likely don't know about every dog this guy has got his hands on."

"One occurred way out east in Las Padres National Forest."

"The next along the coast."

Twelve Moons nods. "We have a serial killer out there. Bouncing back and forth across the region. But for now, he's just killing dogs."

"We think. Let's hope it's just dogs."

We spend the day crisscrossing Ventura. We interview each lawman who'd been on scene at each crime scene. There are photos that we don't like seeing. Our killer is a sick bastard.

In Sitas Springs, we hear something new.

"Old Ralph Newman, he saw the fella. He has a pond that sometimes young fellas like to fish on without permission. Day we found the dog, he saw somebody on the pond's east side. Old Ralph, he lives about a half mile or more south of the water's edge. He comes through the valley and he sees somebody near the dock on the east side. He yells and scares the fella off. Guy heads north away from Ralph. Ralph follows, but he's getting up in years and don't move all that fast-like. He does get close enough to see the fella is a big guy, lumbering like. And Ralph is laughing as he heads toward the dock on the east side. Seems the fella left all his fishing tackle on the dock."

"The dog killer was fishing?"

"No, it wasn't a rod and tackle. It was a dog. A dead dog. Crucified like. Pretty terrible stuff."

"Ralph get any kind of look at the guy? A description?"

"Not really. Said he was a big man. Over six feet tall for sure. White, brown hair. Younger than Ralph, but everyone is younger than Ralph. Moved fast, fella did."

"You investigate or send anything to the crime lab?"

"No, but it shook Old Ralph up. He wanted it all washed off the dock right away. He's religious and it bothered him greatly. Ralph scrubbed it away the same day. Buried the dog not far away in the woods. Never knew whose pooch it was. Damned shame. Ralph is still upset to have an evil son-of-a-bitch to do something like that on his property."

In Pirus, we learn the perpetrator might drive a pickup truck as one was seen leaving the crime scene. Sheriff Abbot drives out to meet us on Pirus Canyon Road, and we follow. Once there, we walk a quarter mile off the road. Stopping, the sheriff tells us what he knows.

"Jason Brit, fellow who owned the dog, he didn't see nothing. However, the master mechanic from town who lives in the walled compound to the west, Murphy Klein, he says he saw a big man moving through the trees, get to his vehicle, and haul ass out of there in a F-150 Ford pickup."

"Any details on the guy?"

"No, it was too dark," Abbot replies. "But Murphy knows his vehicles. He said for sure it was an eleventh generation Ford truck, built between 2004 and 2008. The sharp lines, no oval grill. He was sure."

"What color?"

"Burnt orange. I checked about that. That paint color's not listed as a Ford option for those years. So maybe a custom color. No one in Ventura County has one registered with that color. Hell of a bunch of F-150s, though. Most popular vehicle in the whole county, next to the Taurus. Ford must be doing something right."

"Can you show us where the vehicle was? Maybe where they found the dog?"

"Sure. Dog wasn't found until the next day. Brit went looking and spoke to Klein afterwards. Klein told him what he saw. First thought maybe they had themselves a Peeping Tom jerking his knob, creeping houses, but then they found the dog dead. Brit has three daughters. The oldest is a senior in high school. The middle one is kind of a red-haired Tomboy. Great at track and tennis, eighth grade, I think. The little one is only about six. Brit keeps a close watch over all of them. He and his wife are good people. Both Brit and Murphy were upset finding the dog mutilated like that."

"What kind of dog?"

"A Schnauzer, a good little fella. A little small for its breed, Brit told me afterward he thought it would have put up a fight. We saw blood on some sage down the trail. Thought maybe the dog made its mark before going down."

"You collect a blood sample?"

"No, it rained late that afternoon. They called me too late."

"Note any meat used to lure the dog in?"

"Yeah, now that you mention it. Cubed beef."

Abbot takes us to the road where the Ford truck had been parked. The location is secluded under some of California Valley Oaks. The trees are overgrown and limbs hang low over the road. At nearly seven when the man was seen running toward the vehicle, it would have been in deep shadow.

"Sometimes, we get parkers out here. Find a discarded bra once in a while."

"Not that night."

"Oh, no. That sicko don't get his jolly from ladies, I figure. To do that to a dog, it's a sickness."

The sheriff leaves us then, but we see the mechanic, Klein, just pulling up at his mailbox. I honk just after he enters his gate. Klein stops and exits his truck. He reaches in and hits his gate release. The locks pop. The gate opens, and he walks through, closing it behind him. Two big ass dogs, both Rottweilers, cruise up to the gate behind the man. They bark incessantly as we approach, but then Klein turns and gives a command in German. They both silence on cue.

"I help you two?"

"We're investigating the death of five dogs by the same man. Four around Ventura and your neighbor Brit's dog too."

Klein takes a moment to absorb that. "Figures a man who'd do that once would keep doing it."

"Yeah, that's what we think too. Need to stop him."

Klein nods. "Don't know nothing much. Keep to myself. Don't think nobody will be coming after my two dogs. Would be a bad idea."

"They dangerous?" Twelve Moon asks.

"One of them more than the other. Cerberus and Typhoon."

"I know Cerberus," I say. "That's the dog who guards the gates of hell. I don't know the other reference. Typhoon?" I ask.

Klein shrugged. "Cerberus's daddy. Mean animal."

"Worse than Cerberus?"

"Typhoon is, at least in my case. Both got the same training, but Typhoon just seems to have blood lust. Can't stop him once he's on somebody."

"Remind me to not come knocking after hours," Twelve Moons says.

Klein nods. "Be a bad idea. I'm a survivalist. Got me a shelter with enough food for a year. Those dogs will keep anybody from breaching our compound. They're trained to kill. Come the apocalypse, I'm not messing around." Klein turns his body toward his house. "Anything else? Or you just want to tell me you were trying to catch the dog killer? You tell Brit?"

"He's not home."

"I can deliver the message," says Klein.

"You remember the color of the Ford?"

"Too dark. Definitely body style 2004 to 2008. And then the funky taillight."

"It had a broken taillight?"

"No, not for sure broken, but it reflected weird. Like maybe it was cracked and the cheap bastard taped it. Red translucent tape maybe? Couldn't tell you for sure. He lit out so fast I just caught a glimpse."

The sheriff up to Casitas Pass on the coast also has a surprise. He'd recovered the dog's carcass after hikers had found it off trail. However, this time, the dog had vomited the diced beef. The lawman had taken samples and still has it stored in a cooler in his crime lab.

"Can we examine the beef? Maybe have a sample to send to a chem lab to be analyzed?"

"Chain of custody issues. Can't do that. We'd have to send someone to maintain the evidence's integrity," he says, raising his eyebrows. Sheriff Brown is well tanned. His uniform fits just so. He is not the crumbled local yokel we mostly have seen during our travels.

Brown smokes as we speak on the porch out front of his

tiny station. It is a square brick structure with two offices, a conference room and three cells for prisoners. There are two parking spaces out front. Both are taken with shiny new SUVs, white with black doors and cherry tops.

I have an idea. "You be willing to go to Los Angeles yourself if we set you up at a hotel, paid your expenses?"

"I don't know," Brown says, not ruling it out. His body language speaks volumes. "Maybe I could take my wife down for a night."

"Have to be tomorrow. We need results. You wanna take the missus away for a night? Have a nice dinner out on the town?"

Brown smiles. "My time, your dime? Dinner? Hotel? Drinks?"

I nod. "Yep, you just take the samples to our lab, go have fun, and pick up the results in the morning."

"Lydia will like that, so the answer is yes. How we working the details?"

I smile. "Give me your email address. I'll send you your hotel reservation. My wife is a publicist. I'll have her get you into one of those celebrity hot spots for dinner and drinks. But you get the diced beef samples to the lab first. Deal?"

"Deal."

I call the Sheriff over to Santa Clara and ask him if he would need to send a deputy or himself to Los Angeles to get the contents of Lassiter, the Vinmore's dog's stomach, analyzed, chain of custody and all.

He laughs. "For stuff out of a dog's stomach? Chain of custody? No, we're busy running a police department for humans in Santa Clara," he says. "Somebody been pulling your chain?"

I agree with him, but do not mention Sheriff Brown from the next township. "Would you send it in a refrigerated container down to a lab overnight?"

"You got a Fed Ex number? I'll get it there tonight on your nickel."

I give it and we end the call.

The next day nothing happens. I call Animal Control offices around the county for the duration of the morning. Twelve Moons visits shelters and organizations that foster dogs. Nobody knows anything, although there are now rumors around Ventura that somebody is killing dogs. Law enforcement officers talk.

Vinmore calls, requesting a status update. We tell him we know Lassiter is only one of five we now know about. I ask about Winifred. Vinmore says Winnie is somewhat better. At least better rested but still under sedation. I promise to keep him apprised of the situation.

The lab reports from the two crimes, one from Casitas Pass and the other from Santa Clara, are quite different. Ketamine, however, they do have in common.

"Quite a lot of Ketamine in the first sample, the one from Casitas," says Owen Thorsby, the lab tech I know in Sherman Oaks. He is a vet of Iraq and a hell of a guy. "Probably knock a dog out quick. Maybe even kill it. Toxic levels."

"And in the Santa Clara sample?"

"Much more refined use. The dog might be fully sedated. Maybe only slowed. Perhaps reduced to semi-conscious. Depending on the weight of the dog and the other contents in the stomach."

"The dog in the first situation was likely unconscious or dead, but not the second dog?"

"Right. If the drug was administered by a single person, he or she had gained experience. He became more refined in administration."

"Okay, thanks, Owen. I owe you concert tickets."

"Red Hot Chili Peppers coming. I'll take two on the floor up close."

"You got it," I say. "Talk to you later." I start to hang up.

"About the beef," Owen says.

I move the phone close again. "What about the beef?"

"Fine grade steak. Kobe beef maybe? Definitely Wagyu Beef at least. I know a good steak, and this had the marbling, even though it was fucked up with the dicing, being poisoned and everything."

"You're sure?"

"Definitely, primo, man. Best stuff available. And then to cut into bits and use it to kill dogs. Crazy."

"Yeah, the whole thing is fucked."

"Indeed. See you when you get back from the northlands."

We ring off.

Twelve Moons and I discuss things over pancakes at the local diner.

"We got some rich asshole using twenty-dollar-an-ounce beef to kill dogs?"

"Seems so."

"But our killer owns a ten-year-old Ford truck with a broken, taped-on taillight?"

"Yeah, those two facts don't exactly jibe."

Twelve Moons takes a bite of pancake and syrup. He smacks his lips with happiness. "Just a thought," he says, "but I wonder how many places in Ventura sell Kobe beef?"

"Or Wagyu?"

"Is that spaghetti sauce?"

"No, that's Ragu," I answer, laughing.

"More in line with my budget, though," the Rincon opines.

"Me too," I concur. "One more thought," I say. "I was looking at a map of the county after you started your engine running last night."

"Like you don't snore."

"I defer to your superior skill. Anyway, I marked the crime scenes on the map with numbers in order of their chronology. You see anything?"

"Looks like five fingers. Thumb being North Fillmore, left hand."

"What's in the palm where we got nothing?"

"The city of Ventura itself."

'No crimes there, huh?"

"Ever hear the expression, 'Don't shit where you eat?'"

"Think rich guy with Kobe beef in his fridge lives in Ventura, but goes hunting in the country?"

"Yeah, it crossed my mind."

Twelve Moons sits back and takes a sip of coffee. "Shall we visit butcher shops in Ventura today?"

"I think we shall."

It takes most of the day to hit all the grocery stores—Ralph's, Von's, and Trader Joe's—and determine only Trader Joe's has Kobe for sale. We hear a lot of Lakers jokes asking for Kobe. Trader Joe's is, we conclude, one possible location where our killer is buying his beef. However, there are also four independent butcher shops in the area. By 2:30, we visit three of them. Kobe or Wagyu is not in their vocabulary and certainly not in their inventory. One last one remains on our list – City Center Meats.

CCM is attached to a small, but vibrant, IGA store. They share a parking lot. Across the street, the Farmer's Market seems sleepy and slow. It closes at 1:00 pm, and the vendors have pulled up stakes for the day.

The parking lot for the two businesses probably holds eighty cars max in the front lot. More blacktop wraps around the building to the west, for employee parking. It is a narrow strip with two rows of vehicles. While the main lot is only partially filled, the side lot is parked full.

Twelve Moons and I enter the store, splitting up and heading to the back via different aisles. At the meat counter, I take a number—93—and hear the woman behind the counter call 87. I stand patiently—not really, but I can give the appearance of patience after two years of fatherhood. The woman wraps orders in white paper, while a butcher slices meat with the pace of reading *War and Peace* on a winter's night.

The woman with 92 in her mitts eventually steps ahead of me to have her order taken. She has enough Tanqueray on her breath that I am guessing her lime usage makes her an unlikely candidate for scurvy. Her tennis outfit clings in the right places, though, so I don't mind seeing her backside. However, her order of a variety of cold cuts in various half pound and three-quarter pound derivations takes the charm out of our encounter, as it were. I wait. And wait some more.

Twelve Moons steps close and pokes my shoulder. "Follow me," he says.

"I'm next."

"Leave it," he says insistently. "Come with me."

With irritation, I lay my ticket on the counter, seeing joy in the eyes of an old man clutching the 94 ticket to my right. It's the little things, I remind myself. I smile at the codger and follow my companion who is strolling casually toward the west wall of the store. Large picture windows, perhaps eight feet tall, loom above the shelves, except where the meat counter intersects.

"What?"

"Look out the window."

I look, still irritated. "What?"

"The truck."

"Yeah, it's an F-150. But it's bright red. Not burnt orange."

"Yeah, in the shade. Look on the sun side."

I look. The truck's color, with the Californian sun beating down on it, is burnt orange, almost brown in fact. I nod and without speaking, I walk up the bread aisle, past the checkout counters, and out the front doors. I turn right and Twelve Moons catches up with me on the hot sunbaked tarmac.

We rubberneck once to see if anyone is watching. Twelve Moons steps onto the sidewalk bordering the lot. He pauses to light a cig. He gives it to me and lights a second for himself. We stand there, puffing.

"Ta da! A burnt orange truck," Twelve Moons said.

"With a taped-on right brake light cover."

"Our rich asshole isn't necessarily a rich asshole."

"Nope, he is parking in the side lot of a butcher shop and an IGA."

"Where the employees park."

"What do you bet he cuts meat for a living?"

We stake out the vehicle from the Farmer's Market lot across the street. About 5:15, a tall, bulky man wearing a white smock, jeans and black tennis shoes exits the store by the back door. He opens the Ford with a key, gets in, starts the engine and drives away. We wait until one car turns onto the street after him, and then with a vehicle between us, we follow him out of town.

The truck proceeds down the 101, but then turns east on 126 toward Santa Clara. Midway through Santa Clara and within blocks of our hotel, the Ford turns north. It rumbles up 150 into Mud Creek Canyon. The driver, who we stay a quarter of a mile behind, drives the speed limit. He eventually turns right into Steckel Park, right again on Pine Grove Road. We remain well back, just keeping his dust in sight. The truck leaves the main road into the hills before it arrives at the KOA camper ranch. We stop along the side of the road at the campground entrance, watching the Ford truck depart up what the sign calls Mud Creek Road. It is a dirt road and anybody behind him would be easily seen. I am not ready for a confrontation, so I stay back until he rounds another bend heading south. I then meander up the road, going slow enough to not create a dust plume. As we reach the curve, Twelve Moons points for me and I can see the Ford perhaps as much as a half mile up the slope heading into the Las Padres National Forest.

According to our map, there is almost nothing between this dead-end road and the Condor Sanctuary near Hines Peak. There is nothing except trees and desert for fifty miles. You want seclusion? In Cali, this is as remote as it gets.

I don't drive up the road. Instead, I park, take binoculars, and move into the trees. We hike a half mile until we can see a house and outbuildings in the distance. The two of us settle down into the grass. We watch the house, seeing movement inside the windows. There are no drapes on the house in the kitchen and living room. Silently, we sit in the undergrowth for two hours until it is fully dark. Then with the lights on inside the house, we can clearly see the butcher move around his house. There are no signs of other inhabitants or even a pet. I figure he isn't that into pets. At least not in the traditional way.

"What are we doing? Gonna wait until he goes to sleep? Then end our problem?"

"William," I say, using his first name as emphasis, "I told you we can't just go pop the guy. One, we're not absolutely sure he is responsible. And two, the Vinmores need closure. We must be able to tell them we have resolved the case. We can't tell them we just whacked the guy. All those lawmen we spoke to will remember us."

"Okay, then what?"

I tell him my idea. Then I stand and retreat back down the road to my truck. Two hours on my knees in the sticks had done a number on my stumps. We drive back into Santa Clara, which is only twenty minutes away. The two of us eat an early dinner, set the alarm for 3:00 am, plug in our two tasers for a full charge, and make an early night of it.

It is dark as hell in the hills of Mud Creek Canyon at 3:30 am. We park up the road a quarter of a mile from the butcher's mailbox. Just beyond it, a turn-in ruts into the trees. The drive is barely passable, and a bramble of trees is spaced randomly along the front of the drive toward the road. Closer in, a large unkempt hedge hugs passage right up to where car doors would be. I imagine the limbs would scratch a vehicle going in and out.

I tell Twelve Moons to help me and we push on a small

bushy tree to bring it down across the drive. I am a strong, burly guy, and the Rincon is no slouch, but we can't budge it, even though we can both hear roots snapping underground. It is no dice on moving that tree.

Twelve Moons takes a chance and backs my truck up the driveway. He fastens the hook of the cable for my winch around the tree trunk. The wench engine is whiny and loud, so we can't use it, but the Rincon puts the Ram in tow gear and he pulls forward slowly. The torque is more than the tree will bear, and it eventually topples across the drive. Twelve Moons returns my vehicle to its shelter down the road out of sight.

Now we wait.

A thermos of coffee and two pee breaks later, the sun is peeking over the ridge to our east. We hear movement at the house, perhaps a football field away up that long, narrow driveway. We assume our positions in our planned hiding spots, crouching down in the trees and brush. We put on rubber gloves as we wait.

Eventually, a truck engine roars to life. We peer up the road in both directions. Nobody else seems to be about. The red Ford descends the drive to our location. The butcher brakes and exits the vehicle.

"For fuck's sake," the butcher says, staring with disbelief at the tree across his drive. He approaches and again considers the situation with another f-bomb. He then bends and tries to lift it from his trail. No dice.

I hear the man curse once again under his breath. Now he moves to the truck and reaches behind the seat for a tow rope. Rope in hand, the man, whom I estimate at a good 6'3" and who has eaten his share of pork chops, bends at the tree, struggling to get the rope around its base. With our butcher boy kneeling, Twelve Moons and I step from hiding and tase him twice in the ass.

Butcher boy gives just one grunt as he topples into the downed tree limbs, unconscious.

"So far, so good," the Rincon says.

"Let's hope the son-of-a-bitch lives alone."

Inside the butcher's house, it feels like a messy bachelor's place. Newspapers, mail (addressed either to occupant or Mr. Steven Celedon), and empty beer cans litter the living room. The sink is clear of dishes from the previous night's meal. The remains of a steak, cut from the bone, lay on a skillet on the stove. The freezer is filled with beef. I am guessing Mr. Celedon's cholesterol is in bad shape.

Twelve Moons backs the butcher's red truck up the drive. Then we move my truck up beyond where anyone could see it from the road. We turn off his cell phone, taking out its battery and ensure there is no landline. We cover the windows with towels and duct tape. The room is dim, even with the lights on now with the windows covered. Steven Celedon lies on the floor. I take a glass of water and splash the man's face. He awakens slowly, his eyes becoming wide with fear as he discovers his arms and legs bound with security ties. Twelve Moons and I both wear Zorro masks, and our captive looks at us with terror as he regains his senses.

"Hi Steve, my buddy and I are here because we think you've been a bad boy."

Celedon tries to yell but ends up gagging a little with wadded sock Twelve Moons earlier put into his mouth.

"Shush," I say. "This won't take long. We're going to search your house and see if we find any evidence of your interaction with dogs. It won't take long and if you are clean, we'll be on our way. Sorry about the tasers. Most people's hearts don't stop when they get shot, but it was a risk we were willing to take with you."

His reaction is again the wide-eyed Betty Boop thing, but he doesn't try to speak this time. At least Celedon is a quick learner.

The two of us wear dark clothes and gloves, guns on pancake holsters on our belts. Our masks are stylish, I think. I guard Celedon as he lies on the floor of his shack. Twelve Moons tosses the place.

There are guns in the closet and some pretty traditional porn on the nightstand, but nothing perverse. We don't find any evidence he has been killing dogs once a month for the last two-thirds a year, though.

Until we do.

Under a rug at the entrance to the single bathroom, the wooden floorboard rattles as Twelve Moons steps across onto the tiled floor of the smaller room. The Rincon nods at me, kneels and moves the rug. Twelve Moons tugs at the loose board, but he can't move it. He removes a serrated blade from his boot's sheath. He flicks the tip of the blade under the board and pops the slat free. There in a space about eight inches wide and a foot deep, my partner withdraws a vinyl three-ring binder from the hidey-hole.

"Ah, methinks we have found our treasure!" I say.

Celedon lunges upward, but my bindings are secure and he falls backward like a fatted calf.

Twelve Moons approaches, giving the bound man a wide berth and sits beside me at the kitchen table's only other chair. He opens the binder. Inside there are a dozen tabs. He flips the first open. It is a sketch of a dog. A healthy-looking dog. It is a good sketch in charcoal and pencil. Steve Celedon has talent. It does not mean he is not a bad apple. I remind my partner that Germany once had an art student who went off the rails too. Artistic traits are not always a good sign when dealing with psychopaths.

Twelve Moons turns the page and things go downhill. On the facing page, the same dog is depicted in the same charcoal and pencil. Now it is damaged and dead. The Rincon shakes his head and turns the page again. Now we have an actual photo of the dog, and on the fourth page, an actual photo of a fatal wound.

There are nine filled tabs and three blank. We flip through each, finding the same pattern for the eight dogs. However, we come to one that chills our bones. At the tab where we expect to see a sketch and a photo of a gray Schnauzer belonging to Brit, we instead see a drawing and then a photo, grainy from enlargement, of a little girl.

Twelve Moon closes the book and his eyes. "The Brit guy has three girls."

"One of them six years old," I say.

"Celedon here killed the Schnauzer, but maybe he was thinking about moving up in species."

"Looks that way. Eight tabs of dogs, all with sketches of dogs. All with photos of dogs. Then kill shots. One with a sketch of a little girl, one with a photo of a little girl."

"But the kill shot is still of the dog."

"Probably lost his nerve." I look down at Celedon and see that he has wet himself.

I take my taser from my waistband. I switch it on and the hum is loud in the room. "Moisture makes it hurt more," I say. Then I turn out his lights once again. I can hear a little sizzle as the taser hits his groin.

It takes three more hot shots to keep Celedon out until sundown. By then, we find a bottle of Ketamine in the meat drawer of the refrigerator. One baggy of chopped Kobe beef seems to have been tainted; one seemed pure, deep pink and plump.

"I could put a little A1 on that with a slice of onion and not even need it to touch the grill. I like good beef mooing at me," Twelve Moons says.

"Make sure you grab the right bag," I say, laughing.

I notice Celedon is stirring. This time rather than hitting him with the taser, I reach down and remove the sock from his mouth.

"You shout, and both of us will give you a jolt to the scrotum, got it?"

He nods, and I can see fear had him. Cold sweat is forming on him and he smells of it, perhaps even stronger than the urine on his jeans.

"You can't do this," he says. "I did bad things. I killed dogs. I admit it. I just couldn't stop myself, but I'm ready to fess up. I'll pay my debt to society. You can't just torture me with a taser forever. Can't imprison me. You have to turn me in." He bobs his head up and down. "I mean to the law. Take me to the police."

I laugh and look to Twelve Moons. "I'm thinking that isn't something we're planning on doing. See, the photo of the little girl in that book fundamentally changes our perspective. But I do figure you are probably hungry. We'll give you some food. I mean we're not animals or anything."

The Rincon is in line with me without us having to discuss it. He goes to the fridge and gets the Ketamine-laced diced beef. He stuffs a handful into Celedon's piehole despite him trying to avoid it. The Rincon holds the man's nose until he opens him mouth. It doesn't take long and Celedon is snoring softly on the floor. No need to gag him again. But we do.

"The plan still a go? Or did you change what you want to do?"

"All systems go, Houston," I reply.

We wait until after midnight and then take care of it. We are tired after carrying Celedon through the woods. Lifting the unconscious man over the wall is even tougher, but I am a strong fellow. I can also be quite determined.

It is 2:00 am when we make it back to the hotel. We sleep until the sun comes up, ready ourselves for the day, check out of the hotel, and drive back toward Los Angeles. I call Vinmore and tell him we believe we can do no more and are headed home. He sounds angry, but I tell him it will end with the man's capture eventually.

∽

Sheriff Abbot of Pirus calls us just as we hit L.A traffic at the Tejon Pass south of Bakersfield. I put the lawman on speaker through the truck. Twelve Moons is driving and he raises an eyebrow upon hearing the sheriff's voice. He gives me a poker face.

"Figured I'd hear from you two fellas today," he says. The sheriff's voice sounds pleasant, almost happy.

"Why's that?" I ask. "We gave the case up. Used up our five-day retainer. To be honest, we hit a roadblock. We found enough to know for sure that some perv is out in Ventura killing dogs, but that's as close as we got. Five dead dogs."

"I got more than that," he says. I can hear his bemused smile through the phone.

"And what would that be, Sheriff?"

"I got me a dead dog killer. Guy named Steven Celedon, a butcher in Ventura, who lives up in the sticks in Mud Creek Canyon."

"You caught him?"

"No, didn't catch him. His dirty deeds caught up with him."

"How so?"

"Well, you fellas remember that Brit fellow. Lost Teddy, his Schnauzer. You remember him?"

"Yeah, the guy with three daughters."

"Right. And next door, the neighbor Klein has the walled compound. The survivalist plumber fella? I believe you spoke to him."

"Yeah."

"This dumb son-of-a-bitch dog killer, Celedon, climbed Klein's wall. Had a camera, a carving knife, and a five-foot snare-em. You know, like dog catchers use. Found a bag of poisoned beef on the outside of the fence. Must have fallen out of his pocket as he climbed over. Guess the dumbass thought he would take on Klein's Rottweilers. Didn't work out for him."

"Klein called you."

"Only after it was too late. One of those Rotties, Typhoon, the mean one, got there first. Klein heard the racket and came running with his over under, but it was too late. Dogs ripped Celedon's throat. Bled to death before the ambulance could get there from town."

"You're sure it's the right guy?"

"Yeah, damn sure," Abbot said gleefully. "Found a note-book on the seat of his Ford parked under those same trees as before. Same broken taillight, right year of truck, like Klein said. Notebook had photos of the five dogs in it and more besides. Also, had a photo of Jeannie, Brit's little girl in it. That gave me a chill to see that. Celedon got his due. We're well rid of him."

Vinmore calls and tells us that he is elated to hear the man who'd killed Lassiter and the other canines is dead. Although we weren't directly responsible, he is happy with what he calls our inertia which seemed to push the perpe-trator to make a fatal mistake. He pays us the bonus in full. I give Twelve Moons half, a full five grand extra. He made ten grand in the week. The agency received fifteen.

Vinmore tells us one of the policemen has questions for

us. He finishes the call, saying Constable Mullins will be contacting me.

It isn't an hour later, and the law enforcement officer, whom I remember as no dummy, calls. I am home now. I take the call, but step out by the pool, so his words are private. I know our subject matter is bound to ruin an appetite.

"Hello, Mr. O'Malley, it's Constable Mullins, up here in Ventura County."

"Yes, sir," I say, "Mr. Vinmore said you would be calling. What might I do for you, sir?"

"Wayne tells me you had decided to quit the case after your five day's retainer was up."

"Yes, we were on the way back to L.A. when Sheriff Abbot called to let us know that Celedon had been apprehended."

"Not quite apprehended. The sheriff recovered the body."

"One as good as another," I say.

"Not exactly. We don't do dead-or-alive these days, not so much."

"I was just expressing my opinion that the world is better off without his kind."

"On that we can agree. I did wonder about a couple of things on the morgue report."

"What's that? And why would you want to ask me?"

"Just a curious constable, shall we say."

I laugh. "Okay, shall we say. Ask away."

"The body was found with five distinct burn marks indicating the man had been tased in the previous day or night. You know anything about that?"

"Perv's have strange turn-ons," I respond. "Any signs of any perversity at his home? Auto-asphyxiation? Porn?"

"None that would explain self-harm. And no taser was found in his vehicle or home."

"Perhaps a prostitute paid to provide some sado-masochism?"

"Perhaps." His end of the line is silent.

"Anything else, Constable Mullins?"

"Wayne says he paid you a ten-thousand-dollar bonus for the case's permanent resolution?"

Now it is my time to be silent.

"You seem like a very strong man, Mr. O'Malley. Able to hoist a man over a wall, especially a man who is drowsy with Ketamine poisoning."

"I work out. And I'm naturally big-boned."

Mullins' laugh is dry and mirthless. "You don't seem much like a quitter, not when you have a client with a big checkbook. I was surprised to hear you had packed up and went back to the city without resolution to the case."

I come back at him. "I told Vinmore from the start he would do better offering a reward than paying me to look for Lassie or whatever. I didn't want to take his money. I didn't want to come north, not until I saw the photos he sent of his dog. Even less so after. But after seeing those photos, I knew whoever killed that dog would end up killing humans. You know the FBI stats on serial killers spending time in the minor leagues with people's pets. Somebody needed to apprehend that evil fuck. I volunteered to do it for a price. I didn't end up finishing the job, but Celedon is dead. I think everyone, especially the Britt family, is glad of that fact. Vinmore is certainly grateful."

"How much did you make this week, Mr. O'Malley?"

"My associate and I were extremely well paid. Plus expenses. And we're worth every penny."

"I don't believe your story, nothing personal. I don't want you back in Santa Clara, Mr. O'Malley," Constable Mullins says in a flat tone.

"Yeah, that won't be a problem," I say. "Nothing personal, but I don't think it's small enough for the both of us."

"We like our small town ways," he says. "Don't need your city poison up here bothering the good folk of Ventura. Celedon's injuries and death kind of feels like a case I could investigate, but I won't for Winnie Vinmore's sake. My wife and her are close. I don't think Winifred could take any more stress. I will let things lie."

"You take care of yours, Constable Mullins. I'll take care of mine," I say flatly.

I hear him grunt and the call ends. I nod, knowing there is now one more place I am not welcome. Shrugging, I go back in and join the family.

We have an eventful evening as both Gracie and Jerry get peanuts stuck up their nostrils. Four nut alarm. Eventually, I make them cry by squeezing their noses until the peanuts break into pieces Karen can remove with tweezers. Both monkey and kid are mad at me when I send them to bed early, but it is better than a trip to the emergency room ... and the vet.

MAN ABOUT TOWN

The next morning Karen corners me in the kitchen. Jerry is reading the paper with his roller, headphones on, and the little imp still seems miffed with me.

"Outside," she says, pointing to the sliding glass doors. I follow her out. I figure I am in trouble for how hard I squeezed our daughter's nose. Or did I leave the toilet seat up? Did I leave the refrigerator door ajar? I have no clue about my crime.

"I have an idea," she says.

"That is always scary."

Karen smiles deviously. "Oh, you like my ideas sometimes."

"Oh," I say, winking, "we'll have to hurry then. Gracie will be up soon." I take Karen's arm, aiming her back toward the house.

"No," she says. "No pony rides. I have an idea for Jerry."

I pause, liking the previous idea better. "What about Jerry?"

"You know my starlet?"

"Sassy Spencer? Yeah, her movie deals pay our mortgage."

"That it does," Karen reflects. "I just signed her to a major horror flick yesterday. My cut will pay that mortgage of ours down considerably."

"Very good news," I say, "but what has that to do with Jerry?"

"The horror flick is called *Phantom Pain*. It's about a wing of soldiers at a military hospital. The V.A. tries out an experimental drug on them for their phantom limb pain and it goes wrong."

"Documentary, I take it."

Karen nods. "I thought that too when I read the script, but I was under a nondisclosure, so I couldn't say anything."

"Back to Jerry," I say, no longer amused.

"Sassy plays a nurse who ends up running for her life when the amputees grow invisible limbs back. They can't control the invisible appendages and become homicidal."

"Still not seeing any Jerry," I say.

Karen raises a finger for me to be patient. "Well, it's a year before *Phantom Pain* will start production, but there's going to be a big press conference on Sassy's signing. Everyone there. *Entertainment Tonight*, *Variety*, *L.A. Times*, *New York Times*, the foreign press, you know, the whole nine yards."

This time I just raise an eyebrow.

"You know Sassy just broke up with that guy in that band?" Karen adds.

"Yeah, I just downloaded the first album, whatever it's called, by that guy in that band."

It is Karen's turn to raise an eyebrow. Pause. Then she says, "Sassy doesn't want her break-up to be the focus of the press conference. She wants it to be about phantom limb pain."

I laugh. "Sassy wants it to be about Sassy."

Karen nods. "True. But super not about the ex. She wants to bring Jerry to the table with her."

"Jerry?" I say. "On national television? What, in a little tux?"

"Oh, that's a great idea. No, wait. We need to be able to see he's lost an arm. Maybe just a cute little vest and a bowtie around his neck."

"You're wanting Jerry to speak with his little box? Bob Lee won't like anything about this idea at all, but least of all if Jerry speaks."

Karen looks horrified. "No, Jerry doesn't get to wear his little box. He would just be there as a prop. Cute little monkey with one arm gone. To draw attention to phantom limb pain. Sassy will do all the talking. The presser is about her first major role in a feature film."

I shrug. "I'm sure Jerry will groove about being on TV. But he's unchained mayhem, take it from me. But you ask him yourself. Tell him what the gig is. He's savvy enough that you'll have to pay him. Buy him a box set of some vinyl. That will keep him happy." I lean in and kiss her cheek. "You sure you want to buy what's Jerry's sellin'? It'll be trouble."

"I think Jerry will be pure gold in publicity," Karen says, smiling and putting her arms around my neck.

"What could possibly go wrong?" I say, laughing. "What could possibly go wrong?" But she starts kissing me and I don't care about Jerry anymore.

"Wanna go back upstairs?" Karen whispers in my ear.

I am willing.

MAN ABOUT A MONKEY

It is the year of early morning phone calls. This one on a Wednesday. Karen is already up. Her starlet has just been cast in a horror flick. Contracts are to arrive today. It is a big payday for both, said soon-to-be movie star, Sassy Spencer and my baby. Up and Adam. Cash the check.

I am still in bed, but kind of dimly lit. The house phone rings. I pick it up. Bob Lee's voice. I barely can form words. "Rod here. 'Sup?"

His reply is curt. "Get on the scrambler. Secure the line. Call me back in five."

"Ten," I say and hang up.

Karen comes out of the bathroom. "What was that?"

"Work," I reply and head downstairs in my apelike method. I am missing both legs above the knee, so my arms, long anyway, are longer than my stumps. I scrunch my calloused knuckles into the carpet, swinging my torso along. I usually slide downstairs on the seat of my hemmed-shut compression shorts, but I sleep in unhemmed cotton jammies, so no slide. I descend on knuckles here as well. Bangity-bang, bangity-bang.

In the kitchen, Jerry, my one-armed monkey, sits on a barstool, drinking coffee—I am glad he'd made some. The Rhesus dude wears my headphones, which are plugged into his roller/scanner/reader. He runs the device up and down over *Rolling Stone*, which is spread on the counter next to a half-eaten croissant. The device rolls over a copy and translates it into speech. Right now, that speech is piped into his head by my headphones. I can see he is reading the personals, searching for what? Monkey hook-ups? I appreciate him using the headphones. Gracie, my daughter, is still sawing logs.

"Morning, Hot Rod," he says, waving his one arm. He speaks by typing on the symbol keyboard on a device wrapped and secured on the stump of his left arm. It translates the message into audible English or he can choose to send it as text with the press of a button. He is in a good mood, I can tell, as the Pee Wee Herman-like voice of his device is registering normal. His armband also has sad and excitable modes.

I pour a cup of coffee. "Morning, Monkster," I reply. We are big on nicknames this week. "Thanks for brewing the coffee. I have to make a call. Need to set up the scrambler and get a secure line. I'll set up in your bedroom. 'Zat okay?" It wasn't really a question and Jerry hardly takes notice anyway, but then he turns to me.

"Big Boss Bob call?"

"Yeah," I say, slip into Jerry's bathroom, use the facilities, finish, wash up and then prepare the phone set-up with the scrambler plugged into the landline. The landline is plugged into a laptop, and the desktop phone jacked into the laptop. I check the connections, log on, test both the phone line and the internet connection. All good. With a gulp of coffee, I judge it has been about ten minutes and I call.

"We secure?" is my greeting. Bob's voice is his all business one. Which is what you get ninety percent of the time. He is generally not good at parties.

"Yeah, what's up?"

"Sending you a video."

It is one weird vid. It was recorded in a warehouse or basement of a garage. Concrete wall behind and poor lighting to boot. In the foreground, a juvenile gorilla stands. A man in a black ski mask, long sleeve white shirt, suit, but no tie, holds a pistol to the ape's head.

The gorilla is blubbering. His hands are in front of him and his fingers are gesticulating in rapid fire. He is scared. That much is obvious. I freeze the screen for an instant to gather more data in my head. I pinch the touch screen to increase the image size. I examine the gun by expanding the screen even more. The gun is a rare one. A Shadow Hawk, government issue, if I remember correctly. Five-inch barrel, Trijicon night sight, and an extended mag. Very expensive gun. Five grand or more in pristine shape, but maybe not this one. This one has a gouge on the side of the barrel. Cut deep and curved like a dick with Peyronie's disease. Not good in all the ways you might imagine.

I start the video again. Not much else. Nothing in the background of the shot to indicate anything. Nothing I can tell about the man, except that he is slightly taller than the gorilla. His hand is steady with the weapon.

The ape continues to blubber, but then a human voice floats in. We can still see the gorilla's head with the gun to it, but now just the hand with the weapon. In the movie business, the shot would be considered an extreme close-up. The voice comes in from off camera. "Three million in forty-eight hours. By 5:00 pm Friday, or we kill Gorgeous George here. We'll be in touch with the arrangements. Plan on a wire transfer to an offshore account. More on that later."

That's it. End of video. My screen fills with my boss's face.

Bob Lee's voice: "The gorilla was taken from the Philadelphia Zoo last night. There has been no public announcement yet, but it will leak today—too big of a story—so the zoo and the police are going to get ahead of it and make an announcement within the hour."

"And why does Welmar Security give a shit?"

"We hold the contract for security at the zoo."

I laugh. "That seems out of character for Secretary Welmar."

David Welmar is Secretary of Defense for the current nutjob in the White House. He owns a billion dollar munitions company and a very sketchy pharmaceutical firm. Welmar is not a good guy, but he is my employer.

CEO Robert E. Lee clears his throat before responding. "Rupert Mendelson is the zoo director. He was Secretary Welmar's roommate at Yale. They have remained close."

"I'll bet," I say, still amused. "Why the scrambled call if the story is going viral today anyway?"

"The Secretary wants us to be hands on from the top

down on this one. He doesn't care about the gorilla, or even the three million, which could be paid by insurance, but the publicity could be tricky. Blowback in the press is the last thing the administration needs. Thoughts right now are this ape-napping is an eco-terrorist group wanting the President to look bad."

"Yeah, the orange cheeto has been perfect up until now."

"This operation is non-political."

"Top down mean me or you?"

"Both of us. I will send a limo to you. I am in San Francisco. My team will leave within the hour. Touch down in Las Vegas in two and we'll wait for your shuttle. The limo will arrive at your home within the hour. Bring any equipment you need for a quick solution. There will be a Lear at Orange for a private flight. No one will be checking your bags. You should bring one man. I have already informed the Philly police and the FBI that I will be bringing two investigators. How soon can you be ready?"

"Got to get somebody to watch my daughter Gracie. Get my second lined up. Shouldn't take too long. I can call you back on the cell with an ETA."

"Do so. We need to get this ape back home before CNN has a fucking field day."

"Animal Planet too," I retort, but Lee has already hung up. I start to unplug the scrambler, but I hear a shuffle on the tile behind me. I turn and Jerry is standing there in his little red satin robe. His eyes are big ovals.

"How much of that did you see and hear?"

"Jerry see all."

"Well, you weren't supposed to. This stuff is secret. You can't discuss it with anyone, okay?"

"Jerry speak gorilla."

"What?"

"Jerry speak gorilla. You want know what George say?"

I raise an eyebrow. "You're telling me the gorilla was communicating? It sounded like a blubbering baby."

"Two messages."

"Two?"

"Yes. First is Gorilla Sign Language. I use same for my arm pad. George is sad, yes, but he is signing message with hands."

"And what did George say?"

"He say food no good. People bad. People mean. Cage cold, no blanket. Say he want back to Jan."

"Back to Jan?"

"Yes, name. Jerry no know Jan."

"What was the second message?"

"George say with mouth. No eco-terrorist. He say gangster. For profit. Otero gang in Philly behind ape-napping."

I spill coffee in surprise. "You got to be shitting me! Are you serious? He said the Otero crime family is behind this hair-brained steal-the-ape thing?"

"Yes. He say."

"Jerry," I warn, "this is serious shit. No joking. Did Gorgeous George really say the Oteros grabbed his monkey ass?"

"Yes. Jerry sure."

I call Bob back. I tell him what Jerry said. Lee swears for a while. Then he says, "Get things around on your end. I have contacts who can verify the sign language part of Jerry's cockamamie tale." His voice falls in pitch as he takes the receiver from his face. "Fucking monkeys," he says in exasperation, hanging up.

I tell Karen I am leaving town for a couple of days. Then I call Father Eric, my defrocked priest buddy who is now a Hollywood life coach, and he volunteers to watch Gracie for a couple of days. I act like it's a huge favor, which it is. He reacts humbly. In truth, we both know he needs the money. He says he'll Uber out within the hour.

Next, I call Twelve Moons, but the Rincon reminds me he is back on the reservation seeing family. Rat is gone too, playing in the World Series of Poker this week in New Jersey. My partner Clayton Grace still doesn't have his head on straight and is up in a trailer in Topanga, catching up with his inner coyote. RoBo and Penny, the last I heard, are back in Florida. St. Clair and the Moor are in Belgium. My options are limited. Fortune is here, but his experience with gunplay is extremely limited. That kid is just A-List Security and not up to battling the Oteros. Yeah, Fortune is out. By process of elimination, only one of the team is available right here, right now. The Chechen rebel, Vakha Bahaev.

I call him. Tell him Bob Lee has called our numbers. We are going into the game. A driver will pick him up in thirty minutes.

"I be ready," he says, with his Slavic accent. "Need to bring weapons?"

"Yeah, sidearm, plenty of ammo. Wear a suit. Pack for a few days. I will bring the rest."

Bob Lee calls back. "The monkey's story checks out. The

hand signals say essentially what Jerry told you. Jan is Gorgeous George's caretaker. Nothing in there about it being cold or the food bad, though."

"Maybe he got that from the verbal," I say, then pause. "I'm bringing the Chechen."

Lee swears again. "Vakha Bahaev," he says in disgust. "You're bringing a contract killer to find a monkey?"

"Bob, I'm a contract killer. You called me, remember?"

"Don't make me regret it." Then it is his turn to pause. "Aw, hell," he finally says, "bring the goddamn monkey with you."

Vakha's limo dumps him at the private airstrip at Orange fifteen minutes after Jerry and I arrive. The Chechen raises an eyebrow at the monkey as we board the Lear, but he asks no questions. I like that. He wears a dark gray suit with a bulge under the left arm. I like that too.

I show him the video on my laptop on board, explain the mission and tell him about Jerry interpreting Gorgeous George telling us that the Otero Crime Syndicate is behind the ape-napping.

"You have bad blood with Oteros, yes?"

"Yeah, they shot Grace from a rooftop a few years ago. I took it personally. Killed the man responsible. They know and don't like me."

"Yes, that would be bad blood," he says approvingly. Then he tips his seat back and sleeps the remaining forty minutes to Vegas.

Jerry, however, is way too excited to sleep. "First fly, Jerry," he says. "Well, first fly up top. Came to America in cargo hold. This better. Way better."

"It's cool, huh?"

"Yes, Jerry like. Look out window. Would be good with weed. That okay?"

"No, and I told you that you weren't to bring any. We're working."

"Jerry just make joke."

"Not a funny one."

The monkey ponders that for a moment. Then says, "Jerry now no badge police with you, yes?"

"Yes, you are officially a member of Welmar Security's Secret Assassination Team." I laugh. "It's very prestigious. Except you can't ever tell anybody. Not even Gracie or Karen."

"Save Gorgeous George, get picture in paper?"

"Probably not."

Jerry nods and looks out the window for a while. As we start our descent, the simian turns and speaks. "Jerry get benefit package?"

I throw him a second package of peanuts, laughing. "That's it."

Jerry smirks, pleased with his joke. He tears open the nuts. "Good start, but Jerry need three week vacay first year."

Bob Lee rendezvous with us in Vegas, his jet idling on the tarmac. Besides the pilot and one steward on board, Lee's two security guards, Miles and Vernon, wearing spiffy navy suits with pancake holsters on their belts, greet us at the gangway. Just inside the door, Lee's personal secretary is a slim, scary guy with a pencil-thin mustache and what looks to be a petite .28 caliber semiautomatic stuck in his belt. Orson mixes an old-fashioned for Bob Lee. He makes eye contact with me but doesn't speak. I avoid that guy. His eyes are set too closely together, and he seems to be looking at me over his nose as if sighting in on a target. I wonder vaguely if I punched his nose I could un-cross-eye that guy.

"Keep the monkey aft in the office," Lee orders from his captain chair. He doesn't look up from his reading.

"Aye-aye," I say. I hustle Jerry to the back. We discover that the furniture moves and locks on the rear wall. I move it. A full double Murphy bed swings down from the wall. I set Jerry up on the bed with a huge seatbelt over him. He takes out his roller and begins to scan the Spiderman Annual. I remind him to wear my headphones. He nods and goes back to Peter Parker's exploits.

I go forward with Vakha for takeoff. We grab a beer and try to schmooze with Lee and the boys, but Lee is in such a foul mood, I excuse myself and go back to Jerry. The Chechen sleeps. The monkey is sitting on the desk against the bulkhead looking out the window at the brown desert receding in the distance. He looks forlorn.

"What's the matter, little guy? Are you queasy? Flying upsets some people's stomachs."

"No. Jerry belly fine. Bowel movement this morning real good."

"O-kay," I say, "TMI."

He does not smile. Something is wrong.

"What's bothering you?"

"Jerry confess."

Now it is my spidey-sense going off, not Parker's. "What do you need to confess about?"

"Gorgeous George not speak. Jerry make up."

I almost punch him. "What? You made that stuff up about the Oteros?"

"No, that real. Jerry know gun. Recognize gun. Dark gray. Green on sight. Deep scratch, curly on end like feather."

I am still furious. "You lied to me. I am going to have to go up there and tell Big Boss Bob. You'll be lucky if he doesn't throw you out of the plane." I pause, then add, "Mid-flight."

Jerry leans forward and bumps my chest. I am ready to clobber the little troublemaker. "Roddy man. Listen Jerry. It was gun at park when my pills bad. Last man out of car. Pointed gun at Jerry. Shoot at Jerry. Jerry drop grenade. Dark gray gun. Green button end of barrel. Big gouge. Curl like feather."

I take a step back. I reflect. That gun was very unusual. A collector's piece. A Nighthawk 1911 style with a night scope site and an extended mag. Long, deep gouge, distinctive swirl at the end of the damage. It might be traceable. And I know people getting shot at do generally remember details about the gun, maybe more so than the shooter. It could be true for a monkey too.

I don't speak but instead leave the cabin. I go and sit down next to Lee. "I think I might have an angle to find the guy in the video."

Lee raises an eyebrow. "I'm listening."

I tell him about the gun. That it is a museum piece except for the damage to the barrel. That a gun so unique might be noted somewhere in the Philly PD Organized Crime files. Lee doesn't speak, but he motions for his secretary, Orson, to make the call.

Then I go back to the bed and sleep next to Jerry until we land in the City of Brotherly Love. You never know when the next time you'll get rack time during an operation.

As we taxi in and stop, there are two dark Mercedes waiting for us.

Vakha, Jerry, and I are escorted to the sedan. Bob and the boys to the stretch.

"Where we heading?"

"You are expected at the Four Seasons Hotel Philadelphia at Comcast Center. Johnny Otero is expecting you. Leave the monkey in the limo."

"And what am I supposed to do?"

"Just tell Johnny we have evidence that one of his men has taken the monkey and the full force of the federal government will be used to resolve the issue. Tell him to cut his losses. Return the monkey. We can let any arrests slide. We want the monkey back unharmed and we will not be paying a ransom. Tell him if he doesn't, shit will rain down." Bob Lee bends to get in the back of the stretch, but I stop him.

"Do we have any evidence?"

"Not yet," he says, "but I'm checking on your weapon lead as we speak. I should know soon. The FBI is now involved."

"Where are you headed?"

"Franklin Square. Philadelphia Police Headquarters. I want an update on any developments since we've been in the air, plus I want their Gang Detail laser focused on the gun. We'll see you at Le Meridien. We have a block of rooms. I will text you your room number after we check in."

"Any advice?"

"Don't let the Oteros frisk you and take your weapons. I hear the Chechen is good. I hope we don't have to find out."

"Me either."

Then Lee is gone.

On the sixth floor of the Four Seasons, the Chechen and I exit a private elevator to a private lobby, brightly lit and decorated with bamboo-paneled walls and deep-piled Persian rugs. Two thick-bodied Italians named Tony and Anthony, I imagine, are waiting. One approaches, arms raised. Hands forward as if he intends to grab my partner. He wants to feel us up for weapons. Or at least feel us up.

Nothing doing on that score. Vakha Bahaev shrugs away the man's advances. The Chechen is not giving up his weapon. Vakha's facial expression makes his position plain, but he does not speak. I like that. I grin. The thug looks to me. I shake my head no. He frowns to match my grin. He acts like he is going to pop attitude, but his partner says, "Wait," and makes a quick call. We are cleared to enter with our weapons. Electronic locks pop loudly. We leave Mutt and Jeff behind. I'll bet their little brother is named Tony too.

We step inside to a huge reception area in a monstrous private suite. I recognize Johnny Otero seated on a bar stool. He tilts there against a fully stocked bar, a bottle of Johnnie Walker Blue within reach. It looks as if he is having scotch with his coffee. I think about recommending Jameson.

It is late afternoon, nearing dark. The streetlights from below provide meager light through the tinted windows. Otero is at least sixty, I suppose, and he looks it. His face is pitted with ancient acne scars. Johnny's hair is starting to recede, much thinner than any arrest photos I saw while researching him earlier. His eyes are dark. They are venomous, and the poison in them does not look like he has lost his edge. Johnny Otero is head of the third largest branch of the mafia in America. His eyes know evil and they reflect it. I see it and it makes me wary. Otero is short, thick at the waist. Lots of pasta. His legs dangle as he stares across the room at us. Think Joe Pesci on a bad day on steroids.

But of course, we are not alone. Johnny has friends, if a man such as he can have friends. One man sits below Johnny in the sunken living room area. He is nearly swallowed by the cushions of the pit's circular couches. His suit coat is open to show a sidearm under his left shoulder. His jowls leak a shadowy smirk. A gold tooth gleams like the barrel of a gun.

However, it is the two other men, one at ten o'clock and one at two at the edge of the room, who have my attention. With the man on the couch, Vakha and I are standing in a triangulated kill zone. I can barely see the two hidden in the gloom of the large room. The edges around the recessed pit group are dark and I cannot see much of them, except below their knees. The Chechen seems to recognize the danger too. He focuses up that way as well. I spread my hands subtly, ready to reach for my firearm and dive toward the floor. Vakha moves away from me. Tension rises in the room. I half expect the tune from *The Good, The Bad and the Ugly* to start playing until a voice from the shooter at ten o'clock interrupts the emerging Mexican standoff.

"What the fuck are you doing here, Roddy?"

The man who speaks steps forward. He is extremely short, but I know him extremely well. It's Penny. He's one of my band of brothers from Iraq, a bro from back in the sandbox. I rotate my head enough to see the other hired gun is RoBo. He holds his maimed arm in a sling in my general direction. I know it holds a weapon aimed at my heart.

"Same question to you, I guess," I say to Penny. "I thought you two just worked for the Cosa Nostra in the Sunshine State."

RoBo steps down onto the carpet. His free hand grips mine.

Johnny Otero interrupts our homecoming. "Robertson Bonney, you know these men?"

"Yeah, this one is Roddy O'Malley. He was in my unit in Iraq. The other I know just in passing. He is a contractor from Chechnya." RoBo looks at me, raising an eyebrow. "You brought a gunner? Why? I thought this meet-and-greet was over some bullshit monkey caper."

"It is. I was to bring one man. Only found out seven hours ago. V was the only man in town."

"Bad move. Ratchets up tension. His rep is bad medicine. Shoots first and doesn't even bother to ask questions later."

"Yeah, I know. Your reticence to use violence is also well known."

Penny pipes in, "I still like our odds."

Vakha Bahaev gives him a look to say who gives a fuck. "Yes, Penny, we start shooting, you might kill me. Because I will not shoot you." He nods at Johnny Otero. "Anybody grabs gun and I kill Otero before I die."

Johnny doesn't like that much and says as much. "Simmer the fuck down, everybody. I don't need a game show cluster with hired guns in here. This is about the monkey. I mean, what the fuck anyway? I don't know nothing about no monkey."

"Yeah," I say, "I thought you might not. We figure it was one of your capos or somebody going freelance. But somebody high up in the organization. He's not a soldier. We know he was in San Fran on the pain killer caper. He might have even been in charge. He carries a high dollar gun. A Night Hawk, green site, cut on the barrel. Stupid that. Carrying an identifiable gun on camera for a job. One of a kind gun like that in a video. Stupid. You're well rid of him."

Johnny looks vaguely interested.

I continue, "Your renegade is holding out on you, Johnny. Running a three million dollar scam right under your nose. You know nothing about it. He's skimming three mil and not cutting his boss in? Stealing a monkey from the college roommate of the Secretary of Defense? Your boy is a real stupid bastard. I'd deliver him to David Welmar in pieces if I were you."

Johnny Otero's eyes get really scary. He tips his head back to look down his long nose. "Might not be the only dumb fuck delivered to Welmar in pieces. I remember you. Fucked us in California on the pills. Burt told me all about you."

I laugh. "Burt? Not the sharpest knife in the drawer, Johnny. You know that. I wouldn't put my business on the line on Burt's word."

RoBo puts oil on the water to soothe things down. "Johnny, let's slow things down. You'll let us check on the gun thing? Let's end this soiree before it goes way wrong. Penny and I will sit down with these two. Break bread. Have a couple drinks. Keep things calm. Get things figured out peaceful like. Nobody hurt." RoBo looks to me. "Where you staying?"

"Le Meridien, ask for Robert Lee. The big man is here himself with a full team. Welmar has decided this one is a pissing contest, and he's standing on top of the Pentagon to make sure everyone is downwind of his stream. Johnny should avoid taking on Secretary Dr. No. He's a different level of crime lord. Not worth it. Give up the fuckwad who took the ape. We can all go home."

Penny laughs and throws his hands up in the air. "Maybe another time," he says to Vakha.

"Damn, Penny," RoBo replies, "put your dick back in your pants. These are friends."

Penny nods at Johnny. "Not when I'm on the clock."

That makes Johnny Otero smile.

"Come on by for a drink later," I say to my brothers-in-arms. "We'll get pizza or some cheesesteak sandwiches."

"Both?" asks Penny. That little man is always hungry. But

his comment is good news. I know we are still good and that his B.S. macho play had been an act for his employer. It is all copacetic.

Back in the limo, Jerry is all questions. "Who you kill?"

"Nobody, it turned out to be Penny and RoBo."

The monkey eyes get big. "Who Penny and RoBo kill? Otero? Did you free George from his captors?"

"No, this was just act one. We still don't know who's got George. Got to let Johnny Otero calm down and figure out he doesn't want Welmar up his ass until the end of time. Easier to give the monkey back than fight the FBI, the CIA, the NSA, Army, Navy, and scariest of all..." I pause.

"Us," Jerry says. "We bad. We nationwide."

Vakha narrows his eyes and nods. "Worldwide. I am from Russia. I will not die without bringing others to the devil with me."

I shake my head, not liking that talk. Gunners always have their dicks out. "Let's just reel things back in, bad boy. We'll get to the hotel and order some grub. Deal?"

Jerry grins. "Yes, Jerry hungry. Jerry take full pill. Get easy. Lots of tension today. Jerry no arm hurt bad before. Not now. Jerry feel good. Pill good."

I nod. Phantoms haunt us all. I am glad the little guy can find a way to dodge his phantom limb pain for a while. Me? I still am feeling on edge. I'm hoping Gorgeous George is spending his last night in captivity. Well, at least in Otero captivity. After all, the gorilla's goals are modest. He just wants to be returned to a better jail.

Bob Lee spends the afternoon at the Philly Police Department. The local cops, he is assured, are checking on the gun. The fancy gun with the scar is nothing anybody on the Gang Detail can tell him about off the cuff. Teams will work on it in the morning. Time is running out. We are all aware of the ticking clock.

In the meantime, the ape-nappers have sent a text message from a burner phone with routing instructions for the wire transfer of three million bucks. There is no text, just a routing number to an account in Switzerland. Three million to be transferred before the 5:00 pm deadline on Friday. That is 21 hours away. George has less than a day. He won't have to suffer through bad food and a cold jail for much longer. Either way, I figured he isn't sleeping as a hostage tomorrow night.

Vakha, Jerry, and I stop by Bob Lee's suite of rooms at the Le Meridien. Orson, his secretary, opens the door. He wears no jacket and the .28 caliber is shiny on his hip. He is doing a very good impression of Doc Holiday without the cough. His vest is paisley across his slim back. I expect he has a derringer up his sleeve, and just maybe the ace of diamonds.

"Lee's this way," Orson says, stepping aside for us. Vakha,

Jerry and I march past, and I note Orson's nose is turned up at Jerry. *Yeah, the Rhesus doesn't like you either, ya priss*, I think.

Lee's living area is full. Besides Security detail Miles and Vernon sipping water and packing heat, and the priss, Orson, Lee is entertaining one other man. Bossman Bob introduces us. "This is Detective Evan Marsi. He has been assigned to sit in on your pizza party tonight."

I laugh. "That's not necessary. RoBo and Penny are my guys. It's like having somebody on the inside. We're fine eating pizza downstairs by our big selves."

"Will they be giving you intel?" Marsi asks. His voice reveals disapproval and aggression. He does not like us. The detective is a stout man, bald with a heavy five o'clock shadow. He is wearing suit pants and suspenders, but no suit coat. Instead, he sports a Sixers jacket, loose enough to cover his service weapon. He looks competent and smart, but he is out of his league with our weirdness. He waits for me to answer, so I pause a long bit to get his goat before responding.

"No, no intel. RoBo and Penny won't cross the mob. You don't do what they do for whom they do it and then cross people. Penny and RoBo ride for their brand. But they aren't gonna kill us. That's a bridge way too far. If it comes down to shooting, we're good to go with two more guns on our side of the ledger."

Marsi wrinkles his lip. He likes all of us none whatsoever. "My orders are to accompany the three men registered as Roderick O'Malley, Vakha Bahaev, and Gerald Monk. I am to stay until the two Florida hitters leave your suite."

Jerry starts laughing. "Roderick! Funny."

"That's not my name. It's Rodney," I respond.

It makes the monkey laugh more. "No more. Now all I call you Roderick," the monkey says, laughing.

The detective stares at him with a gaping mouth. Evidently talking monkeys are rare in Philly.

I intercede. "Detective, meet Gerald Monk, monkey consultant for Welmar Security."

"What the fuck?" Marsi replies fiercely, standing and stamping his foot.

It makes everyone laugh, especially Jerry. "Me Gerald in disguise. Really Jerry. Jerry and... Roderick." He points to me with his one arm waving to a crazy dance.

Everyone laughs again, except, of course, Bob Lee and the detective. I think even Orson cracked a smile. Maybe there is hope.

"Okay." Bob Lee stands and snaps his words, ending our comedy bit. "Back to business." He looks to me. "How can we leverage Otero enough to make him rat out his boy?" Lee asks.

"Johnny will never do that. He might kill the ape-napper and leave the body with the Night Hawk in his mouth for us to find, but he won't rat him out to us or the police. If the offender's a capo, somebody far enough up the food chain to afford a five-thousand dollar gun, then he knows too much about the organization to turn in to the cops. That is not our play."

"Then what do we do?"

"We need the name. Detective, we need to know what capo in the Otero ranks was in California for the pill steal and who owns that gun. It's someone with balls enough to steal Gorgeous George, but still stupid enough not to think through the consequences."

The detective shrugs. "Gang Detail is already looking. I got nothing you ain't got. Now, let's move and get you into your rooms before Thing One and Thing Two arrive."

I nod in appreciation of the Dr. Suess reference.

As we sit in our L-shaped living room in front of a big screen two floors down from Bob Lee, Detective Marsi reads us the riot act. We listen as we wait for pizza and hit men to show up.

"You's three would be downtown in a holding cell without the sway of your boss upstairs." The cop points to Vakha. "You are wanted by Interpol for a murder in Poland."

Vakha shakes his head, amused. "I have never been to Poland. That was my dear departed brother. God's blessing on him. He is gone now. Killed by the Iranians in Turkey."

Marsi says, "Yeah, right. It was your dead identical twin who did the killing. Right. That's handy."

Vakha shrugs and sips his beer.

"And you." Marsi points to me. "You're a person of interest for, like, thirteen dead gangsters up in San Francisco. You and your partner Clayton Grace. Where's he? Lurking around with a sniper rifle?"

"No, he's living with a coyote up in Topanga Canyon," I reply.

The doorbell on the suite rings.

"Like a human trafficker coyote?" asks Marsi of me, unde-terred by the bell.

"No, the dog type. Named Dapper. Kind of a mind reader coyote. It's a complicated story."

Detective Marsi flips me off and goes to get the pizza. He peers out the peephole before answering. But he's hungry, and we ordered dinner. Cops gotta eat too.

Penny and RoBo arrive minutes later. Detective Marsi wants to frisk them. No dice. Hitters don't like that. Penny has never liked people to touch him much and shrugs off the cop like a flea. The detective is a big guy, but Penny is like a fireplug on steroids. Penny shakes his head, not backing away. Marsi looks offended, and I intercede. I warn the copper to just let it go. No violence is occurring here. It is all copacetic. Just a pizza party for some international contract killers from out of town. And a talking monkey.

Penny is funny all evening and holds court, trying to get the cop riled up, which is easy money. He skirts on drug trade, then being a mercenary, then suggests we call some hookers. None of it plays well with Marsi. After riffing on loose women in Miami for a bit, the conversation takes a darker turn with our short hitter from Florida.

"You know," says Penny to Vakha, "I *could* take you."

"Where he take?" Jerry asks, munching on cheese-stuffed crust and drinking a beer.

"Maybe prom," I answer.

Vakha laughs along with everyone, but I notice his hand

flick to his jacket buttons. He lays his lapel back. Chechens don't fuck around as much as we do, I am thinking.

I change the subject. "I know you guys don't do stuff like this," I say to RoBo, "but we need the capo's name. The one with the gorilla. The one who carries the Night Hawk."

"One, we don't know the name," answers RoBo. "Two, we give that up and they find out, there'll be a contract on us."

"What a shame," Detective Marsi says. "Two dirtbag hitters for the Florida drug mob get whacked in the City of Brotherly Love." He sneers. "Wouldn't even make the newspaper up here. Small time punks, all of ya's."

"You have a newspaper? I mean, Ben Franklin is dead, right?" Penny cracks.

Jerry shakes his head. "Not good joke, Penny. Need to up game."

That makes me laugh. The cop too. Penny frowns.

RoBo raises his good hand, slowing the roll. "Johnny and Burt are having dinner. They're going to talk. Decide, I mean. I think they know who you're after. They know for sure who was in Cali with the pills. They probably know the gun you've identified. Probably deciding if they can get their hands on the three million without too much heat. But it will be hard for them to decide to whack their own guy. It's hard to take out someone high up in the family. A made man. All the soldiers below take notice. Instability is bad for the organization."

"But so is freelancing," I say. "Express to Johnny when next you speak to him that if they don't assist us in the return of Gorgeous George, shit will rain down in Philly until Rocky has to swim up those steps at the museum."

Jerry says, "Good movie. Me like Apollo Creed."

Penny turns back to Vakha. "You never responded when I said I could take you."

Vakha finishes his beer, belches, and sets down the bottle. "Chechens don't talk much about killing. Rarely with friends. Never with police in the room. Maybe we talk someday. Maybe there will be no talk."

I wave my hand. "I'm going to call the dick measuring contest a tie for this evening. I'd like to thank the contestants and ask them to place their members back inside their pants."

Jerry laughs. "Jerry tiny dick," he says.

We all laugh at that.

The detective looks around the room, shaking his head. "Just a bunch of punks sitting around playing the dozens. Nobody's got the balls to do anything. I am wasting my time here."

"What is the dozens?" asks the monkey.

"The dozens is what he do to your momma," Penny says, laughing.

Jerry frowns.

The detective nods in appreciation. "That there is the proof. Just punks playing the dozens. And talking about mothers is a sure sign we have moved to round two. I'm out."

Detective Marsi stands, shaking his head. "I'm going home to my wife. It seems pretty clear that you's are not going to shoot each other. It is far more likely that all of you end up in a circle jerk." He points at Jerry. "He seems the sanest of the lot. Yeah, I'm not any part of you's circle jerk. I am out."

RoBo stands, laughing, raising his bottle of beer with his good arm. "Yeah, guys, and remember to pivot left. I have one arm in a sling after all."

That gets a reaction. "Sick fucks," the cop mutters as he strides to the door, but I am thinking RoBo got a smile from him. Marsi's bluster is an act, and as if to prove it, Marsi slams the door on his way out. We all laugh again.

"Good riddance," Penny says. "We've got problems, but nothing cops are going to solve. Right?"

I nod. "Right. RoBo, get Johnny Otero to give us the name. Tell him if he lets us know who, we'll do the wet work for him. The four of us. He can wash his hands of it."

RoBo nods. The room is silent. We have agreed to kill someone. It is solemn for a heartbeat or two. But the monkey breaks the tension.

Jerry looks to me. "Jerry have to confess again."

I narrow my eyes. "What now? More lies?"

"No, no more lies. Jerry smuggle your marijuana bag and pipe in a pair of socks in my suitcase. Me want smoke bowl before eat pizza place brownies."

"You hid them in a pair of socks? You don't wear socks," I say.

"And yet *Roderick* not check them in my suitcase," Jerry says, scolding.

Everyone laughs at me. Tomorrow's violence forgotten for now. One team again. Rolling around, laughing, on the cushions of a pit grouping in a hotel suite that costs five grand a night. Everyone laughing at me. I nod at Jerry, letting him know I am not mad.

"Bring it on," RoBo says. "I think all of us could use a

buzz to smooth the waters."

"Especially Marsi. Cop boy too intense for Jerry," the monkey nods.

"Weed can indeed smooth ruffled feathers, Jerry," Penny says wryly. "Even mine. Go get those socks."

And he does.

Later, with everybody gone, just after I turn out the lights, my phone rings. I pick up. It is RoBo.

"Johnny took you up on the job. We four move on it tomorrow. It will have to be in daylight. Deadline's tomorrow at five pm."

"Got a name I can give the boss?" I ask.

"Salvadore Razutti. Johnny decided to cut him loose."

"Mañana," I answer. I decide to walk two floors up to deliver the news personally.

False dawn. I am drinking a cup of bad coffee at the bar in our suite. The room is quite dark. I can hear the Chechen snoring. But then Jerry is there beside me.

"You awake?"

"Yeah."

"You scared die today?"

"Not so much that. The guys we're going after are not nearly as skilled in combat as the four of us." I pause. "But there is always a chance."

Jerry begins to look freaked out.

"I'm not dying today, little guy."

"Then why sad?" Jerry asks as I pour him a cup.

"Knowing you're going to kill someone should be sobering. Let me give you an example. You know Clayton Grace, my partner?"

He nods.

"If I could describe him to you two years ago, the three words I would use would be 'happy,' 'steady,' and 'focused.'"

Jerry scratches his head. "Grace not like that now."

"I agree. He spent two years with people trying to kill him while he himself perpetrated violence on a regular basis. It damaged him. I think violence injures you either way—if you are killed or if you kill. Either way, you are diminished."

"Jerry understand."

"Good. Now you promise to stay here while we go get Gorgeous George today?"

"Jerry promise. Can you leave credit card? I shop vinyl and have Uber deliver. Good record stores here."

"Limit at a hundred?"

"Two?"

I frown. "Okay," I agree.

"Pretax, right?"

I nod in surrender mode. Then I go and wake Vahka. In a half hour, we are both ready. Jerry is at the bar using the headphones and his reader with the newspaper which had been delivered to our door. I open the door. "Stay inside, okay? I'm putting the 'Do Not Disturb' sign on the door. You can order room service if you want. That is the only time you use the phone, okay? Order your records by text."

He nods, then he pauses and a solemn look fills his eyes.
"What?" I ask.

"Don't fuck up, Roddy. Come back Jerry."

I have to smile. "Deal," I say.

Vahka just laughs. Then we exit and put on our game faces.

Johnny Otero is not stupid. You don't stay head of an Italian crime syndicate for 28 years if you're stupid. The cops are after you. The FBI is after you. The Russians want you dead. The Haitians want you dead. The Mexican cartel wants to cut off your balls. The Columbians would do the really bad stuff to you.

To stay on top for 28 years means you're smart, you're brutal, you stay out of the news, and you don't take unnecessary risks. Last night, Johnny and Burt had dinner, accessed the risks of fucking with a friend of the Secretary of Defense for a one-time score. Stealing a monkey and making it the number one story in full rotation on every newscast in the country is stupid. *"Where is Gorgeous George?"* is the headline in every newspaper. Hell, the *Go Fund Me* page for George has more than the ransom price pledged after one day. The Oteros make the smart choice—have the out-of-town talent handle the problem and then have them leave.

RoBo and Penny pick up the Chechen and me in front of the hotel. They have spent the night casing the scene of our target. RoBo gives us the lowdown on the way.

Salvadore Razutti is the capo with the Night Hawk. He

has three men with him on the caper. They are hiding in an abandoned car repair shop on 30th and Ridge in a shithole neighborhood called Strawberry Mansion. It is two blocks from the Schuylkill River and the Hiking Trail which goes through the neighborhood. We meet Orson there. Miles, one of Bob Lee's security detail, is in the van too. The four us, grim-faced, get in the van. Penny hands Miles the keys to his rental. Miles exits. Momentarily, he drives Penny's car away. I don't think we're going to see it again.

Orson is tight-lipped, which I respect. He is wearing a deep brown three-piece suit with a burnt orange pin and a bow tie with a black shirt. I figure he still has his cute, little gun on his hip too. Orson's killer attire is different than the rest of us who are wearing jeans, black sweatshirts and work boots. Penny has a large duffel of weaponry he disperses to us. Vakha gets two Glock nines. So do I. RoBo takes his weapon, a customized Charles Daly PAK-9 semi-automatic with an extended mag. The gun has two grips, and it comes with a sling to keep it from flying out of control as the shooter releases the cache of twenty rounds per mag. Penny takes his two Glocks and reaches in his pocket and begins to insert two metallic inserts into his weapons' slides.

"What's that?" I ask.

Penny smiles. "Called a Glock switch. ATF calls it an 'auto sear.'"

"And it does what?"

"Keeps the gun firing until I let off the trigger. I put on extended mags. Fires the 30-round clip in 1.9 seconds."

"Get it at the toy store?"

"No, brought mine which are metal in Miami, but you

can 3D print these things at home out of plastic. Template's on the internet. Either of you two want one?"

Vakha and I decline.

The play is simple. Our target is an abandoned building at the end of a block. It is barely six in the morning. No one is about. RoBo and Penny have cased the property overnight with an infrared heat-detecting device.

"Gorillas run at a lower temp," RoBo explains, "so we got him pegged in the garage. They have him stuck in a bay with the car lift up over him. Netting or something to keep him in."

"It's structured in a big 'L' with a reception, waiting room, and manager's office in the front. Bays in the leg of the L. Restrooms and rear door off the back beyond the bays."

"Our play?"

"I blast the fuck out of the front window. Two guys up there. Two back with the ape. Put forty rounds through it," RoBo says.

"I am on the dumpster lid looking in the window opposite the bays," Penny adds. "I fill the office and hallway with sixty rounds. Nobody from the front is going to the bays."

"And Vakha and me?"

"You," RoBo says, and points to me, "you just walk in the front door. It should be clear after the havoc I'm going to create. Vakha kicks the rear door. Comes in hot. Hopefully, nobody is back there taking a shit."

The Chechen nods. I do too. The four of us put on black latex gloves and ski masks. We are good to go.

Orson drops us and without a word drives away. He'll be at the corner waiting. Our getaway vehicle—an unmarked van.

There is no waiting around. Vakha walks around back with Penny. Penny leaves him at the back door. He goes on around the side and climbs onto the dumpster. Even on top, he is barely tall enough to fire in the window. I am crouched by the front door. RoBo stands on the side, watching Penny's ascent. Penny waves him the okay. We are a go.

It is loud. I mean like dropping a hymnal during a prayer loud.

I think RoBo starts the shooting, but Penny joins in almost simultaneously. RoBo fires twenty rounds, pauses, slaps in a second clip and lets fly again. Penny has a momentary pause as he switches guns. He lets fly with another 30.

When RoBo finishes the second magazine, he nods at me. I step in. The door is locked, but it is glass and little of it remains. Inside, the forty shots have done extensive damage to pretty much everything. My ears are ringing and things have slowed down. It seems everything is broken. Except for a certain Salvadore Razutti who'd been sleeping on the couch in the waiting room. He is on the floor, gun out as I come in, low and then to the wall, using the gum machine for a shield. Razutti squeezes off two rounds, but they are behind me. Gumballs fly like asteroids. I am not in a hurry. I fire with both guns when I'm sure.

Vakha comes in the back door. A man is indeed in the bathroom or at least he was until the cacophony of gunfire occurs. He heads for the backdoor. Vakha greets him. The Chechen fires a trilogy of shots sounding like one short trill. The man drops, his weapon skidding down the hallway tile.

I meet Vakha in the hallway. At the opposite end, the Chechen offers a grim smile to me and holds up one finger. I hold up one. We turn to the bay. Still two bogeys out there. We peer around the corner.

The gorilla is peeking up from the far bay. His cage is six pallets leaning against the metal car lift, its greasy silver pole in the middle of the bay. George is babbling in fear.

Two voices call to us from the other bay, the open pit. "We're not armed. Don't shoot us. We're not armed. We're just here to keep the ape healthy. We own a pet shop. Don't shoot us."

By now, Penny is inside. RoBo too. I keep Penny from tapping one into each remaining man's ears. No more killing. Instead, we quickly zip-tie their arms and legs to the lift pole in their bay. For good measure, Penny pulls down their pants. It makes me laugh and I remind myself to tell Jerry that detail.

I look to RoBo. "How do we get Gorgeous George home?"

"We don't," he replies. "Orson will call Bob Lee. Lee will call Detective Marsi. We let the police recover the beast."

RoBo leads us back to the front door. He stops and takes the Nighthawk handgun from Salvadore Razutti's stiff hand. RoBo unzips the capo's fly and inserts the gun in so the barrel pokes out like a five-inch woody. Penny laughs. We exit.

I find out later the operation took less than three minutes.

We change clothes in the van. Guns, clothes, gloves, and masks go in the duffle. Orson drives us to a place called Delaware River Steel. Penny walks to the front door as the seven o'clock shift begins. The director of security is waiting for him. Penny is given a visitor's badge, walks with the security man up two flights of metal stairs. Then they walk down the long ramp where the man unlocks a steel door onto a large metal platform. Below them, Penny can see the slag heap, glowing deep red at 2300 degrees Fahrenheit. Penny tosses the bag two stories down. It is too loud in the foundry to hear the weapons hit the molten metal. There is a brief flame. The man nods and Penny hands him an envelope. He is back in the car in five minutes. He tells us about it in the vehicle. "Guy was wearing a Welmar Security shirt."

"Steel is a vital manufacturing process," says Orson. Then he drives.

Orson takes us to a private runway somewhere west of the city. Penny and RoBo get in a Florida bound jet. Vakha and I get in the other. Jerry is in ours. I smile when I see he is drinking champagne. "George safe, radio says."

"Yes, let's go home. Where's Bob Lee?"

"Lee talk police. Say he send us home this morning. He drive me here. Lee say he will talk to Otero. All good. Police take credit."

"Detective Marsi will be a star."

Jerry points at the cop on the television screen built into the seat back. "Marsi smile good on TV."

We will be home by noon.

MONKEY GRINDER

I call Karen from the plane.

"There's got to be some changes made," she says right out of the box, her voice full of gravel.

I am thinking about having just killed a man. I agree but don't think we're on the same page right this second.

"What happened?"

"Gracie was at Montessori. They were at story time. It was Gracie's time to tell a story."

I groan. "Did she reveal bad shit?"

"Oh no, not that. She just was rambling on about living with a monkey. Each child gets five minutes max. Our girl went way long. The instructor asked Gracie to wrap it up, and she says, 'Shut your piehole, you wheezy bitch.'"

"That's unacceptable," I say, stifling a guffaw.

"You think?" Karen says, exasperated. "And where would she have heard words like that? From you? From Jerry?"

I don't think either Jerry or I have used 'wheezy' as a

curse, but I don't want to tell Karen that Gracie might have been freelancin'. Her technical prowess at swearing is already at a high level. "No idea," I say. "Definitely not me. I'll have a talk with Gerald Munk."

"You do that. There's got to be some changes made."

Karen hangs up. I tell Jerry to get his ass in line. He just nods silently but then flips me off. We both laugh. We are still high on life, having survived a firefight. I open two Miller pony bottles and we clink a toast to flying home after a gig.

Some change, and some don't.

GRACE AT WORK

"I should have been there to back you."

That is Clayton Grace speaking to me in the kitchen. I am getting a stack of ribeye steaks out of the fridge. Those beauties have been marinating in Italian dressing all afternoon. The gang is here. Well, the gang minus our cop friends.

Immediately after a mission or a case, there is euphoria. Call it a survival celebration. A soldier celebrates coming home. That's the immediate. A catharsis. I've lived to tell the tale. Yahoo.

But there is an after. The comedown from the euphoria. Karen, my fiancé, knows after I come back from one of those missions I cannot talk to her about, that I need downtime. I have already celebrated living. Now, I want to curl up in a fetal position and hold close all of those who mean the most to me—Gracie and Karen, and I guess, now Jerry. That is stage two—realizing all I hold dear could be ripped away by my choice of employment and the random inherent nature of violence. Wait. Did I choose this violent path, or did it choose me?

No matter at this stage. We are entangled. And knowing that, I curl into my ball like a centipede in trouble. Eventually, however, I must emerge. Life must be lived. I want to reach out to my compadres. I want to feel the zest of life with those who understand my feelings. There needs to be a confessing of sins and forgiveness by those who know and understand what we do. That is the stage we are experiencing this evening. My return to the zest for life. Thus, the gang is all here.

Grace is on hand and he is earnest. He is ready to come back to the agency. I am ready too for him, but I will hold out on him a bit. Not to make him beg, but to make him think deeply about the dark world we enter every time we take a case. The madness of it. The violence of his last two years has likely caused a renewal of his PTSD from the war. It has likely caused his symptoms to worsen. I want him back by my side. Who wouldn't want to work with his best friend? To go into the fray with the partner best in the world at having your back? I want him, but I know the line of work we do is not a great idea for him. I don't think I can stop him. I don't *want* to stop him, but I have trepidation on whether I will let him back in for him or for me.

I nod at Grace's statement, smiling patiently. Grace believes he is best at keeping me alive. I happen to concur. We discuss it openly. Nobody else is in the house. Karen has taken the kid and the monkey out to see the movie *Dumbo* on the big screen. Jerry has never been to a theater but is looking forward to the live action version of the film. Gracie showed him the cartoon version on DVD. Jerry is quite curious how the filmmakers intend on soaring a real elephant through the skies.

"Jerry know about elephants," he says. "They big and fat. No fly."

"Movies are always fake," I tell him. "You just have to believe for the time you are at the show."

Jerry shakes his head. "Fat pachyderm, no fly." But he is excited to attend. I stare at the monkey, wondering how "pachyderm" came out of that armband he wears. Gracie gives me a look and she rolls her eyes, like I got her into this, now get her out. I laugh, and they are gone.

I shower, shave, and put on cargo shorts and a fresh t-shirt. This one says, "I'm with stupid" with an arrow that points down. The house is clear, so I put on "Bittersweet" by Big Head Todd and fire up the one-hitter. All is good.

An hour later, the bar is ready outside, the ice chest is full of beers, the coals are stoking, and the appetizers are on the counter in the kitchen. The boys arrive – Fortune, Twelve Moons, Vakha, Rat, Father Eric, and Grace all join me. Father Eric is not a soldier, but we include him after I get a guarantee from him that all that is spoken this evening will be considered as words in the confessional. He agrees. The priest is in.

It is a cool L.A. evening for December, but the pool is heated. The guys all swim a bit and then as the coals get to the right shade of red, I head in to grab the steaks. Grace joins me in the kitchen.

I know he wants to further discuss his return to the

agency, but I need to get the steaks on the grill. First things first. I leave the house and Grace trails along. I grill the steaks while Father Eric heats the beans and gets the picnic table set.

Dinner is good. The weed is good, and now my Weller on the rocks California style with fresh lime is good. Everybody is leaned back. Bellies full. The booze works its magic.

Father Eric throws out a question. "Can I ask what led all of you to this profession? I mean, do you consider yourselves at this stage to be mercenaries? Soldiers of fortune?"

"Are you asking if we are paid killers, Father?" Grace asks with a raised eyebrow.

"Do you consider yourself one?" is the reply.

Grace nods. "I would have to say yes after the last two years. How did I get here? Joined the army to show my asshole brother that I was as tough as him. Got a leg blown off. Ended up working where they would have me. A private eye is a profession with very few rules and low entry requirements."

"As for me," I add, "I was given the choice of the Army or the state penitentiary. After that, same as Grace, except I lost both legs."

Rat nods, his toothpick firmly in place. "I figure I've done dastardly deeds, sure enough. Definitely when Grace and I did the Russian mob job for the gang banger, Thiago Reyes, but I don't consider myself a paid killer. I am a professional gambler. I work for Fortune when he is overbooked at times, but I play cards. When I list my profession for the IRS, I write 'gambler.'"

That makes everyone laugh.

I ask, "You think RoBo and Penny list 'hit man' on their tax forms?"

"They file taxes?" Fortune quips. Then he shrugs. "I don't consider myself at all in the category of mercenary. I run a security firm to keep the paparazzi away from Hollywood A listers. To my knowledge, I mean in absolute certainty, I don't know that I ever killed anybody. I have fired upon enemy combatants in Iraq and once here in L.A. defending Karen and Vio Landaugh at her father's place when the cartel sent some hitters. I was no doubt trying to kill that night. Don't know if I did, but I definitely don't identify as a contract killer."

Twelve Moons, the lanky Rincon tribesman, jumps back in the pool. His bronze skin holds the last of the sun's glow as he reaches out and hangs on the diving board. "I guess I was temporarily a paid assassin for the government over the last two years," he says. "Even though my M.O. was simply to keep Grace alive. Almost fucked that up, but he's here tonight. Feel bad about Khasan not making it out of the Grand Bazaar in Istanbul, though." The Native American smiles sadly, but then brightens. "However, I do have an announcement. I decided it is time for me to strike out on my own. Working the assorted case with Roddy or covering a side security job for Fortune ain't getting it. I've been looking for a law enforcement job. Bob Lee put in a good word. I got an offer. I've accepted. I've joined the U.S. Marshals. My first posting is in Oklahoma. Place called Woods County. I have to be there in a month."

Everyone shouts out congratulations. Twelve Moons smiles and ducks under water to avoid the attention. The news calls for shots and I serve the dessert chocolate pie Karen made along with them. Fortune helps me with the plates, spatula, and forks. Everyone is happy for Twelve Moons. He was born to be a cop and is going to be great as a U.S. Marshal. It is quiet while we eat. There is generally a good vibe. This night is what I need after Philly.

Father Eric brings us back to the topic at hand as the chocolate quickens our pulses. "Do any of you worry about the mortal consequences of your actions? Does it interfere with your faith?"

Vakha Bahaev, the Chechen gunner, laughs. "God? Am I worried about God?"

Father Eric shrugs. "Yes, if you want to put it like that. Do you worry that God will judge you for killing other humans, even bad ones?"

Vakha takes a sip of bourbon. "My family is from outside of Benoy. That is a large city. Over a million. In a district called Nozhay-Yurtousky, along the Russian border of Chechnya. My grandfather on my father's side was conscripted to fight for the Soviets in 1942. He died at the Battle of Stalingrad. My grandmother, protected by the people of her village, took her son, my father, to the forests when the Germans fell back, killing all as they retreated. The forest was very cold and very hard to survive, but my grandmother and my father, they did.

"In my grandmother's fear of both the Russians and the Germans, she kept my father in those remote lands. He grew up there and became a lumberjack. A very strong man. A very tough man. He stayed with my grandmother in the eastern forests until she died. She was the only of our clan to die a natural death.

"My father married late. My mother was twenty years younger than him. I am now thirty-nine. Born in 1980. My father was 38 and my mother but 18 when I was born. My twin brother Khasan and I were the oldest of four. In 1994, the Russians invaded. By then we had moved back to the city. My father and mother were killed by a mortar round in the first weeks of the war. Khasan and I got our brother, Rashad, and my sister Makka out of Benoy back into the forest. My father had taken us there in the summers and we knew those remote woods well enough to hide. I returned and brought others. We remained there. A meager existence, yes, but existence was not assured in those days. Survival under Russian siege was enough.

"Two years later, our band of rebels was found by Russian soldiers when Khasan and I were foraging for supplies. We were not there when the Russians came. They took Makka, our sister, age twelve. Rashad was wounded and left to die. He did survive."

Vakha pauses, his memory all too real to continue.

Father Eric breaks the silence. "Do you know what happened to Makka?"

Vakha shakes his head. "I have no news of her since that day. The fate I imagine her makes me wish for her a quick and painless death. I doubt that was the case." Vakha finishes his bourbon. Twelve Moons pours him two more fingers and pats his arm. The Chechen nods thanks and speaks again.

"Rashad, Khasan, and I lived from that time as feral dogs," he continues. "As the war slowed, we crossed the border into Russia. Soldiers did not hunt us there, only lawmen. The Russian police were unmotivated and terrible at their jobs. We stole and killed to make our way and survive. We would raid a farmhouse, steal what we needed, kill if we had to. Carjackings. Mug the wealthy for money. And everyone looked wealthy to us. We had nothing. Sometimes for fun, we shot police from tree stands, like hunting deer, but there was karma to be paid for that.

"War began again in 2004. Rashad was killed in the third year of the second war in 2007. By this time, we were back in Chechnya in the border regions of the North Caucasus mountains, hiding in the Chechen Republic of Ichkeria. Rashad died from a sniper rifle. I was with him when the bullet struck his chest. Khasan too. Our younger brother died quickly. We never even saw his killer. Rashad was 23 and had been fighting since he was ten. I remember seeing his face relax after he stopped breathing. He looked so young in death. I had not remembered until then he was young. None of us were allowed to be young, except in death.

"Khasan and I left Chechnya when the war concluded in 2009. We had only the clothes on our backs and our rifles. Our only skills were theft and killing. No village wanted us. We called ourselves war heroes. War heroes without a home. And without empathy. We were too damaged for anyone to want. Too uncivilized for even our destroyed country. So, we became like you." He points to Grace and me. "Mercenaries because no one else would have us. Khasan and I had nothing, but we had more than most Chechens because we were twins born together. Khasan knew my thoughts before I did, and I his. We had each other."

There is quiet in the gathered darkness. We can feel Vakha's pain. He has spoken more in the last ten minutes than in all the time any of us have known him. He seems to realize it and seeks to close the chapter.

"And now my other half, my Khasan, is gone," he says. "Killed in Istanbul by a cowardly Iranian who blew up all his cell and family, hiding in a cistern, rather than facing defeat. That cur took the only thing I had of value—my brother. Now for me? There is nothing. I am nothing. I kill because there is nothing left except to kill."

Father Eric makes a sign of the cross upon his chest. "I shall pray for your solace, Vakha," he says softly. The priest stands and moves to the Chechen. Father Eric places his hands on the man's shoulders. Vakha shudders as if the touch brings nothing but pain.

I look to Grace, his face in distress over his friend's sorrow. "You sure you want back in?" I ask. "Our work is a fucking train wreck waiting to happen."

"I'm betting not," Clayton says solemnly, "with you at my side."

I smile my approval, but there is no joy in it. My partner is back. It will end badly. Because that is the only conclusion to the stories we know.

Just then Jerry the monkey strolls in, his one hand linked with my daughter's. "Jerry like movies," he says. "Still don't believe elephants can fly but want to go to theater with a buzz on next time."

The monkey looks around. All our faces are grim. "Not much fun party," he says. "Where's the one-hitter?"

HUNTER, THE NAZI

Grace's first full day back on the job does not start until evening. It is full dark as Grace and I amble out to Toluca Lake for an appointment with a new client. I watch my speed. The cops here stop people if they aren't Scandinavian enough, and for sure for "driving while black." Grace and I are as white as it gets, but cops immediately get a vibe off us that we willingly befriend people of color. We also tend to drive too fast. Even driving over twenty-five mph will get you a flashing blue light special here. Strike two. If I told them I am trying to eat less beef, they would give me a quick escort out of Tolucaville.

Toluca Lake is in the San Fernando Valley, northwest of downtown. The neighborhood is tucked in nicely between the Warner Brothers Studio lots to the east, the 101 to the west, Universal City to the south, and the Ventura to north. It is small, exclusive, and despite being in the center of things, removed from all the worst Los Angeles has to offer, except maybe smog.

Bob Hope lived in Toluca way back when, but he was far from the only celebrity with a home along the lake. Bette Davis, Jonathan Winters, Audie Murphy, Bing Crosby, Frank Sinatra, and even Amelia Earhart have lived there. Those celebrity homes now are owned by studio executives these days. The most exclusive are along the lake or on the golf course, Lakeside Golf Club, or both. However, we are heading away from those, turning off Valley Spring onto a little spur of a road called Navajo. The lake recedes to our right, hidden in inky darkness, except for a few small boats with running lights blinking at their moorings at private docks. It is all very picturesque. I note that I can see stars here. That is unusual in Los Angeles. Light pollution and air pollution are in a running battle to hide our skies.

It is unusual for clients to ask to meet us at their homes at ten pm, but the neighborhood is toney enough that we really didn't hesitate to accept the appointment. Cash talks, bullshit walks, and big stacks can set calendar appointments.

The address is not marked, but the GPS slows my roll. I look right. A black gate folds into a large wall and blocks our passage. We have been given a numeric code for entry. I put down the window and poke the keypad. The electronic locks pop and allow us to proceed. I tool on down the black tarmac drive which ends in a roundabout with a spewing fountain. A golden goddess extends a lance in one hand and a wreath in another. She spouts water from her mouth. She wears wings and looks victorious, except the gushing hydrant from her mouth looks as if it would get old really fast.

A large mansion hovers on an immaculate lawn just beyond the fountain. There are no lights visible inside the home. A blaze of porch lights, however, show us the way to the front door.

"Tell me about this guy again, Gracer," I ask.

"Not much too tell. His name is Herman Hunter Vanst. Old L.A. money. His father and grandfather were land and water barons back when Huntington Beach was an oil field. Bought up land cheap when L.A. was the size of Dodge City. They brokered oil leases on the land for all those wells on the beach you see in the old photos. Made piles of cash in the oil boom of the 40's and 50's. Then capped the wells and sold the land again to real estate developers in the 60's and 70's. Both of the old timers have passed on. But before they kicked, they bequeathed their wealth to their one living descendant, Hunter Vanst. Maybe a half billion smackers. He's now not quite seventy. Word is he's doubled his family's coffers. A billionaire. But a quiet one. There's not much news about him. Quiet life. No hint of why he'd want our services. There is one photo in LexisNexis from eight years ago."

Grace shows the image to me again on his phone. The photo is in no way remarkable. White guy, mid-fifties, balding on top. Prominent nose. Flaring ears. Sharp eyes, thoughtful almost. Doesn't look like a dummy, for sure. The man in the photo is wearing a gray suit. Windsor knot. A dark navy tie with white dots. The photo shows Vanst sitting before a painting. The caption says, "Angeleno purchases Paul Klee painting for The Getty." The painting behind Vanst is what I would call "Picasso-esque" if I called paintings I didn't like names like that. Plus, it probably isn't "Picasso-esque" since I don't know anything about art.

"Well," I say, "I guess the thing to do is go in and find out why he needs the Purple Heart team on his side."

Grace smiles. "Must be bad shit."

"At least he's got the best there is."

"Fuckin' A," Grace replies.

I wonder if we are still serious when we play this "pump me up" game. "Ready?" he asks.

"Born that way."

We amble up the steps and I ring the bell. It plays Wagner, which is an eyebrow raiser in itself. Weird. I can't say as if I remember anyone's doorbell playing the "Overture to Tannhäuser" before, but I know the tune. Why? I have no idea. Weird shit sticks in my head is my only explanation.

As I recall, the song is really long, so I am relieved when relatively quickly we hear a lock turn and the door opens. It is not the stuffy butler we are both expecting. It is the man himself. Vanst is smaller, more wizened, than in the photo, and his eyes are more intense.

"Welcome. You are the Purple Detectives?" His mouth curls as he finds humor in the line, and I have the impression he rehearsed it.

"Yes," Grace says, extending his hand. "Clayton Grace here. My partner is Roddy O'Malley." My partner is quite pleasant. We are clearing $1500 an hour for taking this late meeting. Each. Cash gets a smile and a firm handshake. Damn straight, Skippy.

"I am H. Hunter Vanst. Please enter. Thank you for coming at this entirely uncommon hour. I hope it wasn't too jarring to your schedules."

"Not to worry," I say, shaking his hand. "I am hoping we can be of service to you."

"I'm sure you will," he says, ushering us inside. He closes the door and then leads us down a dim hallway to a large living area. There is a hearth roaring with crackling logs. There is not a hint of chill in the air outside, but you know old folk. Gotta have it hot enough to peel paint off the wall.

Vanst begins to sit behind a small writing table. He is nearly settled in, but he changes direction, mid-squat and rises up. "Excuse me. I am a poor host," he says, standing. "I am out of practice. I meant to offer you a drink. I have some very fine wines. Perhaps a bourbon?"

We agree on the bourbon. I see he has Pappy Van Winkle open at the well-appointed bar. I am thinking the fifth is a bottle worth about three grand. Things are looking up.

"You said H. Hunter?" Graces asks, accepting two fingers of the liquid gold.

"Yes, the newspapers get it wrong. My first name is Herman. I go by my middle name, Hunter. Both my father and grandfather were also Hermans. Early in my life when both were still living, I was called Hunter. It was expedient. It is habit now."

We settle in the chairs by the tiny desk. I am opposite Vanst, Clayton to his side. The arms of their respective chairs are nearly touching. Clay looks quite large to this curious fellow.

"I apologize for my remiss hospitality. I usually have servants attuned to keeping guests comfortable, though I entertain seldomly. I don't worry too much about it myself when the staff is here. However, given the nature of the subject matter tonight, I have sent them all away for the duration. Even the live-in maid and my personal valet are absent."

I nod. "I see. Well, you can depend upon our discretion."

Vanst smiles grimly. "Oh, I'm afraid that won't be good enough." He draws a couple of two-page documents from the leather folder at his left. He hands one to each of us. They are non-disclosure agreements. They are quite nasty. The terms, if I understand them correctly, confirms a $300,000 penalty for each of us for revealing any information disclosed by the client in this meeting. No exceptions. And unusually, if either of us reveal info, both of us are in jeopardy.

I read both pages and put the document down on the desk. "Pretty hefty penalty."

"Very private information," Vanst counters.

"What's the job?" asks Grace.

"Sign the documents and I can tell you."

"What's the payout?"

"Ten times what you are being paid for this meeting for each of you, plus I'll pay the two of you a thousand an hour for any time expended. I doubt there will be even a day's work involved in completing the task."

"We cannot agree to terms which might include illegal activities," Grace says, quietly.

"Given what I know about your past exploits, I know that to be a false statement." Vanst laughs. "But I will not ask you to commit any illegalities. However, to alleviate your worries, I'll make the bonus upon completion a cool one hundred thousand. American." He smiles, takes back the documents and switches them for a second set. Vanst has been prepared to pay the higher fee from the outset. I am not sure whether the feint makes me like him more or less.

Grace looks at me and I nod. We both sign. The documents require we verify the signing of each other. We do so. Vanst then signs below each of our scrawls. He takes the signed copies and inserts them back inside the leather binder. He places the folder in the center drawer. Then he stands and crosses the room. His dark wardrobe seems to shun light. He fades into the gloom, a creature of the night, nearly disappearing. The optics are strange, but it goes with the whole scene. I try to enjoy the spectacle.

Just beyond the fireplace, Vanst steps to the wall and removes a book from the mahogany shelf holding perhaps two hundred volumes. I notice the title. It is *Mein Kampf.* Behind the book, Vanst presses a button on the wall. One half of the shelving unit creaks as it revolves outward. The gap beyond reveals a dark hallway and a stairway heading down. Rough granite steps curve into darkness. Vanst takes the rail and begins down, his black leather-laced boots clicking on the stone.

"Follow me," he says.

Grace and I descend the stairway with apprehension. When we are far enough down to see the room ahead, I give my partner a sneering grin like "This is going to be on Sports Center tonight," but Grace has a furrowed brow when the bookshelf slams shut behind us.

The basement, I guess, could be called a safe room, hidden as it is from the first floor by the door behind the bookshelf, but it would be the largest safe room anyone could imagine, it is safe to say.

The room is at least forty feet square. Floors, walls, and ceiling are all cut from the same rough stone as the stairs. The back wall appears to have two more doors—a wine cellar, I later learn, and a restroom. Long red velvet tapestries, perhaps four-feet wide hang from three of the walls, interspersed by large paintings, a foot gap between each. I suppose the tapestries are to soften sound bouncing off the stone walls. They work. It is deathly quiet down here as we watch Vanst switch on lights. As he does, the room's eccentric décor has Grace—and me—all the more concerned. The tables, including a full-sized billiard table, are covered with felt emblazoned with the logo of the Nazi SS.

However, the Nazi memorabilia would not be the high-light of the room. No, those tapestries, eight per wall, each punctuate paintings, each lit with exquisite lighting recessed in the stone ceiling above.

Vanst looks at Grace's visage. My partner's face shows

amazement at the scene in front of us. "Don't act shocked. The fee I am paying you for your services came with your pledge of secrecy. The amount of the fee should have led you to assume the secrets I would divulge would be large ones."

The old man gives us a chance to take in the room. There are three tables covered with the red and black logo of the Schutzstaffel, the German secret police. The light hanging over the billiards table is emblazoned with a swastika. A glass case displays a mannequin wearing an SS uniform; a cap; and a belt holding both a holster for a Luger on the right and a short dagger on the left. The jacket collar supports two stickpins—one of the swastika and the other the familiar SS logo. The assembly is completed by a large velvet cape with what looks to be wolf fur trim. The eyes of the mannequin are covered with motorcycle goggles. Soft light inside the glass case illuminates the ghostly figure. I know Grace and I are both agog, but my self-awareness does not mean I can turn my eyes away.

"My grandfather's uniform from his days in Paris," he says with a nod to the glass case. "Herman senior was familiar with the city of light, even before the war, as he attended the Sorbonne in the early thirties. He planned on becoming an art historian. The rise of the Third Reich ended that career path. Grandfather, Herman the First, returned to Germany after the Munich Agreement in 1938. He could read the tea leaves and joined the Nazi Party that year."

"I take it the family name was not originally Vanst?" I ask. Grace and I are now standing at the table nearest the stairs. Vanst bids us to sit. We do.

"No, Van Sticke. He was Herman Van Sticke, Sr. He was a member of the Einsatzstab Reichsleiter Rosenberg, the ERR unit of Paris. He was also thought to have been killed by French Resistance on August 19th, 1944, days before the Americans recaptured the city. That name died that day."

"I assume he managed to get a few paintings out in his departure."

Vanst smiled. "Yes, quite a number. You are familiar with the ERR?"

"No."

"Very early in the war, soon after even the fall of Warsaw in '39, Hitler's commanding generals began to steal art en masse. There was so much taken, it required an agency. They formed the Einsatzstab Reichsleiter Rosenberg, which was tasked with the systematic looting of art and cultural artifacts across Europe.

"The loot was at first stored in the Parisian museum, Galerie Nationale du Jeu de Paume, but soon it was decided art would be stored in salt mines in the homeland. Did you know salt mines have perfect pH levels? They are ideal for storage of delicate canvases and old paints."

I simply nod. Grace sits, still in a trance, it seems.

"Hitler, a painter himself, wanted to build a private museum called the Führermuseum in his hometown of Linz, Austria. Much of the artwork was sent near there and stored inside a church in Ellingen, Germany. My grandfather was a key determiner of what was to be in the museum. The Führer had great confidence in my grandfather's selections."

"So many people don't get to use their college training. How lucky for Herman Sr.," I say.

Vanst smirks but continues his tale, "But there was so much artwork. The chapel at Ellingen would not hold nearly all that was taken. From that site, the ERR expanded its warehousing to the famous Neuschwanstein Castle in Germany."

At this stage, I stifle a yawn. It appears we are in for Art History Lecture 101, and it is past my bedtime.

"My grandfather reported to the SS general in charge of Paris operations in October of 1940. His name was Otto von Stülpnagel."

"I know the name," I say. "Nice guy. Killed himself in his cell during the Nuremberg trials if I remember correctly."

"Yes," says Vanst. "You know your history."

"Read it in a Phillip Kerr mystery. Bernie Gunther is totally the bomb."

The old man laughs. "You are a flippant one."

"Indeed."

"Your partner seems rather dim," Vanst remarks.

That does get Grace to blink. "Just trying to retain my humanity. You'll have to give me a minute," Grace says, coming back from Zombieland.

Vanst shrugs. "As I was saying, the booty from these incursions across Europe netted works by master artists Rembrandt, Picasso, Matisse, Vermeer, Van Gogh, and countless others. They acquired Michelangelo's sculpture, Madonna and Child. The best collection of art ever assembled."

"Stolen."

"You say tomato," Vanst replies with a grin, then continues with his tale. "My grandfather lived in Paris throughout the war, the zone occupée. He was quite valuable to the Reich, receiving accolades from the top brass, including the Führer himself. Many ingratiated themselves to him as Herman Sr. was the best appraiser in the ERR and was able to assist those in search of art for their homes back in the Homeland.

"Hitler's right hand man, Hermann Göring, traveled to the Jeu de Paume in Paris twenty times to shop for the masterpieces he desired most. Göring needed two train cars for his art alone."

"Which brings us to the 'train' itself," I say.

"Yes." Vanst nods. "The train made so famous by George Clooney. The Monument Men did return a large portion of the Nazi art to the Americans, Brits, and French, but not nearly all. The haul was enormous. U.S. officials found 30 miles of galleries and over one billion euros in Nazi gold in the Mekers salt mine. In the Altaussee mine, U.S. reports were that almost seven thousand paintings, over two thousand drawings, a thousand prints and over a hundred statues were reclaimed. 'Madonna and Child' was found there and van Eyck's 'The Adoration of the Lamb' was also there. The estimate of value in 1945 dollars was $3.5 billion recovered from Altaussee alone."

I look around the room at the 24 displayed works. "I take the Monument Men did not find these."

"No, nor scores of others. Do you recognize the two works facing you?"

"No. I take it that they are expensive?"

"Priceless. The first is Raphael's 'Portrait of a Young Man.' The second is 'Portrait of Gabrielle Diot' by Degas. Both are worth millions." Vanst smiled broadly. "On the far wall is Pablo Picasso's 'Naked Woman on the Beach.'"

I start to speak, but the old man points to our left. "That entire wall is Matisse. Six by Matisse. Seven went missing. My grandfather sold one to get funding for his flight from Paris."

"I imagine that even in a war-torn city there are those who will buy masterworks on the cheap."

"Oh yes, many French were collaborators."

"I think they hung about two thousand of them."

"Only the sloppy ones."

"I see. And where did your grandfather go once Paris got too hot for him?"

"Mexico. Mexico City specifically. There he sold the bulk of his liberated art. Once there with a new name and papers saying he came from Switzerland, he established himself as a broker of antiquities. His clients were New Yorkers who flew in for auctions. Provence was less important than price. A wink and a nod was all it took. Buying a Vermeer to decorate a condo overlooking Central Park is very chic, especially if you can do it in Mexico on the sly."

Vanst smiles before continuing, "Herman Sr. moved to Southern California in 1948. He had a French accent after all, not German. He moved to Huntington Beach, threw big parties, and began to buy oil leases."

Grace breaks up the old man's story. "What do you want us to do? And why wouldn't we just turn you in and pay your forfeiture of confidentiality? The reward on the artwork would be millions."

"I will answer the latter first. Your non-disclosure document as signed upstairs requires you to relinquish any funds received from information gained from our meeting. Thus, you turn me in to authorities, you surrender your livelihood, all the money you currently have, and any you would make from your betrayal regarding the art would also be returned to me. You will find I have broken no laws."

"It is a big gamble on your part."

"I am an old man. My son lives with another man in San Francisco. I have no grandchildren. I can risk it. I have a billion in the bank as it now stands. Public shaming would matter little to me. There is no crime here. I've sold no paintings; I've stolen no paintings. I just discovered this secret room filled with art. Or at least that would be my story."

"And what are we to do for the one hundred K while we keep our mouths shut?" Grace's voice has a bit of an edge, but the words are what our host wants to hear.

"That is more like it. I want you to find the living heirs to a sculptor whose work stands there in the corner. I want that statue returned to them."

I look into the dimness by the door to the wine cellar. A white marble figure, holding a javelin and a chalice, stands in solitude. Solid looking dude, free-lifter, I'm thinking.

"Beautiful, is it not? The artist is Josef Thorak. He was German, born in Vienna. Most of his work was destroyed in the Allied Bombing of Berlin. He was the best sculptor of the Third Reich."

"How did that piece become part of your grandfather's collection?"

"A present from Göring. A thank you for my grandfather's

assistance in finding the proper decor for the Göring palatial estate. Brought to Paris in the rail cars which took the General's treasure trove back."

"And we are to find Thorak's descendants and return the statue to them?" Grace asks.

"Yes."

"Without explanation?" I inject.

"Yes."

"Why?"

"Because he was a good Nazi. My art collection is either that of Jews, or that which Joseph Goebels deemed 'degenerate art.' Goebels mandated that this art be sold to support the Reich's efforts. However, Thorak's was not among that ilk. I have all I need and more. I feel perhaps I can serve my grandfather's cause by returning the sculpture to Thorak's family. It is surely worth millions."

"To serve the memory of the Reich?" Grace asks.

"Yes." Vanst is tiring of Grace.

"Do we know the sculpture is authentic?" I ask.

Vanst laughs. "I would pay you thousands to return a fake? Why?"

Then he reaches into his coat pocket and removes an envelope. It is sealed and stamped with an SS pressed into red wax. The old man, his heels clicking, moves to the glass case. He opens the case door and flips up the leather flap to the dagger on the belt of the mannequin. Vanst retrieves the blade and returns to us. He sits beside Grace.

"Göring," he says, pausing to carefully select his words, "was a meticulous man. Very exacting. The provenance of his art was not taken lightly. The general provided multiple sealed proofs for the statue that it might be appraised correctly at a future date. Here is one of them. You see it is marked with Göring's seal."

Vanst takes the dagger's silvery edge and slips it into the envelope's flap. He cuts through the wax and the glue holding the envelope. Removing the two pages from the envelope, he hands them to me. "You will see, all is in order. The statue was carved by Thorak and gifted by Göring to my grandfather. The provenance cannot be questioned. And since this art was a product of the Reich, not stolen, it is clearly mine to give."

"When are we to do this?" I ask.

"Not until my death." Vanst smiles. "An easy job for you. Nothing to do now, except to take my fee and drink a shot of schnapps to my long life. Go home. Do diligence. Find the heir, and then you wait until I die. I am sixty-nine and in good health. It may be twenty years before you must earn your fee." Vanst lays the dagger on the table's blood red logo for the Schutzstaffel. "Shall we drink to my health?"

Grace raises a finger, keeping the old man in his seat. "Before we shake on it and get all chummy, let me make sure I understand."

Vanst smiles derisively. "It is all very simple."

"Then let me paraphrase for my clarity," Grace says. I am looking at my partner with amusement. Grace can be a little intense, but it all seems copacetic to me.

"Proceed," says Vanst.

"You are the grandson of the biggest undetected art thief in history. We are sitting in a treasure trove gallery of perhaps a half a billion bucks or so in stolen art. Most of it is considered degenerate art, but your grandfather didn't mind selling *Jew* art to fund the oil boom of mid-century Los Angeles. However, one of the pieces of art you still have is by a good Nazi, so you want us to return it to the man's Aryan grandchildren, or great-grandchildren. And we do so with no explanation of how we got the statue. For that, you will pay us a hundred thousand dollars. But we don't have to return it until you die?"

"Yes. *Ist das verstanden?*" Vanst sneers.

"Not till you die?"

"Yes, is it so difficult?"

Grace picks up the dagger. "How 'bout we return the statue tomorrow?" And he plunges the dagger's double-edged tip into the old man's chest.

Vanst's eyes register surprise for just a moment before he dies. He slumps down, his head on the table.

I rise and gaze in amazement at my partner, his hand still holding onto the blade.

"I did not see that coming," I say.

"What the absolute hell, Grace?"

Grace shrugs, his eyes are huge. He cannot believe his own actions. He releases the grip of the weapon still stuck in the old fart's chest. "I don't know-ow," he finally stammers. "I don't know why I did that. Why I killed him."

Grace's face is blank and pallid. Blood has drained from around his eyes—and from Vanst's wound.

I am furious and very frightened, but I go into survival mode. "Stand up, Grace."

"What?"

"Stand up."

He does so.

"Stay right there. Do not move. Do not touch anything until I get back."

Grace does what I say. I run to the vehicle, reach behind the seat, and bring a tacklebox back into the house. Downstairs, I hand him a set of rubber gloves. We both put them on.

"Now, we have to be very precise and very smart. Otherwise, we are both going to prison for the rest of our lives."

"You didn't do anything," Grace says, objecting.

"Cops won't care."

I reach into the case. "Here," I say, handing him a bag of wipes with an alcohol solvent on it. "Start wiping the wood edges to the table and chairs."

I watch him to make sure Clayton is doing a competent job. He is diligent. I take the dagger and wipe away any prints and DNA my partner might have left on it. Then I place it back into the wound.

"Next, wipe the stair railing all the way down. I can't remember if I touched it or not. Bookshelf door too. Pour the whiskey down the toilet. Flush it three times. Wipe down the glasses really well. Then bring them back upstairs."

"What are you going to do?" Grace asks me as I leave the basement.

"I have to find the home security system. We're surely on camera someplace. I am going to pull the hard drives."

Once upstairs, I go to the table where we first signed the nondisclosure agreements. I take the first copies and the second from the center drawer. I place them in the fireplace with care. I stand there and make sure they are fully incinerated. I find a laptop in the desk. I study the files stored there. I find the two nondisclosure docs. I stick the laptop inside my shirt to take with us. We can dispose of it later.

Then I scour the huge house, finding a small room on the second floor. Two computers seem to be recording six different cameras of the estate. I have to pray neither computer is set up to upload to the cloud. A quick examination tells me that is not the case. A straightforward record to the hard drives. I pull open the covers and smash the motherboards, pulling the hard drives. I place them in my back pockets.

Back on the first floor, Grace is wiping the table where we first sat. I join him and together we each crisscross each other's work, leaving wet trails of alcohol over every surface.

"Do we leave the bookshelf door open or closed?" Grace asks.

"Closed, I think. Might take the staff a bit to find him."

"You think they know about the Nazi room?"

I smile grimly. "Yeah, I'm guessing the staff here is onboard with the whole Third Reich thing."

I check the glasses we drank from. I rub them with the wipes so hard they are of thinner construction before I place them back on the shelf. I locate them back among the other six above the bar. I put them at the back and rotate two others to the front.

Next, we use our wipes to erase prints on the front door,

including the doorbell button. I am satisfied we are leaving no evidence of our presence inside, but cops today can find a hair—you just never know. Plus, today the whole world has cameras. The cops will likely have my truck on camera somewhere in Toluca Lake. I cannot come up with any reason for us to be in Toluca Lake at night—or anytime truthfully—so we are in for trouble.

Grace puts words to my fears. "When the cops review the stoplight cameras in the surrounding area, they'll get your tags."

"Yeah."

"No good reason to be in Toluca."

"Nope."

"We get caught, I'll take the fall. I'll confess. This is not on you."

"We'll cross the bridge if we come to it."

"You mad?"

"Hell yeah, I do not plan to spend Gracie's next fifteen years in San Quentin."

"Sorry, Roddy. I don't know what happened. I guess for the last two years I was just so used to killing bad guys I just did it automatically."

"Yeah, you just came back too soon. I pushed to get you back to work. For me. I wanted my partner back. It's my bad as much as yours. You had a PTSD-induced trauma event. You weren't in control."

Grace nods, his face fallen. Defeated.

We drive home by way of the Santa Monica Pier. At the far end, overlooking the surf, I destroy the hard drives with the butt of my sidearm while Grace stomps the laptop to pieces. Then we throw it all into the ocean. I know the water is about sixty feet deep here from having fished it in the past.

Grace comes home with me. He curls up on the couch. I go upstairs and slide beside my slumbering bedmate, Karen. I cannot sleep and wonder if she will be sleeping solo soon. We are in deep trouble.

PIN UP GIRL

I wake up way before dawn—well, I can't say for sure I ever slept, but I do come down the stairs way before dawn when I hear Jerry open the front door. He does that every morning after the *L.A. Times* is delivered.

He has the coffee going when I arrive in the kitchen. The little monkey is staring at the front page. Jerry's face is contorted. It looks as if he might cry. "So sad," he says and looks up at me with red rimmed eyes.

"What's so sad?" I say, although I can name a few things myself.

"Kidnapped girl still missing. Kidnapper kill cop, then himself after police surround him. Bad man already kill three girlies. Bad asshole."

"Let me see." I skim the story. The story is sad and terrible. A serial kidnapper, who has previously killed three times, took a girl two days ago, but this time police got a plate number from an insomniac who noticed a car parked up her street. She thought it strange enough to write down the license plate of the car, but she didn't hear about the kidnapping on her street until the next day. She didn't call the cops until she got home from work on Day 2.

The call goes out for a residence in Glassell Park. First cop on the scene, a rookie named Garinger, is gunned down. There is a standoff. The police don't go in blazing because the girl might be inside. But then, the perp comes out holding a gun to his own temple. He says, "You want the girl? Figure it out. I left you all you need to know." Not great last words, but they are his. Bastard blows his brains out. The article ends by saying the department is conducting an investigation, but the girl's whereabouts are unknown.

I hand the paper back to Jerry and give him a hug. Then I pour us both a cup. We have our communal drink. Waking up a bit, I remember Clayton is asleep on my couch. I return to the living room. No Clayton Grace.

I reenter the kitchen. "You see Clay?"

Jerry looks up. "He leave very early. Take your truck."

That raises my eyebrows—and my dander. I call Grace on my phone. I am irritated. I mean, I am more pissed about him killing the Nazi than stealing my truck, but things compound, you know?

I call him. He answers.

"Grace?"

"Good. You're up. I'm almost back. Put on some clothes. We have to make a quick run."

"Why? What are you up to?"

"Just get dressed. I'm turning into the driveway. You got coffee on?"

"Yeah."

"Bring both of us a go-cup."

He hangs up.

I get in the car, hand Grace his java, and ask him what the hell is going on. The clock has not yet reached six a.m.

"I didn't sleep. Kept thinking of a reason we might be in Toluca Lake last night. Came up with a good one."

"What's that? I mean, besides murder?"

It is Clay's turn to raise an eyebrow. "I went by and saw Fat Amos. Woke his fat ass up. He wasn't too happy, 3:30 a.m. and all, but I told him we wanted to go back to work for him. Doing repossessions."

"And he was enthused you informed him at that particular hour?"

"No, but I told him we'd do the first one for free, but we had to have been hired back yesterday. Then he gave me yesterday's list. Got lucky on location. There's a car we're going to pick up. A 1995 Rolls Royce Corniche, Red Convertible. Owner is an old comedian, lives in... wait for it... Toluca Lake. I never heard of him—some comedy rapper named PeePee McGee. He's more than ninety days in arrears. North of where we were last night, but close enough. I got the listing. Got Fat Amos' master set of keys. Got a fifteen foot ladder. Checked out Google Earth from Amos's laptop. Walled estate, electric gate. Car parked out under a carport. Should be easy. That is if we beat the traffic."

I got to admit, it is a reasonable explanation—back in the

day, we often did recon before taking a car. If we didn't leave any DNA or photographic evidence or something of our visit to Vanst, we might be good to go. Cops might come knocking, but we could rock them an alibi. I feel my chest start to allow oxygen in again.

Grace's recon is right on. We pull up along the road, not far from the entrance to PeePee's McGee's estate. My partner extends the ladder. I hold it as he goes over. Once he drops to the other side, I pull the ladder back, lower the extension, and put it back in the truck. It doesn't take a minute. In less than a minute, Grace starts the car, hits the remote control on the visor and comes cruising out. The car is a beauty. Rolls Royce makes a fine automobile. Grace waves as he passes me. I flip a Uey and follow him to Fat Amos.

Inside, I refill my coffee cup and let Fat Amos pour a little whiskey in it. He is glad we are back working for him. And we'll have to stick with it to make our alibi stand up.

"First one is free," I say to the big man.

He nods. "Grace told me when you came by and I rehired you two nights ago."

"Stick with that story," I say.

Fat Amos smiles. "Like I tell cops shit."

Outside, I tell Grace it was good thinking and he may have kept us from jail.

He nods soberly.

"I am still not a happy camper," I say.

"Nor should you be," he agrees. "I need more time and more therapy. Obviously, I am pretty messed up."

"Yeah," I concur. "I saw your work."

Grace nods sadly. "I know. Hopefully my screw-up won't end up with us in jail."

"Hopefully. What's next?"

"I'm headed back up to Topanga. Hang with Dapper. Cook us some burgers."

"Call your therapist, but don't confess anything. Some things you can't tell anybody."

Grace nods.

"I'm out," I say, getting in my truck.

"Love ya, brother," he says across the gulf of our lives.

I feel emotions in my gut, but I put the truck in drive. I don my shades in the morning light and put on Bob Marley to get me through.

When I get home and enter the house, Karen is looking at me with a jaundiced eye. She is going to be late because I am supposed to watch the kid. But I had disappeared with no warning. She is hurrying around. Jerry and Gracie are playing Chutes and Ladders at the kitchen counter.

"What gives? You were home last night, right? I didn't dream you tossing and turning all night?"

"Roger that. Too weird to even explain. Sorry. Grace and I had to make a morning run. We've decided to try to break away from Welmar. Going to do repo work in the short run. Started back with Fat Amos."

Karen smells something hinky. I would have discussed a change like that with her, but she will be late now unless there is a helicopter out front and there is not. Instead, she kisses my cheek and says, "Good. Welmar is an evil asshole."

"Evil asshole," both Gracie and Jerry say in unison, laughing.

I pour another cup of coffee but wait until Karen leaves to add the Jameson.

The phone rings just as I'm getting out of the shower. It is Captain Janelle Jackson, Head of Robbery Homicide for the Los Angeles Police Department. I pick up, thinking, "Jesus, they got our plate numbers up in Toluca damn fast."

"Roddy?"

"Yeah, hi Janelle. What's up?"

"It's a Captain Jackson sort of call," she says.

"Gotcha. What can I do for you, Captain?" I am drying off. My phone is on speaker and lies on the bathroom counter at head height. I do not have on my prosthetics.

"Is Grace with you?" she asks.

I laugh. "No, I'm getting out of the shower. That would be awkward."

She laughs. "When's the last time you saw him?"

"Just saw him. We worked last night. He's headed back up to his trailer. Might be sacked out by now. I would be too, except I'm watching the little lady and monkey today."

"Grace is not answering."

"Might not even have the phone on. He was pretty tired."

Janelle pauses. "Well, this is sort of a Roddy thing anyway. Can Speedy and I come by? We need to see you."

Okay, the two of them are there in, like, two minutes. I mean, I have a flattop haircut and it isn't even dry when I come downstairs. They had to have been waiting down the block. I believe I will be arrested.

I open the door with their knock, expecting the worst, but they are cordial. Janelle and Speedy enter the kitchen. I offer to put on more coffee. It is still just a smidgen past nine. Gracie and Jerry are riding trikes around a little track they have made with cones in the garage. The two cops stick their head in and say hello. They get only waves from the racers.

"You think Speedy could watch the kids? You take a drive with me?"

My nerves are tingling. "What's up? Am I under arrest?"

"Should you be?" Janelle laughs, then adds, "We both know the answer to that question—a dozen times over." She pauses. "No, we just think you might be able to offer some insight into the Janey Mansfield case."

"The missing girl?"

"Yeah, we want you to look over the perp's residence. You might have insight we don't."

I raise my eyebrow in skepticism.

"It's kind of a rock-n-roll thing," Speedy says, explaining but not telling me specifics.

What can I say? I nod yes, tell the little maniacs that Speedy is in charge, and go for a ride with Captain Janelle Jackson. It has been less than twelve hours since I saw her old partner, Clayton Grace, commit murder, but I don't bring it up.

Owen Pursig, killer of three girls and kidnapper of four, lived in a small ranch style home in Glassell Park, which is only fifteen miles from us in North Hollywood. It is right down 134, but there is no way with morning traffic to make it quickly.

"Los Angeles is an hour drive from Los Angeles," she says.

I just nod. I realize I am weary. Janelle does not use her lights and siren to expedite our travel time. She uses the slow roll to inform me about the case.

"We know Pursig took the four girls. He held each of the first three for a few days before killing them. He dumped their bodies in various places around the metro area. We know a little from the first three bodies. He took Janey Mansfield three mornings ago. She was getting ready for school, we think. Maybe she was at her bus stop or on her way there. Her mom had already left for work. No cameras, no witnesses. Woman who saw an old Dodge sitting with a driver in it thought to write down the plate. She thought he was a perv. But she didn't hear about the kidnapping until the next day. Didn't call until she got home from work."

"I read all that in the paper. No sign he took the girls to his residence?"

"No. We've inspected it top to bottom. Plus, the neighbors would have seen or heard. And they did hear him. A lot. He's a rocker. We've had noise complaints about his music volume. Owen Pursig was not a popular neighbor. Windows open, music blaring at all hours."

"I still don't see how I can be of help. Your technicians...."

"Pursig said he left us all we need to know. We have turned the place inside out. We have no clue where Janey is. Time is, of course, of the essence. Mr. Pursig has his walls covered with memorabilia. Rock-n-roll posters, ticket stubs. You know as much about that as anyone I know. Thought you might give it a look."

I don't answer, and we are quiet for the next fifteen minutes.

The house in Glassell Park looks normal for the neighborhood, which is a little worn at the seams, but is coming back. This home, probably a 1100 square feet ranch, is worth over a million these days. It is beat up inside. Wood floors scuffed and unpolished, but the place is generally clean. I can tell the police techs have done their due diligence. The place has been dusted for prints. Everything has those telltale smudges. The house looks like everything has been fingered and poked through. But the police didn't tear the house apart. It looks like someone could be living here.

I remind myself that no one is. Owen Pursig killed

himself on the front lawn yesterday. The crime scene is out front. The house, though, I can still imagine as a home, albeit one for a serial kidnapper and killer.

The stereo is monstrous. A great looking Marantz amp, two Infinity towers, two Bose 901s. Nice Audio-Technica turntable. Lots of vinyl. I mean, three thousand or so. Mostly classic rock. There's a TV, but it doesn't appear that watching *Nick-at-Nite* is what this dude did.

The walls are plastered with posters and photos. But there are windows or doorways on three of the walls in the living room, so the heavy-duty poster effect is on the north wall. It is fully covered with corkboard. The posters are standard issue rock god images, mainly of rockers of the seventies. In order from left to right above eye level, it is The Rolling Stones, The Beatles, The Who, and The Eagles. The aforementioned are butted against the ceiling. The second row is directly under the first. They include Santana, The Kinks, Jimi Hendrix, and oddly, Farrah Fawcett. It is her most famous pose—red one-piece, swirling hair, head tipped back, toothy grin, hard nip.

Janelle lets me absorb things. I take out my camera. I give her a look like "May I?"

She nods and then says, "No sharing."

I acknowledge her directive. Then I take full wall shots, then close-ups of each poster. They are clean. Pristine even. No markings. Each is attached to the wall with colored push-pins. There are three colors. They appear to be random. Some are black, some green and some pink. Most posters have all three colors. The Farrah Fawcett poster is a little different as the pins are not neatly in the corners like the others. They are stabbed into the poster in random locations. Nothing kinky, just random placements. I take photos of each. Farrah's photo comes last. I note there is something written in the narrow top margin of that poster. Black ink, neat print: RM-GT-C-CA-LA.

I go through the house. Concert tickets galore are stuck around the edge of the mirror. The closet is filled with rock t-shirts. The dresser, Janelle assures me, holds jeans, undies, and socks. Work boots rest on the floor in the closet. Pursig died wearing Chuckie Taylor high tops, black.

I examine everything for a good hour and a half, but I got nothing. Janelle thanks me for looking. I shrug and apologize. She gives me a ride home. On the ride back to North Hollywood, Janelle inquires about Grace. I tell her he may never be ready to conduct detective work again. I tell her we have decided to repo again for a while. She knows we resorted to that kind of work during the recession in '08. Janelle also figures it would not be something I would do if Grace was back to himself and says it is good of me to do. I do not share all that I am feeling.

When Janelle and I enter the homeplace, there is a dance party going on. Gracie and Jerry are shaking their good thang to Wu Tang Clan. Speedy is lounged back on the couch, taking in the show. I am surprised by the music selection and tell Jerry as much after I turn the amp down from a seven to a two. Once we can hear to talk, Jerry responds without any hitch in his bugaloo.

"Speedy say I only listen to dead rockers. Me sad. Decide to go modern with live musician music called disco."

"I am not sure I'd call Wu Tang Clan disco," I reply with a grin.

Janelle and Speedy are laughing as she thanks me and they leave. They have a girl to find. I am no help. They are not concerned about me. No arrest. No murder rap for now. I am glad of that.

I fix the crew lunch. Fried baloney and wedge salads. We all three eat. I can see dull eyes on my daughter. She will be down for the count soon. I carry her to her bed.

After putting dishes in the dishwasher, I print out my photos and tape them in order across the wall, representing the corkboard wall at Pursig's residence.

Jerry asks about them. I explain the police asked me to look at the house. I tell him these posters were in Pursig the bad guy's house hung on the wall just as Jerry is seeing them. My monkey knows all the artists. He ponders them for a bit, but then is bored. He begins to scan the newspaper. He has his scanner on audio. I can't hear myself think and tell him to plug in the headphones. He purses his lips, annoyed, but does so. I stare at the wall.

Janelle calls and says she is sending me Pursig's social media posts. I get the email in a minute and spend an hour looking at them on my laptop. There are posts of photos of the posters. I get to the Eagles poster. I get up and get a Coke

Zero. Jerry raises his hand once I open mine. I go back to the fridge and get one for him.

I hand him the drink. He sets down his scanner and takes it. He looks at me. "Jerry glad he now start listening to not dead rockers. Dead singers make Jerry sad."

I look at him. I turn away and look at the posters on the wall. "Dead rockers," I say.

"No dead," Jerry says. "Jerry want to be more with it. More live rockers. Get progressive. Listen disco."

I ignore him. I go to my laptop. I zoom in on the Eagles poster. I look at the date of the entry on Pursig's Instagram posting. Summer of 2015. I zoom in further. I look at the pushpins holding up the poster in the photo. They are pink. Four pink pushpins, one green in the center top. I turn and go to the wall where I have taped the images from today. Three pink pushpins, one black, still the green one in the top.

I turn to Jerry. "When did Glen Fry die?"

The monkey looks at me like I'm crazy. "Jerry no care. Jerry like disco now."

I google it. January 18th, 2016. Black pushpin now, but not before Fry's death. I examine other posters. The Who has two pink, two black. The Beatles too. The Stones have six pins – three pink, one black and two green. I smile. I get it.

"Jerry, look at this. The pins in the posters indicate if the members of the band are alive or dead. Pink is alive. Black are dead."

Jerry screws up his mouth, swishes Coke Zero around, gargles, and swallows. "What green mean?"

"Left the band or was replaced."

Jerry looks at the Rolling Stones poster. "Green mean Ronnie Wood in, Mick Taylor out. Bill Wyman out, Darryl Jones in. Black is Brian."

"Yeah."

"But make no sense with hot woman," the monkey says, referring to Farrah.

"No, we have the pushpins randomly stuck across the poster, Three black and one pink."

"Is hot woman dead or alive?"

"Dead," I say. Then it hits me. "Oh shit, three dead girls, one live."

I go look at the Farrah poster again. I go to the close-up on my phone. The little coded phrase is there. I read it out loud. "RM-GT-C-CA-LA."

"Jerry no understand."

I am already googling travel stores. I find one called Away on Melrose. I call the number. A young woman answers, "We are Away. Where are you going?"

It makes me pause, but for only an instant. "You sell maps?"

Her answer is perky. "Yes, we do. We have a very good selection. What country are you interested in?"

"Greater Los Angeles," I say. "Specifically, a Rand McNally map. Stock number might be GT-C-CA-LA."

"Let me check," she replies, her voice disappointed with my domestic choice. The young lady is gone for a short time. She returns. "Yes, we have several copies of that map."

"What is the map's size?" I ask.

"Two by three," she says.

I tell her to hold one for me. I will be right down. I call

Janelle and explain. I give her Away's address. Complication. I am watching the kids. There is no time for me to find a sitter. I wake Gracie and have Jerry in tow. We take off and I go as fast as my responsibility to the kiddos will allow. Janelle has already arrived when I get there. I run in and buy the map. Speedy is at the wheel of the unmarked cruiser as I carry my daughter from my truck to the cop car. Jerry, right behind, climbs over me to the other side. I buckle us all in. Janelle turns on the siren and lights. We run hot to Glassell Park. The trip with lights and siren is much quicker than our last trip.

Inside, I hand my daughter to Speedy. Janelle hands me gloves. I put them on and unwrap the map of Los Angeles. Jerry sits on floor cross-legged and starts flipping through crates of albums. Janelle is too intense to notice. Speedy does, but he doesn't admonish the monkey.

I make note of the placement of the four pushpins on the Farrah poster, taking special care to note where the pink one is placed. Then I take them out one-by-one and place them on the floor. I put the map up in its place, using green pins from other posters to hold it in place. Once I have the map of L.A. on the wall, I place the Farrah poster over it. I trace the pin holes with my gloved fingers. I reinsert the pins into Fawcett's image. Each is placed in the same hole as before. Then I remove the pins again, take down the poster, then replace the pins into the map. Three black and one pink.

Janelle steps up. "Three black. Pins are located in Los Feliz, Atwater Village, and the Fairfax District."

Speedy nods, stroking my daughter's hair. "Yeah, that's

where we found the three deceased. They match. Where's the pink one?"

I kneel down. "Vasquez Rocks Natural Area Park."

Janelle examines the pin placement too. "Just about as remote as you can get in the L.A. area. What's the closest city? I will call ahead. Get teams out there to look for Janey."

"Agua Dulce," I say.

Janelle stares at me like I'm an idiot. "I meant with a police force."

Speedy says, "Santa Clarita or Palmdale, but the Sheriff's Department is your best bet."

Vasquez Rocks is a roughly thousand acre park out near Sierra Pelona in the northern part of the county. It is an unimproved area. Rough and tumble. Rocks and rattlesnakes. Mostly, people go hiking out there in cooler weather, or at night to lie on the tilted rocks and get high. I suppose lucky peeps have gotten laid out there too. Right now, we're hoping a bad guy hid a little girl out there.

"It looks like the pin is at the very top of the park. Might need a dune buggy or something to get there."

Janelle nods and we all pile back in. We're headed north. Again, we run hot. I have the three of us in the back and I notice Jerry has a stack of albums on the floor, the little thief. He gives me the shush sign. He says to me softly, "Jerry not really like disco."

They find the girl within the hour. Little Janey Mansfield is dehydrated, traumatized, but not sexually molested or otherwise injured. She had been chained inside a camper trailer, half-submerged in sand. We are there, Gracie, Jerry and I, when they find the girl, but we are at the trailhead, far from the remote site where deputies rescue little Janey.

Gracie just wants to go home. Jerry too. He is worried he will be busted for grand theft and transporting his stolen goods in a police cruiser. However, they assign a uniformed team to take us home. For once, nobody is concerned with a monkey's misdeeds.

When Karen gets home from work, we are all in the pool. The coals are nearly ready for me to throw on burgers. She asks what we did with our day.

"Just rock-n-roll," Jerry says.

Karen nods and says she is going to put on her suit and join us. It is all copacetic. Rock on.

NOT GETTING CAUGHT DOES NOT INDICATE INNOCENCE

Karen has the week off for the Christmas Holidays. I take the fam to Cherry Canyon Park and we walk the grounds of the Japanese Tea Garden. It is beautiful and the scenery soothes my mind. My brain is still tumbling. What do I do about Grace? Can I work with him? Can I chance it?

As if on cue, he calls. I send the other three ahead. I maneuver down a path alone. No one needs to hear our craziness.

"Roddy?"

"Yeah, bro. What's up?"

"Janelle called. They picked up your plates out by Toluca Lake."

"Yeah, did you explain?"

"I recorded it. I'll play it for you."

I hear a click and then the conversation between Clayton Grace and Captain Janelle Jackson begins.

JJ: Hi partner. Been trying to reach you all day.

CG: Sleeping. Had the phone on vibrate but couldn't hear it over the air conditioner. Slept most of the day. Worked all night.

JJ: You feeling okay?

CG: Oh yeah, just wiped out. Not used to staying up 24 hours. Don't have my stamina back after the.... [pause] after my hospitalization.

JJ: I've been worried about you. I still want to buy you a meal some day soon. I'm worried about you.

CG: I'm fine. Just trying to get back to work. Roddy and me keeping busy.

JJ: I care about you, Clayton.

CG: Thanks. I appreciate it.

JJ: I do have to put on my captain's hat for a sec, though.

CG: What you need?

JJ: We got a murder out in Toluca Lake. A guy named Hunter Vanst. He was found stabbed in a Nazi bunker, as crazy as that sounds. Sheriff got Roddy's plates on a stoplight camera near there. Plus, your phone number came up on the guy's cell. What gives?

CG: He called us all right. I got the message off the office phone. I returned the call. We didn't take the case.

JJ: What he want?

CG: Wanted us to investigate his son-in-law up in San Francisco. His son is gay. Vanst did not like that. Wanted us to get him dirt on his son's husband. Wanted to leverage things to break them up. Wanted to find a way to deprogram his son. De-gay him, so to speak.

JJ: Sounds unpleasant.

CG: Yeah, I told him we don't work domestic cases. I also told him I thought his plan was a bad one.

JJ: You tell Roddy about it?

CG: I think I did in passing. Just said we got a call about a domestic case. Said I declined. I don't think I even mentioned a name.

JJ: Why were you two out to Toluca two nights ago?

CG: We've decided to try to ween ourselves off the Welmar teat. Financially, that will be tough. We've gone back to work for Fat Amos. Had a recon a repo. We found out what we needed and picked it up the next morning.

JJ: You were in Toluca on a repo? Really.

CG: Yeah, not ideal, but we have to eat. At least I have to eat. Karen is making good money. Roddy is secure. He is working for Fat Amos more for me. It's good of him, but I have reservations about it.

JJ: People care about you.

CG: I know. You need the name on the repo?

JJ: You know I do.

CG: PeePee McGee, some rapper/comedian.

JJ: I saw him once at a club. He's not bad. But I guess he's fallen on hard times.

CG: Mansion was pretty sweet in Toluca Lake. So was the Rolls we returned to Fat Amos. But I guess PeePee wasn't making payments.

JJ: How much you make on that repo?

CG: You working for the IRS too?

JJ: [laughs] No, just curious.

CG: Eleven hundred, cash.

JJ: So, for the record, you never met Hunter Vanst?

CG: That name is not right for the guy I talked to. He said he was Herman Vanst. But no, we only spoke the once by phone.

JJ: Herman *is* the victim's full first name. Thanks. And by the way, I'm glad you're severing ties with Welmar.

CG: Yeah, us too. But we might have to get real jobs.

JJ: It happens.

CG: Thanks for calling.

The call ends.

"That's how I remember it," I say.

"Yeah, me too," Clay replies. He hangs up.

THE ANSWER TO WHAT COULD POSSIBLY GO WRONG

"So that's it? You just say I'm out, so I'm out?" Clayton Grace asks, glaring at me.

He holds his coffee cup that says "Boss" on it in his hand. He'd brought a thermos of coffee and two breakfast biscuits with sausage from Eggslut. But I am not being bribed by breakfast. I mean, I will eat the biscuit. I will drink the coffee. In fact, I will drink it in copious amounts, but I will not budge. Not on this one.

"That scenario is not how it has to be. Grace, you own fifty-one percent. You decide what happens here. Not me. You can decide you want to keep the business. But I'm telling you this—only one of us is going to work here after today. You or me. You get to decide."

"Because I killed that Neo-Nazi asshole?"

"Clay, you stabbed a client to death with a Nazi dagger in his house without provocation."

"Without provocation? You were there. You heard the

things he said. Have you ever met a worse human? I mean, ever?"

"We don't get to kill people we don't like," I reply. "The legal guidelines are pretty clear on that one. You killed Von Licked Meinself without hesitation. Without regards to me. Without regards to my family. If we were caught... if we *are* caught, we'll spend the rest of our days in San Quentin. You did not include me in that decision. That is not okay."

Grace nods. "You're right on all those counts. I'm sorry. He triggered me. I spent two years on the tip of the spear for the NSA. I got to decide life-and-death in real time with no repercussions. My job was to kill assholes. I just reverted back to that for one instant."

I nod, understanding, but not relenting. "And that is why I can't trust you in the field. I will always question your judgement now. I love you like a brother—more than any brother. Certainly more than your brother loves you, but you can't undo what you did. You can't just say you won't do it again. I can't trust you to not do something crazy again. Can't you see that? I have to protect Karen and Gracie from something like that ever happening again. I can't risk losing everything because you snap again sometime. Revert, I mean, Jesus. I still cannot believe you killed Vanst with that letter opener. I just can't."

"Nazi dagger," Grace interjects.

"Murder weapon," I say with finality.

I set down my coffee. Things were at an end. Grace seems to realize it too. He leaves my desk in the lobby area. He walks into his office to the window. We are one floor higher than we had been when I'd come to work for The Purple

Heart Detective Agency, but except for an additional fifteen feet elevation, the view is the same. The corner of Third and Figueroa looks the same. The same traffic is stuck at the same light. I have looked out that window a million times. It now looks like we have made no difference. Los Angeles is still as fucked up as it ever had been.

Grace turns to me. His face is full of sadness and regret; his eyes have tragedy written in them. "Then if only one of us can stay, it has to be you. The agency can't run without you. The security contract with Welmar can't work without your computer expertise. I will step aside. There's not enough income if it's just me, plus this is all my fault." He pauses. "I am so sorry, Roddy. I love you, man."

"I love you too, Grace."

He nods. It is quiet for a while.

"I'll be out after today, but there is one more thing to handle."

I raise an eyebrow. I almost say, "No backtracking." Almost.

Grace doesn't let me and speaks first. "I told you I had scheduled a client in. He's a Chinese national. Chang. First name of Si-le—pronounced 'sigh-lee.' Si-le Chang. He's due at eleven. Been on a plane for a day coming from mainland China but wanted to come straight from the airport to talk with us. I spoke with him on Monday. He knows me, so I'll stay for the initial meeting. To make sure he's comfortable. This client could be a rainmaker. Lots of yuan. Didn't bat an eye at dropping nearly thirty grand for us to take a meeting, plus a two week guarantee of fees. My last function as CEO will be to turn over a profitable client—*and* I can clean out my desk before Chang gets here."

"That's not necessary," I say.

Grace waves me off. "Roddy, you should be sitting in the big desk when Chang arrives. Chinese are big on ceremony. On symbolism. You sit behind the big desk when he arrives. I'll deliver him to you. That way he'll know he is talking to number one."

"You don't have to do that," I insist. But Grace is adamant.

"Just so he's comfortable. That's all I'm saying," he counters. "Chang already filled out the standard contract and transferred the retainer. Two weeks. Twenty eight grand. A thou a day for each of us for two weeks." Grace pauses. "That reminds me. As a silent partner no longer working with the firm day-to-day, do I get a residual?"

I narrow my eyes. The transfer of power is going too quickly and I do not like it. "Stop being a dick. Nothing has changed. You still own fifty-one percent. That's what you get. Fifty, plus one, of the profits. Most months it won't cover your check at Eggslut."

Grace laughs. "We'll be fine for this month."

"Maybe. If we can take the case. I get nervous when Chinese nationals come calling. We can't do any corporate spying—industrial espionage—not for the Chinese government. The FBI will throw us in the hoosgow for that. In an L.A. minute."

Grace smiles. "That's a smidgen longer than a New York one."

I nod. "What's Chang want us to do? Get Apple's business plans?"

Clay shakes his head. "They already have those. No, he said one of his company's labs had been broken into, samples taken. He thought the person responsible had brought them to Southern California."

"Samples of what? Chemical?" I ask. "Like a weapon?"

"No, he said a biologic."

I take a sip of coffee. "Germ warfare shit? I'm not sure I want any part of this contract."

"No worries, mate. You're not drinking the stuff. Just finding the guy who took it." Grace smiles, but there is a sadness there. He pauses after looking around. "Thanks for all of this." He waves around the room. "It has been a hell of a ride, but it's time for me to do something else."

I nod. Yes, Grace needs to get out of the pressure cooker. Maybe I do too. I say as much.

"No, Roddy," Grace insists. "You got this. But for right now, get out of your office and let me pack my shit before Chang gets here."

At eleven, the Chinese man has not arrived. And not at noon either. I get on the LAX website. "Maybe his plane is late," I ponder, looking at incoming flights.

Grace bobs his head, two boxes of flotsam and jetsam at his feet. "Maybe there was a delay clearing customs."

"You're sure he said today?" I reply. "I'm not seeing a flight from Beijing due this morning."

"No," Grace replies. "Not Beijing. Wuhan."

I look again. "Yeah, there was one of those. No Si-le

Chang listed as a passenger." I have access to passenger lists for all the major airlines, although they don't know it. I strum through all the Chinese flights for last night, today, and tomorrow. "Nothing. No Si-le Chang."

"Try San Francisco and John Wayne."

I do. No dice. I shrug. "We deposited the twenty-eight grand?"

Grace nods.

"I guess the next move is his."

Later that afternoon, after Grace has left, I sit at my big desk. All mine. King of Nothing City. I reflect on the whole shit-show and Grace's final departure. I'm not going to write about that scene. Yes, there were hugs and tears and all that. I can't go into it. Sad beyond belief. He was defeated, and it was me who threw him out. Of his own business. It sucks. I feel like a schmuck. Let's just say, I am hitting the Jameson with the remainder of thermos coffee, no whipped cream, when the phone rings.

I answer. A pause. A time lag in transmission. The voice sounds far away. The Chinese accent is strong. "You Grace?"

"No, I'm his associate. Roddy O'Malley. Is this Si-le Chang?"

"No, him no come to America. No meeting. No need for contract. I his boss at company."

"I see," I reply. Something feels fishy. Bad vibes echo over the line. "It will be necessary for me to speak with Mr. Chang to cancel the contract," I say. "He contracted with us personally, not through a corporation. Only he can break the contract."

"He work for company. No work for you from company. Got it?"

"I will need to speak to Mr. Chang."

A short silence is followed by mumbled voices in the background. I can't understand the language and quickly grab my recorder and hold it to the phone. I get only the end of the exchange before the voice comes back.

"No refund necessary. Sorry for your trouble. No Si-le Chang to America. No work. Okay?"

I start to speak, but the voice is gone. The line is dead.

I run the recording through Google translator and get a little from it. "Money not important," the voice says. "No refund. Just end it. If detective have money, he no look."

That makes me angry. "That guy doesn't know me very well, now does he?" I say to the bottle of Jameson. It smiles back, and I pour the rest of its contents into my mug.

The phone rings again just as I am closing up shop. Again, there is a tinny tone once I answer the call. The ringing echo on the line is the same, but the voice is a woman's.

"Hello? Is this Mr. Grace?"

"No, I am Roddy O'Malley. I am President of the Purple Heart Detective Agency." I startle myself with my promotion.

She starts to speak, but whatever she starts to say croaks into the receiver and I cannot make it out. It sounds as if she is crying—or eating jello. The woman tries again but then stops and a few jagged, wet coughs hold her back. I wait. It takes a good thirty seconds, but then she is back with me.

"Excuse me, Mr. Malley," she says mistakenly. "I have been ill. I am calling to inform you that my husband will not be coming to America. He will not be meeting with you." Then there is another burst of tears.

"I understand. The man who called said as much. Is everything okay?"

"No," she replies haltingly amid more coughs. "My husband died of pneumonia today. That is why he not come. He sick for last few days. Hospital, but then dead soon. I sick too but not as bad."

"I am so sorry."

"You say there was other call? A man?" Her voice registers surprise.

"Yes. About two hours ago."

"What was his name?"

"He didn't give it. He just said to keep the money and forget the contract."

There is another pause. Then she speaks again. Her voice is different. Alert, alarmed. Scared. Deeply frightened. "Yes," she says. "That is good advice. Keep the money. Forget my husband. Forget Wuhan if you can. If any of us can."

Then she is gone. I hear the echo of the dead call. I stare at the receiver for a bit, but then hang up and dump the rest of the cold coffee in the bathroom sink. I rinse the cup and set it on the sink. Weird shit, but weird shit is what we, I mean I, do. Weird shit is what *I* do. Tomorrow will be another day.

Just on my way out the door, the phone rings a third time. I almost let it go but relent. I have to be a responsible president of the firm.

"Hello?"

"Roddy?" It is my boss, Bob Lee.

"Yeah?"

"You put that fucking monkey on TV?"

I laugh. "Yeah, busy day. I completely forgot it was going down today. Why?"

Lee's voice is cold fury. "I just heard from David Welmar. The Secretary told me in no uncertain terms that you were done as of today. For good this time. I will send you your final pay. You no longer represent us in any fashion. Fired. Understood?"

"Yeah, but slow down. What happened?"

"Watch the news, Roddy. Watch the news." He pauses, then adds, "Fuck you." Then the line goes dead.

I turn on NBC in time to see Lester Holt begin his telecast. "Today, at a press conference in Hollywood, a one-armed monkey stole the show and grabbed in one hand, his fifteen minutes of fame. For more, Hallie Jackson."

"Hi Lester," says Hallie. "Today at an event supposed to be the coming out party for a promising young actress named Sassy Spencer, her companion on stage, Gerald Munk, stage name Jerry the Monkey, has everybody talking —some with their hands."

Hallie raises her eyebrows, like "Wait for it." I am. We go to the clip with voiceover.

"The presser was to introduce Sassy Spencer, the new ingénue of tinsel town. The film, *Phantom Pain,* set to begin filming next year, is about phantom limb pain and how evil government pain researchers create monsters out of the amputee veterans in a military hospital ward."

Then NBC rolls video from the event. I can see Karen in the background, her client, Sassy Spencer, in front, flashing a winning smile at reporters. Lights flicker with the cameras. It is all very Hollywood 101.

Jerry is alongside Sassy. He stands on the table, so to be at the same height as the starlet. The little monkey looks pretty spiffy. His hair on top is spiked with gel. He wears a bowtie and a red vest. He smiles nice... for the first half minute perhaps.

Then Jerry, eyes jittery, steps in front of Sassy. He wrestles the mic from her. Sassy turns to him in horror. Which is basically what she'll be doing in the movie, so it's working for me. Remember now, Jerry can't really speak without his armband device, so what comes out is just a garbled cry. It sounds like "Welmar" to me, I gotta say.

Then Jerry, in literally a mic drop situation, hurls the device into the pool of reporters with a huge thump. As he does, his one hand begins to sign furiously at the cameras. Over and over. The same message. He is mouthing it as he goes. I am not fast enough to grasp it all. I get enough, though, and I start to laugh.

In the chaos, a security guard attempts to pull Jerry from the table. That does not go well. Monkeys are really strong, and their feet especially so. Jerry cranks back with his right leg and gives the guard a jab in the kisser. The man falls back off the dais into the reporters. Jerry's mouth and hand are still going nonstop.

Finally, Karen steps forward and loops an arm around Jerry's waist. He sees it is her and allows himself to be lifted off the stage. The two of them run directly away from the cameras. I see Karen's cute little backside retreating. Jerry is twisted and in the ultimate act of defiance, he flips off America in a clip which will be viewed one hundred million times by morning. The network blurs the middle finger, but not Jerry's lips which cannot say but can mouth "Fuck you, Welmar" very clearly. It is *so* Jerry I have to laugh. Wow, what a cluster.

Lester asks a question. "And Hallie, it appeared the monkey was speaking in sign language. Do we know if that is true?"

"Yes, Lester, we do. Monkeys and other primates are often taught what is called Gorilla Sign Language. The most famous example of that is the Gorilla Koko."

"And do we know what Jerry's message was?" After the question, he gives a big smirk.

"Yes, I spoke with him through a translator afterwards. Jerry the Monkey accuses Secretary of Defense David Welmar's company Welmar Pharmaceuticals of cutting off his arm. Jerry claims hundreds of monkeys had their arms cut off in the name of research."

Lester seems to pause for an instant. "Is there any comment from the Pentagon?"

"Not at this time. They too are speechless. Back to you, Lester."

Lester smiles at the screen. "Viewers can expect to see

Jerry on *The Tonight Show with Jimmy Fallon* on Friday evening. He will be joined by Sassy Spencer."

I note the actress got second billing.

Then to commercial. I turn off the TV. Yeah, that would do it. I won't be working for Welmar Security anymore. I shrug. Tomorrow is definitely a new beginning.

EPILOGUE

In the car, I call Karen.

"Hi."

"Hi," she says, her voice sounding tentative. "Did you see us?"

"The whole world saw you—and Jerry."

"Are you mad?"

"No." I laugh. "Jerry just did what Jerry does. But it did break the camel's back. Bob Lee fired us. What the hell. Welmar and his thugs are bad karma. We're well rid of them."

"I'm so sorry," Karen whispers back. I could feel her tears through the receiver.

"No worries. Lee never liked me. Was always giving me the evil eye," I say, smirking. "Well, he can't do that. Just has the one, but it *is evil.*"

Karen laughs, relieved I am taking it well. "You'll need to

tell Jerry that things are okay. He's in his room. I think he's scared of your reaction."

"Okay, in a minute," I say. "I have news too. Clayton left the firm today. I told him I couldn't work with him anymore."

"I'm sorry, babe. Is he going to be alright?" She pauses. "Are you going to be alright?"

"Yeah, I think so. Clays needs something new. We both do, really. And we'll have to. I don't really have any income now."

Karen gives a little sigh. "I'm sorry. It's my fault."

"No, not really. It's that little monkey. He farts trouble and lightning bolts."

We both laugh. Then I ask her, "Did you get fired too after Jerry's cluster on TV?"

"Fired?" she exclaims. "Oh, no, the entertainment industry is calling it the most brilliant rollout of a new talent anyone can remember. The phone has not stopped ringing."

That slows me an instant. "Sassy?"

"No."

"Jerry's the new talent?"

"Yes, Jerry. We do own him, right?"

"Well, after today he probably owns us, but yes, I have custodial rights and ownership on paper. I also have an exemption from the city to own an exotic animal. Licensed, and vaccinations on file. Why?"

"Oh, I've already booked Jerry on six talk shows with Sassy over the next two weeks. There's already been commercial offers, a reality series *Shock the Monkey* where they take Jerry somewhere, show him bad shit, and have him lose his temper. The craziness is just beginning. We're going to make a lot of money."

"And they don't even know he can talk with his armband thing yet."

"Yeah, that will cause a bidding war for endorsements like you never saw."

"Jerry can pay our way. That's good, because the detective agency is defunct again, I think."

"For now, you'll be busy. Jerry will need security."

"I can deal."

"Just think about it. Jerry on *Morning Joe* talking with Mika Brzezinski. Won't that be a peach of a moment?" Karen laughs.

I laugh. "Is Sassy pissed that Jerry stole her moment in the spotlight?"

"No," Karen says. "The studio is delighted with the coverage. They moved up the shooting date. Greenlighted the film for another 20 million in funding if the script is rewritten to include Jerry. Sassy has been offered an option for two sequels. *The Hollywood Reporter* issued a statement in the last fifteen minutes saying that Sassy Spencer will be the new Jamie Lee Curtis of horror. Everything is happening so fast."

I shake my head. It was all a little much to take in. "Lester and Hallie said Sassy is going to be on *Jimmy Fallon*. And *The Today Show*. You going to New York?"

"Uh-hum. We have to fly tomorrow. But now they want Jerry too. I'll need you to come along to watch that crazy loon. We'll bring Gracie. Whole family in the Big Apple. Vacay in the city. We'll go by charter. Are you up for it? I hope so because I already said yes."

"Sure, but can we go tomorrow afternoon?"

"Why? What is going on in the morning?"

"I think we should head down to the Justice of the Peace and tie the knot in the am. What do you say?"

"Oh babe, Honeymoon in NYC? I think that sounds outstanding. We'll need a couple of witnesses. I will call Vio."

"I'll call Grace."

"Will that be alright? You think he'll do it?"

"Yeah, it will be excellent," I reply. "That way Clay'll know he's still a part of our lives."

"Good." Karen makes her little surprise sound. "Oh, I have a great idea. NBC asked if we had our own security. They said we could bring someone if we did. I was thinking you, but if you're my husband, well, then we can bring Grace."

"Perfect. I'll call him."

"Hurry home, babe."

"I will. Put Jerry on."

There is a pause. Then that Pee Wee Herman style voice. "This Jerry."

"Hi, little buddy. You had a wild ride this afternoon, huh?"

"Yeah, Roddy mad at Jerry?"

"No, I can't blame you. The guy cut off your arm. I'd be pissed too."

"I tell America Welmar asshole."

"Yeah, I could read your lips."

"Good. Jerry needed to say."

"Had you planned on doing that? If so, you hid it well beforehand."

"No," the little imp said. "Free espresso machine backstage. Jerry had six."

"Ah, yeah, you and caffeine. Your eyes *were* jumpy as hell. Don't do that next time on TV."

"No, Jerry won't. Espresso bad for monkeys."

"I did lose my job today. You'll have to earn the money for a bit."

"Jerry be big star."

"I hope so. *The Today Show* is big."

"Going to meet Hoda Kotb. She hot."

I laugh.

"Roddy not worry. Jerry make lots money and take care of us family."

"Deal."

"It copacetic, Roddy man." He hangs up.

I follow suit with a smile on my face. Despite the traffic snarl, I have this stupid grin plastered on my face as cars crawl slowly north on the Ventura. Light is fading beyond the line of mansion-covered hills on my left. They cannot hide the sun's glow as it falls in the Pacific. We're not moving much, but I don't mind. "Them Changes" is playing and I turn it up. An hour ago, things looked bleak. Now all is right with the world.

January of 2020 begins the best year ever. Guaranteed.

SONGS ABOUT LA AND MONKEYS

L.A. Freeway – Jerry Jeff Walker

Hollywood Nights – Bob Seger

Tweeter and the Monkey Man – The Traveling Wilburys

California – Shawn Mullins

Babylon Sisters – Steely Dan

Desperadoes Under the Eaves – Warren Zevon

Monkey Gone to Heaven – The Pixies

Monkey Man – The Rolling Stones

Los Angeles – X

L.A. County – Lyle Lovett

L.A. Woman – The Doors

Shock the Monkey – Peter Gabriel

What Makes the Monkey Dance – Chuck Prophet

Screenwriter's Blues – Soul Coughing

Los Angeles – Counting Crows

Back in L.A. – B.B. King

L.A. – Elliot Smith

Under the Bridge – Red Hot Chili Peppers

Everybody's Got Something to Hide Except Me & My Monkey – The Beatles

Lullaby – Shawn Mullins

ACKNOWLEDGMENTS

Writing is far from a solitary craft. Many people helped along the way, and each made the final draft better. I am in debt to each of you.

First of all, I thank Nathan Singer, fellow writer. A conversation with him about the damage to the psyche by violence, even if inflicted by the victor, led to this plotline. So it's his fault.

I also want to thank a number of friends and fans for reading an early draft of the book: Julie Mullen Bruns, Terri Eisiminger, Steven Garinger, Ashley Phillips and Nancy Ogle. Thanks so much. Spending a year on a document necessitates a second set of eyes to find mistakes. I appreciate your efforts!

As always, I appreciate Kevin Faulkner and his ability to see and explain the legal entanglements of my fictional characters. I thank Evan Olsen for his eternal encouragement. I thank Brady Lantz for keeping me insane. He makes me laugh more than anyone.

Thanks to Tallie Davis for a great edit to the book. And a big shout out to Tony Acree, my publisher. He listens to all of my crazy ideas, so ya'all don't have to.

I appreciate the boys, Curt and Jake. Our post-movie discussions would not make sense to anyone, except us.

And to my girls, Lucy, Anna, and Kara. Thanks for putting up with me. I know I am a handful at times! Especially if I miss my nap.

To my mom, Peggy, thanks for creating a love of reading in me. I appreciate all those trips to the Hutchinson Public Library. We still go every time I am home. Those visits and my first library card stoked a fire that still burns.

Finally, to my darling wife, Vicki. I love our life together. Thanks for sharing your time on this planet with me. I love you.

Rock